Porphyria's Lover

Also by Maggie Power in Touchstone

LILY

Porphyria's Lover

MAGGIE POWER

SIMON & SCHUSTER
A VIACOM COMPANY

First published in Great Britain by Touchstone, 1995
An imprint of Simon & Schuster

Simon & Schuster Ltd
West Garden Place
Kendal Street
London W2 2AQ

Simon & Schuster of Australia Pty Ltd
Sydney

A CIP catalogue record for this book is available from the
British Library

ISBN 0-671-71941-6

Typeset in Goudy Modern 14/15pt by
Palimpsest Book Production Limited, Polmont, Stirlingshire
Printed and bound in Great Britain by
Butler & Tanner Ltd, Frome & London

For Eliza and Tom

The Resurrectionist Club

My first thought was, he lied in every word,
That hoary cripple . . .

Robert Browning,
Childe Roland to the Dark Tower Came

❧ ONE ❧

A scent of roses and patchouli doped the air that was already singed with heat from too many sweating candles illuminating the woman in white, who was slumped in a chair, her bodice soiled with the sap of dying flowers.

'This air . . . so close . . . I think she suffocates,' someone whispered as heat and perfume thickened the atmosphere and another asked if the woman was in a swoon because she was as pale as parian.

'She's possessed,' a knowing voice explained. 'Keep quiet or you'll spoil everything.'

'Perhaps a loosening of the stays?' a fourth member of the circle suggested with a little cough of excitement but at a sign from the woman in black none stirred. All sat expectantly at the round table staring mutely as the woman in white began to moan, her neck thrown back suddenly, mussed hair spilling to the carpet, so the sitters could see how the woman's throat swelled and a pulse throbbed in a thick blue vein as the voices began to jostle on her tongue, as that ruby stain, as of crushed rosebuds, smeared her mouth when she lifted a pale hand to still the choking medley of voices.

All silence now!

One by one someone snuffed the candles. Then a solitary lamp was lit, the wick turned down low, its lapis shade casting an eerie light on the proceedings.

The air was thick with hot tallow.

The air was swollen with anticipation.

When the first spatter of words shot from her mouth, the woman in white stiffened, sprawling arms and legs stretching, little satin slippers with their splintery heels stabbing the unfortunate gentleman who sat beside her, claw sharp fingers gouging a second sitter's eyes as he drank in a vision of ether conjured from that gloom beyond the mantelpiece; ether materialising as a dumb wraith who mouthed words that sprang uncannily from the throat of the rigid medium and, as she gave voice to the spirit's agony, the woman in white grew paler and stiffer: the voice high and thin, lamenting,

'O whaten a mountain is that,' she said,
'So dreary with frost and snow?'
'Frost and snow . . .'

Then one and all could have sworn the air chilled as

4

the wraith, drawn inevitably as a moth to the flame, fluttered across the room to settle like an incubus on the lap of one of the seated gentlemen.

'Frost and snow,' spectral words again seizing the throat of the medium. The woman in black nodded at the spirit-burdened gentleman who swallowed nervously as a ghostly wreath of lilies materialised in the gloom above him and, conscious of the phantom pressure on his flesh, he tried desperately to recall the lines he'd been given.

'Frost and snow,' insisted the voice that racked the throat of the medium.

The little spirit had slender fingers that worked thrillingly beneath the gentleman's frock coat.

'Oh that,' he stammered . . . pinched all over, his most intimate parts stirred as if by a host of demons. Hell, he thought. Vesuvius!

'Frost and snow,' croaked the voice from its lair in the swollen neck of the medium as the spectre stabbed him in an exquisite spot with what seemed like a small trident, stinging him at last into rapturous recitation:

'O that is the mountain of hell,' he cried,
'Where you and I must go.'

'Must go, must go, must . . . Ooooooh! . . .' his own voice echoing back to him, faint and plaintive, as he broke free from the circle and followed in the direction of the teasing spectre who had dismounted his lap and withdrawn beyond the darkest recesses of the dining-room.

Someone extinguished the lamplight.

Candles flared like jealousy.

The remaining company shifted uneasily on velvet chairs and in the candlelight shadows thrust at the ceiling.

The woman in black poured champagne into shallow glasses and the woman in white, her throat sore with the discourse of demons, recovered sufficiently to swallow a soothing draught as the gentlemen's eyes slid away from each other and fixed glassily on the medium.

Rosebuds withered on her tightly corseted breasts and as the petals shrivelled and fell from her bodice in the singeing candlelight a rosy stain shaped like a heart was discernible on the white silk.

The air so cold now, the night freezing to death around them. A shiver ran like fever round the circle of gentlemen and the colour bled back into the rouged cheeks of the medium. She sat upright on her chair, nostrils flaring, mouth agape, hair tumbling and lifted up her arms as if in surrender.

A low moan from the woman's long white throat thrilled the audience. The moan was soft, moist and drew itself out to a half-suppressed song, a curious hum and then a cacophany of voices competed for possession of the woman's body. Guttural male curses complained from her throat spitting profanities that were torn aside by what sounded to the appalled ears of the listeners to be piteously screaming infantile voices. But when they thought they could bear no longer to hear such cries that reminded them too well of the terrors of childhood, the shrill whimpers were drowned by the siren sighs of breathy womanly tones uttering plangent sentiments: 'Dearest, I've waited so long, so long . . .' and 'Your heart's desire awaits you in the black night of eternity . . .'. Then, 'Passion, and death, no passion without dying . . .' one of the unseen spirit voices reminded them. Other voices began to intrude, shouting down this mournful chorus with cockney lewdness: 'Come ere and see how you can poke yourself right through me dearie and come out the other side again.' More bawdy talk followed and spirit giggles frothed the air.

Then!

Three raps. The woman in white shuddered and the roses strewn in her hair scattered their petals as the promiscuous tongues were struck dumb in her mouth by an urgent orator.

'Yield to me,' this spirit voice commanded her. The ghastly voice of authority. A male spirit then!

The medium's own voice haemorrhaging from her throat, calling weakly:

'Come! Possess me master!'

'Master! Master!' echoes trilled from dark corners.

The voice that answered her was masculine, sonorous and as inexorable as mortality.

'Dare you submit to the grave?' it said.

The gentlemen trembled.

The candles died.

And the room was suddenly crammed full of whispers that sounded like 'Kathleeeeeeen, Kath. Oh KATHY. Be mine!' and the room seemed to shrink, swallowed up by

7

the slither of snaky breath: 'Oh Kathleen, I've dared eternity to return to you.' Cold breath filling the room with gusty draughts, penetrating the thick cloth of the gentlemen's capes and frock coats, insistent breezes that stirred the petticoats of the woman in white and the woman in black who hissed:

'Now!'

Pitch darkness and the candles grew cold.

Then at last a solitary taper glowed from a piano bracket next to an arch linking the dining- and drawing-rooms and, in the debilitated light, there was the medium, naked as the day she was born, laid out like a cold feast on the mahogany table before the hungry gaze of the gentlemen.

A floorboard creaked. The audience panted, then three loud raps on the table interrupted silvery music that tinkled in the background.

The medium prayed a mute 'Hail Mary'.

Full of Grace.

And she had barely finished: 'Blessed is the fruit of thy womb,' when Gabriel was with her, though she had not heard his approach that was muffled by the drugget set down to catch the fall of hot ash from the cheroots of the smouldering gentlemen.

Her eyes shut, the lids pressed down suffocatingly as though death weights secured them. Then she felt the cool shower of earth spilling from his frock coat, which she saw later was brown like a shroud; heard the slither of scarves mimic winding sheets as he peeled them easily from his face and neck, painted white to resemble a dead man.

So the shivering medium waited for her little death on the bare table before an audience of curious gentlemen.

At last he lay over her like a lid on a coffin. Fully clothed, as he was, Gabriel covered her nakedness.

'Kathleen,' his whisper ran round the spellbound circle. 'I've broken free of the grave itself to come for you. Prepare to meet thy doom,' her dead lover warned her. 'When I've embraced you you'll be a fit mate for no other!' He went on: 'No other lover will embrace flesh that death has set his seal on.'

Unfit for true love.

No other lover.

No first love.

No last love.

Only death then.

Kathleen Mangan, stripped of the white dress that would be forever soiled with the bloody heart-shaped sap of dying rosebuds, yielded, to Gabriel Feaver, disguised as a corpse, on the mahogany table in the dining-room.

Submitted with true dread because this was the first time.

Offered up her heart that was cold like a stone as Gabriel swooped: his face pressed close to hers, his tongue in her mouth, his breath healing the ache of spirit voices in her throat. Gabriel's face, shielding her own from the gaze of the gentlemen, his body covering her blushes, hiding the flush of surprise at her lover's astonishing . . . warmth, stoking her like a furnace, . . . fire was it? Too warm for a corpse, after all, as his heat flamed through her veins melting the ice of dread and shame and virginity.

More candles flared like discovery when at last, suffused with heat where she had expected to feel only cadaverous cold, Kathleen's eyes flew open in surprise, flew open to gaze upwards into the glory of burning candles, eyes upturned in ecstasy staring into the face of an angel.

After such heat, the cold again! Always the same cold, the inevitable chill of abandonment.

'You did very well,' her seducer praised her later, much later, when madam, whores and whoremongers had retired or departed. But she only stared at him with a haunted expression. Cold in this shabby room with the puny fire already dying. Gabriel and Kathleen sat before the mean flames drinking hot tea laced with mother's ruin.

The candlegrease and rice powder glistened on Gabriel's face. She saw how his mouth was too thin, too dangerous for an angel's.

His narrow eyes watching her.

Not seduced by an angel after all; the devil perhaps because that limp foot, the other whores had whispered to her, that dead foot he dragged after him almost proudly, was a hoof: cloven. But such a handsome devil! The women were all wild for him. It hardly mattered whether he was an angel or a devil; she was a fool in any case as he quickly made clear to her. A fool to let the devil take her because:

'Bell could have named her price for your virginity.

Why on earth didn't you tell her?' he asked, smiling to himself all the same as if he was pleased to see the old skinflint gulled and given short change for once.

Kathleen: seduced by this hired devil because her looks, her thinness, had impressed Mrs Bell, in spite of the shabby clothes she'd presented herself in (all hand-me-downs which had taken a deal of repairing).

'Not a street whore are you?' the madam had asked her suspiciously.

'I was in service,' Kathleen said, 'as a scullery maid. 'Twas my mistress's husband seduced me and when the cook found out she reported me to the missus and I was thrown out with no character.'

'So you went on the streets?' Bell pursued.

'I sold water-cresses for a time but in winter the work's mortal cruel and when a gent approached me in the Haymarket one day and offered his protection I accepted gladly.'

'He kept you? For how long?' Mrs Bell had walked round and round her during the interview, so Kathleen felt giddy and all she could think of was that the madam looked like a broomstick, what with her stiffness and her hair that bristled.

She had gone on with her tale. 'Just nigh on a year and now it's winter again and I can't bear going back to being half starved, my hands frozen to the cresses, my boots leaking, my spine shivering in . . .'

'All right, all right, don't go on, I don't run a bleeding hearts club. I only employ good girls. This ain't no charity.' Bell pinched Kathleen's waist. 'Eighteen inches! I should think we could lace you

11

down to fourteen. You Irish girls make good corpses. And at least you ain't got no barbarous accent. When did you come over?'

'To England? Oh as a mere girl. I was in service with a naval family and when they left Dublin for Portsmouth I went with them. Then came the posting to London. I was fifteen at the time and the master began to be always after me, wouldn't let me alone until he had acquired my innocence.'

'Hmmm,' Bell said. She had little faith in seduction stories. There were rarely any narrative surprises. All her girls told more or less the same tale with slight variations.

The madam had sat down at last behind her stout oak desk and stared shrewdly at the applicant.

'What made you come to this establishment? Don't you know it ain't the common run of whorehouse?'

Not in the common run of things at all, Kathleen had been warned.

'I heard it's a very good class of house,' Kathleen said.

'You mean the other brothels turned you down 'cause you're too skinny, not enough enticing curves to satisfy their gentlemen,' the madam said grimly. 'And what else have you heard?' Bell went on.

'That you provide a special service.'

A special service! 'But it's only a game,' the whore called Corrie had reassured Kathleen.

'You know what they call this place, hereabouts?' Bell persisted.

12

'The hole in the ground,' Kathleen responded truth-fully.

Bell flashed her an awful look.

'Our gentlemen clients know us as the Resurrectionist Club,' Bell whispered sepulchrally, 'because robbing the grave, as you might say, revives their dead parts just as miraculously as Lazarus was brought back to life.'

She tweaked Kathleen's chin with bitter fingers. 'I only want such girls as make convincing ghosts and corpses. You'll get good clothes, regular gin, the best opium and a starvation diet that'll wither your courses so you can work without a break month in month out and make enough tin to secure an early retirement. Then you can go on to stuff yourself full as a goose at Christmas. Now have you had any better offers? Don't hedge or waste my time. There's a berth for you here as long as you don't go putting any weight on,' she concluded.

'I'll stay thin as a hazel twig,' Kathleen had promised eagerly.

To be warm again. Blessed warmth and shelter after the cold streets. Bell's bordello would be like heaven.

'Why didn't you tell her you still had a maidenhead?' Gabriel tilted his chair so the hot gin rushed down his throat.

'I thought she wanted professional harlots,' Kathleen said. 'And that if she found out I was pure she'd say I was no use to her.'

Her companion muttered something under his breath

about the naivety of an innocence that puts no price on itself. Then he gave a half laugh and said very softly, 'Well if I'd known before I began the business I might even have enjoyed you.'

Kathleen's heart throbbed as if it bled into the mock heart staining her dress. She looked yearningly into the fire that had little warmth in its ashen bosom.

'Why did you give up a place in service for a whore's life then if there was no need for it?' Gabriel looked genuinely puzzled as to why she had left a respectable household when she had been neither ravished nor dismissed without a character.

'Because I don't care for drudgery,' she said. She confessed to him she had thought it would be easier to lie beneath strangers than to endure long years, hopeless decades of going down on her hands and knees scrubbing floors and leading grates from dawn until midnight or developing an ague selling cresses on the winter streets. Wringing her calloused hands as she explained herself. Couldn't he, with his sinfully easy work, appreciate how a slavey such as herself could dream of having hands white as a lady's, of wearing satins and perfumes and lying abed late every morning, she thought, her eyes glazing over like one who has read faery tales too long in a weak light.

They lapsed into a long silence drinking the liquorish tea, Gabriel's chair tilting and swaying, Kathleen shivering and feeling the cold now like a chasm between the flesh of lovers. The gin couldn't warm her but it made her a little bold so at last she said:

'Didn't you enjoy me at all then?' speaking more

brazenly than she felt, looking into his narrow eyes that barely saw her. And as he said nothing, went on drinking his gin, she pressed him, her mouth smudged and ridiculous, 'Is my body too thin for the pleasures of loving? Did you love me and feel nothing at all, Gabriel?'

Nothing? He thought. Of course . . . nothing!

'I can't afford to feel anything or I'd sicken doing this work.' He straightened his chair and sat facing her. 'You are a little innocent after all, aren't you?' he said, not ungently, taking one of her hands in his own and rubbing it solicitously as if she were an infant. 'Don't you know where you are? This is a whorehouse and you're a whore. We worked together tonight. Worked well. It was work not love we made. Rid yourself of dangerous fancies. Though I suppose a few nights here will teach you in any case.'

And though he smiled his narrow smile, the words flicked over her like cold cheroot ash.

'You said, if you'd only known I was a virgin, you'd 've enjoyed me!'

'But I didn't mean . . .'

'What?'

'Whatever sentimental woman's fancies you're har-bouring to delude yourself about cold reality,' he said, reminding her that it was merely his *job* to play a dead man ravishing whores for the amusement of gentlemen. Just *work!*

The tears brimmed in her eyes that even in the gloomy light were astonishing in their piercing blue-ness. Gabriel sighed heavily. He never *could* get used to women's tears. The salt bitterness of their grief always stung him. He would say anything to stop hot tears raining down a woman's face. He straightened his chair and leaned towards Kathleen; curving his arm around her waist with a supple movement, he said, 'How can a man consider the sort of woman he meets here in a romantic light?' He paused a moment, 'Romance is a matter of spontaneity . . . and of . . . purity, yes *purity* of heart. Not something meticulously rehearsed until a flawless performance is accomplished.'

'Do you never put your heart into your work?' Kathleen whispered.

'I'm a perfectionist,' he said. '*Real* emotion would get in the way of technique. How could a man keep the cool head a deft performance requires if he were swayed by the ragged emotions of the heart?' But she looked at him uncomprehendingly. Hadn't she given heart and soul both to this stranger tonight? Hadn't everyone seemed satisfied with the performance?

'Kathleen . . .' The way he spoke her name with a caressing fall on the last syllable made her heart flutter. Gabriel coaxed her hand open and stroked the palm smoothly. 'There may well have been satisfaction in the business . . . if I'd suspected earlier . . . but nothing more. A pleasure of the body perhaps but hardly a romantic occasion.' He smiled wryly at such an imbecile notion. Two spots of blood burned on Kathleen's cheeks where the rouge had faded.

'You think I'm a madwoman to look for sentiment in a place such as this?' Her voice tiny now, hoarse after her choric recitals.

16

'Not crazy, no. A trifle unwordly perhaps.' Gabriel smiled at her indulgently. 'I'm only trying to wake you up to your situation m'dear. What seems like a big thing to you is of little consequence to the rest of us sinners. And really for a novice you did very well. You saw how delighted Bell was with your performance,' he said encouragingly.

Kathleen began to cry more heartily at this praise. Her lips puffed so they resembled squashed roses. Gabriel swigged more gin with just a drop of tea in it. He had seen so many girls come to this house, but none that he could recall had possessed any illusions. None had such eyes, full of dreams. Something about this girl stirred him, reminded him of a part of himself he'd buried deep.

'You'll have to toughen up, harden yourself if you're going to make a success of this business. Bell don't tolerate snivelling unless it's part of the act.'

'That's what I'd really like . . .'

'What?'

'To be an actress,' Kathleen said, wiping her nose on her shawl.

Gabriel stared at her very hard, noting the way her eyes stayed limpid when tears stung them.

'I could maybe help you with that,' he said.

'To go on stage?' she gasped.

His grin flashed teeth like blades.

'Why are you grinning at me?' she asked him suspiciously.

'Takes one to know one.' Gabriel replied. Kathleen frowned. Was he mocking her?

'I'm an actor,' he explained. 'This isn't my only work, thank God!'

'A *real* actor?'

'Of sorts.'

'Then p'raps you can show me how I go about getting on the stage.' She fixed her blue eyes on him as wistfully as if he were a dream, and not a flesh and blood creation.

Gabriel shifted in his chair.

'Well, I don't exactly have any influence at Drury Lane but I might be able to set you up for a few shows in penny gaffs, that sort of thing . . . with padding you'd pass for a pretty piece and you've got a good voice. That reminds me . . .' he paused and looked at her curiously.

'What?' she asked, stabbing her fingers through her disordered hair trying to discipline it into some kind of smoothness.

'Your voice . . . or voices should I say. What kind of trick were you using tonight?'

'Trick?'

'Yes trick. You know what I mean. As a medium you were too convincing. I confess you unnerved me when those babies screamed from your throat. It was you wasn't it? All the other whores were reciting their pieces correctly, hidden in their closets and alcoves. I know because I wrote the script myself. I couldn't account for the extra voices, all those supplicating demons. You improvised Kathleen didn't you?' he asked looking impressed.

'Improvised, what's the meaning of that word?'

'I mean you invented a speech or two of your own. Made it up as you went along.'

'Did I upset the performance?' she asked with alarm.

'No, you didn't spoil the show. In fact, I hate to admit it, I thought your little act was brilliant. I'll have to take care you don't upstage me. I shouldn't care for anyone else running the show.' He smiled his thin-lipped smile at her. 'Your act was wonderful.'

'My act?'

'D'you have to keep repeating me woman? I only mean you seemed just like a *real* medium. You seemed possessed.'

'Possessed?'

'What intrigues me is,' he bent down and rubbed his aching leg, 'not only that you delivered a delicious script to spice up the proceedings but your voice really seemed to come from somewhere outside you. You have the ability to throw your voice like a ventriloquist, obviously.'

Kathleen looked at him blankly. 'I've always had a way with words,' she said.

'Of course I can't promise you anything but if you like I'll put your name up if I hear tell of any suitable acting work.'

His smile warmed her heart. She knotted the fringes of her shawl and spoke quietly so he barely caught the words:

'Would you? Would you?' she whispered. 'You see I don't think, after tonight that is,' she bowed her head so her wild hair spilled into her tears, 'I can

19

lie beneath any other fellow, after all! It's not what I thought.'

'It never is,' he said.

Still with her head bowed, still with the barest husk of a voice. 'It wasn't as I imagined.'

'I'm sorry, as I said, if I'd known I would have been more . . . careful.'

'It's not what you think,' she went on, not looking at him. 'I can't bear to lie beneath any other fellow . . . because of you! All my life I've been cold and you made me warm again. Your loving warmed me.' She jerked her head up. 'To do that . . . with another! You see, I thought I could separate what I was *feeling* from . . . from what I was *thinking*, but they're one and the same, after all,' she said woefully.

Gabriel stood up and moved over to stoke the pitiful fire, his lame foot dragging shards of cinder across the carpet.

'You've taken too much gin,' he said roughly. 'Gin fire in your belly is all that disturbs you. And what you call warmth is only art,' Gabriel laughed shortly. 'I'm a genius in the art of seduction. You're not the first to compliment me by being persuaded my skill was ardour,' he said.

'And you've loved many women?'

'Enough,' he said.

But not one of them the stuff of his desires, the woman of his dreams. He had known dollymops, whores, seamstresses, actresses, housemaids, barmaids, lucifer match sellers, herring vendors, flower girls; he was familiar with all their rough ways and intoxications but in his fastidious heart he knew he could never love such creatures.

Kathleen drew her shawl tightly around her narrow shoulders, collar bones pulling like pincers, hips still aching with his dead weight.

The bloody sap on her bodice had dried to a brownish stain. She began to rock herself slowly backwards and forwards the way she had swayed to warm herself when she sold frozen February cresses.

'Two bunches a farthing mister!' Hunting good fortune in the face of any gentleman who passed by, hoping he'd be the one to sweep her up from the foetid streets to the safety of a crib in St John's Wood. Keeping her splendid hair washed, little torn silken slippers on her feet in the forlorn hope of carnal redemption.

But the man never came.

'So it was all lies, then,' Gabriel's voice was fumy with gin, all lies. 'There was no protector?'

'No.'

'There was no smooth seducer in the case?'

'No seduction scenes,' Kathleen confessed. 'I'm such a scrap of a thing, no gentleman's ever so much as looked at me. They think I'm still a child, I suppose.'

'And what is your age?' Gabriel asked her. His eyes were like stars in the firelight which had begun to grow strong from his ministrations with the poker.

'Seventeen,' she said.

Sweet seventeen with no breasts and no history.

'When did you leave domestic service?' Gabriel was

curious about this odd girl whom he had spoiled so inadvertently.

' 'Tis more than twelve months since I was a scullery maid. I went selling cresses with another girl, but she was stout and her skin was hardened with being out in all weathers much of her life. I couldn't stand the streets any more than I could bear a servant's attic,' she added, the self-pity brewed by gin curdling her voice so she was sulky now, dropping her shawl, the drink fuelling her grievances. 'The costers thought we were easy meat and should go behind a barrow with them for a few pennies.'

'You said no man ever looked your way,' Gabriel broke in quickly.

Kathleen picked up her shawl and glared round the shabby parlour which was at the back of the house away from the reception rooms which received gentleman callers.

'I said I never got so much as an admiring glance from a gentleman,' she averred. 'Those who weren't quality were beneath my notice,' she said grandly. 'I wanted to save myself for better things.'

Gabriel looked at her streaked, mawkish face, the soiled gown with its too short skirts; inhaling her cheap perfume he began to smile. Then he stopped and caught his own white face in a spotted mirror.

'And am I a better thing?' he asked sardonically.

She said bleakly, 'You're not what I expected.'

'What did you expect?'

'I was told this place was the haunt of rich men.'

Kathleen looked at his face that was molten with

22

candlegrease. 'Men who wear fine clothes and drink champagne cold as the beauties who ride in carriages along the Haymarket. I expected some horrors, but most of all,' she continued candidly, 'I expected to be deflowered by a gentleman.'

Gabriel's eyes snapped shut. He stretched out his lame leg.

'My dear,' he drawled, 'you're more like me than I would have imagined. 'But,' his eyes glinting, 'p'raps I'm more of a realist.'

'A realist?'

The rice flour and grease dripping from his strong-featured face, he said wearily, 'Well I'd never be such a greenhorn as to suppose that in this damnable den I'd enjoy the love of a lady!'

❧ TWO ❧

Kathleen dripped hot tallow on to a tin plate, securing the candle which lit the way for her through gloomy passages. A swathe of cold air pursued her up the crooked stairs, almost extinguishing the dismal light. The bordello was spread over two houses linked by draughty corridors. The public quarters, where business was conducted, were supported precariously, as if on a crutch, by the listing walls and sloping floors of the private portion of the establishment where the whores resided. Here were the bare bones of the bordello: unpapered walls and carpetless floorboards. The narrow passages pressed too close for comfort and the ceilings, swollen as dropsy, bulged with rainwater. Kathleen could hear mice scamper and the very joists groan under the weight of night stupor. Gin soaked the

walls, opium-heavy air leaked like gas from the gaps
beneath the shut doors of the whores' bedrooms.

Kathleen climbed the stairs, running her free hand
over the sweating walls to support herself, up to
the room under the eaves she must share with two
other women. The air drowsy and poisonous with
intoxicants. From behind shut doors the thin pipe
of laudanum slumber or the hawking and spitting of
drunkards issued. The air grew thick as pea soup;
Kathleen ascended vertiginous stairs that splintered
beneath her soft tread. Up, up, the air so heavy now
she could have almost spooned it by the ladleful into
her choking lungs. In the meagre light of her candle,
the night seemed to have a damson bloom fading to
indigo where the landing dipped towards a sunken
hollow that marked the entrance to her attic room.

Kathleen opened the door to the bedchamber. A
mirror like a slab of ice covered the window. She
snuffed her candle, removed the bodice and skirt
of the silk dress she'd been lent, unlaced her stays
and slipped into bed, shivering in chemise and two
threadbare petticoats between the doped bodies of her
bedfellows.

Bodies that spilled only the memory of heat; the
sleeping women having so little warmth to spare
because they had been too spendthrift with delirium.
They had drunk so deeply, drawn so wantonly on
liquor and opium, that even desire had turned cold
in them and now they warmed themselves in vain on
its ashes.

Bodies brittle as dead moths. Kathleen was afraid

to turn on the flock mattress in case she disturbed the women. Lying on her back, staring at the night gloom that had acquired a greenish aura with a violet heart, she could almost have swooned with the sweetly addictive pall of opium smoke that laced the atmosphere.

She lay supine, limbs pinned to the bed by the swooping smoky air; languorous as spent love, the drug drifted everywhere as a dim cloud, rising to the cornices, filling the already choked cavity of the chimney flue, even issuing from the lurid sleep of her companions and painting their dreams on the night with sombre tones; dreams that invaded her own. And had they too dreamed of a handsome devil with a cloven hoof as they smoked their opium pipes?

His teeth flashed like blades and cut her heart out.

Gabriel's smile was too dangerous.

Kathleen grew sleepy despite the snores of the drugged women and the lumpy mattress.

One of the women had hard skin on her heels and they chafed Kathleen's thin ankles. The other woman had sharp elbows and they stabbed Kathleen's heart.

Gabriel still smiled through the dark above the mantel opposite. His smile had grown enormous. Kathleen heard a loud tapping like an impatient horse striking flinty cobbles outside her window.

Her eyes had become so heavy, her senses confused. The scenario of the old ballad that the whores had played out earlier, about the mountain of hell in which the devil in the guise of a lover lures a woman to damnation, began to paint itself on the darkness. She felt the bed sway to and fro, to and fro, like a rocking horse on hoops.

. . . *The sea rose and fell. She felt a slight nausea. Seasickness? And dread too! She gripped the handrail as she had done once before, on that violent passage between Ireland and England.*

'It won't be long now,' her companion promised her. His smile flashed like harbour lights at regular intervals until it vanished completely.

And this has all the inevitability of repetition, she thought. Then she shivered as if she had done this before. As if this fateful day weren't being lived through for the first time.

'Where are we now?' she asked him but really she would like this journey never to end. She had succumbed to the intoxicating spell of his company. Beginnings and endings would have no more meaning. This voyage was very heaven.

Bliss to be caught up in his arms. Powerful embraces. His warmth annihilating her past.

The sea churned. An albatross heavy as floods became entangled in the sails and dragged the white canvas awry before it flapped away again.

Still they sailed on and she forgot to repeat her question.

And should you die with no time to speak a prayer of repentance you're damned forever.

They made love shamelessly in his well-appointed cabin.

'I would give all the world for this moment,' she

said and then she repeated herself as if trying to recall a verse of which only the first line is not elusive.

His heat burned into her flesh. His passion scorched her.

'I want to spend the whole voyage loving you,' she said wildly, shamelessly, so of course then he dressed and went up on deck as if to taunt her.

They passed the lovely, green, sylvan isle that lay south of England.

They passed indigo islets of enchanted water.

The sea rose and fell. The boat rocked like a toy horse on hoops.

The sirens who love and live beneath the sea sang to them.

Her lover, tall and proud in his long black cloak, looked away from her. She had no pride. She had left home for him. She would lay her brow beneath his scornful foot and surrender to him.

She threw herself down on the deck of his ship, prostrate, clinging to his stern boots.

The spurs cut her cheek. He limped away from her mad embrace. He limped! Why do you limp, she thought. You never used to; when we loved long ago you walked proud and straight as any gentleman.

Slowly she stood up, staggering now because the boat was tossed on turbulent seas. A mist spumed out of the depths of the ocean. She tried to speak but the only words she found were those of a verse written long ago by others — God knows not her words — but written as if meant for her alone: none other.

'O whaten a mountain is that,' she said,

'So dreary with frost and snow?'

Lo! No sooner were the words uttered than the boat struck something inexorable and shuddered.

She saw a vicious iceberg and a limbo of wasteland ahead of them.

Her love swirled around. His cloak flying open, his boots it seemed snatched by the stormy air, the pretence fell away.

Why, his right foot was supple as any hero's but the left foot! Mark! The left foot was cloven and hairy as a devil's!

She tried to speak again but was struck dumb with terror and could only point mournfully at the icy wastes ahead of them.

For an eternity she waited some signal. Then at last he raised his dreadful snout and the devil answered her!

'O that is the mountain of Hell,' he cried,

'Where you and I must go.'

Must go, must go, must go . . . and she fell into the pit of everlasting unhappiness.

Kathleen was prodded suddenly awake from awful sleep. Two pairs of mulish legs kicked her.

'Yous don't lie flat.'

'You mustn't take all the space!'

Kathleen sat upright and drew her knees in protec-tively. In the wan light she could see the sorry state of her companions. The voice of the first protestor belonged to the whore who had introduced her to the establishment. She knew without further scrutiny that this was a creature whose transparent flesh bandaged rickety bones, her glassy eyes and wasted features indicating a general decline of the corporeal state. Old Corruption her name was and she was remarkable for the mildewed pallor of her skin, its morbid effect much heightened by the practice of baking reddish brown clay into her false ringlets that clacked at her every movement.

'Ain't yous familiar with the rules of bed sharing?' she complained.

'What've I done?' Kathleen said sleepily.

'You laid flat out like a pancake,' the other woman objected.

'Laid flat?' Kathleen puzzled.

'Yous must lie on your side. One side or other,' Old Corruption informed her, 'else there's no room for the rest of us. Ain't yous shared beds before?'

'No!' Kathleen said honestly. 'When I was in service I was the only live-in servant apart from the cook, who had her own quarters. And when I stayed in lodging houses I paid extra to have a straw mattress to myself.'

'Well yous'll have to get used to giving us our bit of space,' the other woman insisted.

Her eyes growing bolder in the pale wash of light Kathleen could make out the moist, waxy complexion of her other bedfellow. Corkscrews of short yellow ringlets frizzed over her shoulders. A long white shift fell from her throat to her toes. Missy, as she was called, looked all of ten years old and her temper burned bright as a candle. Her part in the varying repertoire of Mrs Bell's company encompassed infant corpses, fallen angels, spectral urchins and a succession of child brides felled by death at the altar. She was a noted little tyrant and strong men quaked when she mounted them fiercely in her *pièce-de-resistance* role as an incubus.

Missy looked at Kathleen with contempt. Until Kathleen's appearance she had been accustomed to play the favoured part of medium herself. She thought it should be acted out with more spleen and energy than Kathleen had mustered.

'Be a love and go an fetch the ot water,' she commanded.

'Hot water?' Kathleen repeated.

'Yeah, for us to wash wiv.'

'Aren't there servants to fetch and carry then?' Kathleen objected.

'Only for the general housework and to serve Bell,' Old Corruption said softly. 'We must shift for ourselves. But we don't complain because our berth here is more comfortable in general and we has more freedom than whores is accustomed to on account of our particular services. We give our dark best at nights and in the daytime Bell sets us free from our coffins to wander where we like.'

'Like vampires,' Missy giggled. 'Except we go abroad all day not at nights.'

'Now be a dear and get us a pitcher of hot water,' Old Corruption pressed her.

'What's the time?' Kathleen asked, loth to get out of bed.

'Gone eleven by the last striking of the clock. Get along love I want to make myself look respectable.' Missy pushed Kathleen out of bed with her cold narrow feet, heels hard as riding-boots.

'Where must I fetch the water from?'

'The scullery.' Old Corruption told her. 'Just go down to the front hall, turn sharp left at the foot of the stairs and it's the last door that leads on to the court.'

Kathleen looked at the soiled white dress, tossed on a small deal table. She went over to the press and from the shelf she'd been allotted got down her own gown of earth-brown fustian and the dark shawl she had bought at a dolly shop.

'You need some new duds,' Missy said critically.

'I've no money,' Kathleen said crestfallen. 'I thought this dress was fine. I used the last of my savings on it.'

'Bell will have yous fitted up on account. She doesn't like her girls to look unrespectable like paupers,' Old Corruption assured her, securing her false ringlets. 'I'll remind her at rehearsals,' she promised.

'Rehearsals? Do we practise every day?' Kathleen asked her patron.

'Every day except the Sabbath when we shut up business.' She went on, 'Yous must join us in the dining-room in the premises next door at seven o'clock sharp tonight. P'raps Gabriel won't be there. He has other work and often don't turn up until it's time for the actual performance. The session begins at ten, same as last night, same as every night, because

33

the gents don't care to come until theys had their suppers.'

'The same gents?' Kathleen quizzed Old Corruption as Missy, growing bored, began to lace her drawers and slide under the bed to pick up her stockings that were soiled with cochineal after an evening of revenant revelry.

'Generally a different lot, though some have been known to visit thrice weekly. A few gents have their regular nights in the week. We changes the show every Monday so they don't get jaded.'

Kathleen felt slightly queasy.

'Will I have to learn other parts then?'

Old Corruption laughed, her ringlets clattering.

'We'll be soft on yous yet awhile. Yous can be the possessed innocent for mebbe a couple of months. Bell likes to tease the coves with fresh whores by keeping them at bay for a bit. She won't let them mount yous for a time so the desire will increase with them and they'll grow half mad with lust and curiosity. Then when they can bear no more of Gabriel entering the sweet portals of death that's denied them, she'll grant them access one by one.'

'Or two by two,' snorted Missy, 'like Noah wiv his animals.'

'Gabriel . . .' Kathleen faltered. 'Where does he live? Why doesn't he stay here?'

Missy stood up, whitish balls of fluff in her hair.

'Not another goggle-eyed goosegog,' she whined, sounding vexed.

'Gabriel lives nowhere yet he's everywhere like the

34

good Lord,' Corrie said. Kathleen blushed as Old Corruption informed her that yes, all the girls, every one of them, cherished a grand passion for Gabriel Feaver. All women were fools — even Bell, who swore she hated every manjack who patronised her establishment, had searing vitals when Gabriel approached.

But it was hopeless. He didn't reckon on any of the poor benighted females who could be bought within three miles of the Haymarket. Gabriel fancied his chances. Gabriel was after a respectable woman who could improve his fortunes. A prosperous widow was dangling after him and he was merely biding his time in case bigger fish came along. And they would too because, more than handsome, he was a *dangerous* devil.

'Dangerous?' Kathleen enquired as Missy tutted for hot water.

Old Corruption wore a smile that ached. Dangerous because he was a seducer of imagination.

'Who else do yous suppose knocks out the little playlets we must act out at nights? Bell hasn't got a fancy in her head that he hasn't put there. Her imagination runs no further than a whim for a bit of herring for her breakfast. No, it's Gabriel what's her bad faery and makes up little plots and stories, invents new characters for us to tempt gold sovereigns out of the punters. And he knows well their rum desires that can't be satisfied in other establishments that don't have his imagination to fire them.'

'Why doesn't Gabriel live here with the rest of us

then?' Kathleen tried to force a note of indifference to her voice.

'Again cause he's a dangerous cove, slippery as an eel. He lives in so many places none can get a fix on him and then he plays so many parts none knows what he is. Though he calls himself an actor I says he's a mountebank.'

Old Corruption looked grimly at the gown Kathleen had worn as medium. It was laid out, bodice detached from skirt, on the deal table as if it had been butchered, the stain on the silk dried to dull brown.

'Don't let the devil eat your heart out Kathleen,' she warned her.

↶ THREE ↷

Mattie shivered between glacial sheets. Gabriel insisted on immaculate bedlinen and so the sheets and pillow covers had to be boiled and starched and pressed with a flat iron. He required Mattie to be fastidious about personal cleanliness also and so she was obliged to take a bath and wash the debris of the grocery sacks from her person thrice weekly. Her hair alone withstood his zealous concern for hygiene. She refused to wash it every Saturday night. At certain times of the month it just wasn't natural to dip her head in a tub of water. It would give her a chill, be the death of her. Too much washing stripped the hair of natural oils. She compromised by applying pomades and perfumes so her black tresses looked as if they were japanned like her parlour furniture.

Slithery snails of ringlets trailed over her neck. Her hair was too thin and the scalp peered through pale as chicken skin.

But at thirty she had the hard tight body of a thirteen-year-old.

And her unfussy gowns were always black satin and respectable.

And her grocery shop was prosperous.

She had kept one lamp, the wick turned low, alight at her bedside. Next to it lay a man's silver watch on a chain. Every few minutes Mattie's cold hand would reach out for the watch, and she would peer shortsightedly to discover just how many minutes past three of the clock it was.

Gabriel was late. Very late. And even if she dared she wouldn't begin to know where to look for him if he hadn't turned up by morning.

It was her own fault for striking such an unrespectable liaison. A husband could be called to account for his whereabouts but try as she might Mattie couldn't picture Gabriel Feaver as a husband. Husbands had mutton-chop whiskers and paunches. Husbands performed a certain lacklustre nightly ritual beneath voluminous nightshirts. Gabriel was certainly nothing like a husband. Mattie's blood raced as she thought of Gabriel's almost nakedness. Almost naked, but for those boots which added a touch of devilment. Her cheeks burned, then cooled rapidly as the clock chimed on the landing. The interminable night of the abandoned. She returned her cold cheek to the scratchy pillow.

*   *   *

38

She must have slept at last. When she woke he was beside her. Eight o'clock! Fortunate indeed there were no deliveries this morning. Mattie hurried out of bed sorely missing the early morning kippers and coffee that her little servant usually brought to her. Beth was under strict orders to keep out of the way on Gabriel's days.

When she got downstairs the kitchen stove was lit and there was a kettle on the hob but no time to sup tea yet. She went into the scullery and washed her hands and face while Beth swept the stock room. The boy she employed to assist her in the shop was already at work scooping currants and sugar from the sacks into waxed paper bags. A heedless lad, he needed to be reminded to mix sawdust in with the tea leaves and tip a bit of chalk into the flour or how would there be any profit in selling the stuff?

By eleven when there was a lull in the custom she was half dying with that dizzy sensation, that nausea and exhaustion that was apt to overwhelm her at certain times. She thought longingly of the soft bed with Gabriel still in it.

'Help yourself to a scrape of the plum duff, a *thin* slice mind, and Beth will fetch your tea in for you,' she told Jer who was cutting up bacon on the counter. She'd collapse if she didn't have some bread and tea. Gabriel never ate in the mornings and he generally liked to sleep late before he had an early dinner with her prior to his evening engagements.

'The poverty of my childhood ruined my appetite,' he told her when she marvelled at his weak-as-water lady's distaste for large meals. Else he never spoke of his past. Clammed up he did if she tried to prise details out of him. Nor would he let her come to his shows in the penny gaffs and the thought that other women were admiring his thighs in theatrical hose tormented her.

'Mattie,' he would say in that rich baritone of a voice that made her swoon, a voice he could pitch over the din of Seven Dials when he chose, 'only the merest dabs of girls attend such places. Ladies never dream of turning up nor even working women; they're only children really who come to laugh and romp, watch sensational shows and dance with young fellows.'

'Then why must you work in these low haunts? You know I can help you in the way of a bit of money,' she would protest. 'Penny gaffs are beneath you too, dearest.'

And then he would smile his cautious smile and say of course he would accept charity from no woman and he was a man of ambition, wasn't he, and with his looks (it must be said) and his presence it wasn't long before real theatres yawned their proscenium arches to him.

'If only I had a decent rig,' he said. 'Actors in that kind of circle are often gents. It makes a bad impression when you're down at heel.'

'You always dress with impeccable taste,' she said graciously.

'But in other fellows' garb,' Gabriel went on. 'A gentlemanly cut can't be acquired from a dolly shop or the market at Spitalfields. Bespoke tailoring denotes the true gentleman.' He sighed heavily and his cool grey eyes stared back at Mattie's, small and brown and glazed like currants. 'I shall have to look about and see if I can get more work even if it means I have to see less of you my dearest. I must have a respectable wardrobe otherwise I shall forever be dismissed as a shabby fellow.'

Mattie put down the flowered china cup from which she drank her milky tea.

'If you could only see it as a loan,' she said slowly, 'an investment for your future. I could pay for a new frock coat and . . . ahem, trousers and linen, for you.' She stopped and waited for his demurral but he said nothing, only reaching across the table to clasp her hand within his own. Mattie's slightly greasy complexion flushed. 'If we were man and wife all I have would be yours,' she said.

As she remembered her bold, blushing proposal, that ominous, dragging sensation began to seize her lower parts. The sensation of light-headedness possessed her, dismissing even the embarrassment that swooped in a hot flash as she recalled how he had hesitated before replying smoothly.

'It's too soon after your husband's death. You need time to grieve. What would people think? Consider your customers. While I'm discreet and slip out the back way there's no harm. But when we marry . . .' (did he say when or *if* we marry?) 'it must be all proper and above board.' Gabriel swallowed the last of his meagre meal and left her then.

Beth had set the tea to draw and cut up the good bread that Mattie baked, herself, with unadulterated flour.

She sat down at the kitchen table, feeling suddenly hot and then cool and shivery.

'Are you all right, missus?' Beth enquired.

'It's my curse again,' Mattie whispered. 'The blood seems to flow up over my head. I keep getting queer turns. Think I'll lie down for a bit Beth. Keep an eye out on that young larrikin and make sure he don't pinch the currants.'

Beth looked nervous. Jeremiah Cutts played up to her when the missus wasn't about and she didn't fancy his thieving hands shoved under her petticoats this morning when she too was wearing the rag.

'I'll give you a shout if I see a queue forming, missus.'

Beth's stomach was swollen and ached. She felt a slithery pulse of blood and wished she too might lie abed clutching a warmed brick to soothe her. But there was her daily sixpence to earn and she had to peg out the sheets and then she must press the missus' smalls and even goffer the frills on the fancy man's best shirt. Beth resented having to take on that Gabriel Feaver's laundry too when he didn't even so much as slip a penny of gratitude into her hand.

Mattie walked slowly upstairs, her head down, feeling the clamped sensation begin to tighten her sinus cavities. Gabriel had a horror of her courses so she must make do with an armchair and her feet up on the old sea chest.

He still slept, his light brown hair falling over an ivory throat, lying on his back, one hand thrust above his head, fingers caught in the trailing lace trim of the pillow. Even in sleep he adopts theatrical gestures, she thought.

She was afraid to disturb him. Having tiptoed across the room to the chair that was set on her side of the bed, she arranged a mantle around her shoulders, then a rug across her legs, and tried to make herself comfortable.

Of course as soon as she was securely wrapped she began to sweat heavily, the light-headed sensation forming an alliance with the sinus pains to sustain an attack of vertiginous ferocity. The room span. Her stomach rose up in revolt. Blood leaked in mutinous clots. Her back ached and the battle waging in her spirits as much as her flesh began to exude a bloody spume of rage.

She must lie down. She simply must! Mattie stared at the sleeping Gabriel. He slept quietly, peacefully, but if she slipped in beside him he would recoil at the faint scent of blood, the sulky heat of her loins; a particular man who liked a woman to be, to Mattie's slightly puritan unease, heavily, *sensuously*, perfumed. Her husband of course had never shown any interest in feminine fripperies and Mattie thought how old Ned Holton wouldn't have given tuppence for such extravagances as real silk garters, *scarlet* satin stays and a scented handkerchief slipped between the breasts beneath her intimate garments. So as she went about her business in brisk black satin, Mattie wafted a voluptuous perfume to commingle with the spices of the East Indies, the sweet aromas of dried fruits and fragrant coffee on the tempting air.

43

She had spent a small fortune on the perfume and underthings. Mattie knew well enough that if looks alone could secure a man, she would lose all hope of Gabriel. She needed all the seductive ruses a plain woman could command. And she saw the way other women looked at her lover. First his quite startling beauty. Yes, *beauty*. The strong jaw, the masterful way of narrowing mouth and eyes, the muscular strength in his body that almost drew the eye away from . . . but not quite, not entirely away from . . . For the smitten gaze would fall at last on the maimed ankle, and then the heart would pound, the stomach plummet, as desire met pity and ardour bloomed in the female heart. Then he would open his mouth on to a sharp smile, teeth glinting, razor-sharp teeth that could gnaw right through to the bare bones of desire and hone the amorous point of love; and his smile so ravenous would be fatal. That smile sealed fate because it reminded a woman of her own hunger. And then! Ah then! 'Oh Gabriel,' Mattie murmured as a flood of warm stickiness made a swamp of her undergarments. Surely her brains would burst through her skull! She closed her eyes. A banner of red mist rode across the darkness. A fist of pain struck her across the temples. Mattie opened her eyes again but the brutal colours of the quilt made her shut them again quickly. Behind her shut eyes the red banner was shredded by a thousand cutlasses. Surely through his repose Gabriel must hear the cries of carnage. He must smell the wrath of entrails. Surely now he would awaken and bear witness to the siege of her womanhood. He would ride to her rescue.

But he wasn't a knight, a crusader. Gabriel Feaver was only a man and he simply slept.

And yet he *had* saved her, from horror, from dreary despondency! The pain in her head duller now, a slow thud thud, like the inexorable beat of earth on a coffin. She recalled how she had swayed at her husband's graveside because she had eaten nothing that morning and the funeral service had gone on so long and everyone praised her brave suffering not guessing that her pale face and pinched features sprang from abhorrence at what man must return to: ashes and dust. She had learned nothing of love from marriage. It was death that was frightful to her, not widowhood. But none of the mourners guessed at her feelings and left her for that precious moment alone with the newly interred remains. She stood there just long enough for the others to reach their carriages before turning, a diminutive figure in black, down the long avenue that led away from the cramped but respectable portion of the graveyard through the more spacious area appointed for the wealthy dead – of marble mausoleums, rampant angels, railinged vaults and whited sepulchres, located for convenience close to the entrance. There, what with hunger and disgust, she had fainted. And when she revived it was to discover a man crouching over her, supporting her head in his arms, holding her safe in an embrace that was warm with the vigour of *life*. Real life pulsing through his veins!

She must have fainted away again and when she revived the strong arms still held her as the carriage moved slowly away from the cemetery. It seems he had insisted on carrying her for there were only a few elderly male mourners at the funeral. The undertaker having left, there was no one with the strength to pick a woman up in his arms and lift her into the waiting vehicle. Then naturally, as Gabriel's direction lay their way, it had only been polite for the other mourners to offer him a ride in the carriage.

All the horror of death fell away. Restored with tea and scones, Mattie had glowed as her thankful smile fell on Gabriel's across the fireside. Then her heart missed a beat, for wasn't this handsome man staring at her, *staring hard* as if no one else in the world existed but *Mattie Holton*. And, naturally, he had called again to pay his respects to the desolate widow!

'Were you visiting a departed loved one that morning?' she had asked him not long after that first meeting when she'd tumbled so providentially into his arms.

'Oh no. It's just that I often find a graveyard is the most peaceful spot in which to write . . . I mean *read* scripts. I like to learn my lines there,' he had told her.

How he managed to slip down a half a dozen spoonfuls of her clotted soup, Gabriel marvelled at himself. And then a polite worrying at that leathery chop fried in rancid lard. Mutton disagreed with him, he assured her politely. He was glad at least to be spared the odour of fish. He didn't have to endure any more boiled cod's head or herring gravelly with salt. How those briny odours choked him!

46

'I can't abide the aroma let alone the taste of fish,' he had been compelled to tell Mattie, who was offended by his inability to eat her heavy fare.

Strange how the meals she served up to him, the solid steaming meat puddings, broiled offal, sagging suets leaking treacle made his stomach shrivel with distaste when he knew many a poor fellow would think he had arrived in heaven to sit down at such a repast.

'Good solid food. What a man needs to set him up,' Mattie swore.

He grew restive under her hints that he picked like a lady. He swallowed manfully and the food swelled and burned like quicklime in his belly. Thick gouts of suet lined his gullet. Smoking rhubarb purged his bowels. Only the coffee, hot and piping, strongly brewed, restored him. And her bread was tolerable.

He pushed his plate away, the food uneaten.

Mattie tutted and poured another cup of coffee for him in one of her best china cups. Tiny doll's cups which shivered when they grazed the button-sized saucers.

Through the steam, her face very greasy, her currant eyes glistening, she looked like one of her own sticky puddings.

'You must keep your strength up. How can you work if you don't feed yourself properly? And supping gin at night without any viands lining your stomach will wreck your health,' she warned him.

'You worry too much about me, Mattie,' he said

47

shortly. Then, as her mouth pursed with annoyance, he said more lightly,

'A drink or two after work helps me to relax. Or,' he went on, 'would you set me down as a toper?'

Mattie looked down at her old wedding ring, worn thin on her finger. Gabriel hadn't sworn to love and protect her. She wasn't even affianced to him. They were both free agents. Such freedom frightened her.

'I know you need to relax after performing,' she said, 'but I'm only anxious for your own sake. I worry especially when you're as late as last night.'

'I made it clear, Mattie,' he said, his voice low so Beth wouldn't overhear him, 'I'm in no position yet to offer you permanent companionship. I won't own what I can't afford. And, if I am ever to earn enough to be able to stay with you all the time, I must be free in the meantime to pursue my ambitions. It's often in the hours of leisure over a glass or two that the most felicitous contacts are made, the best deals are struck,' he explained.

Mattie flushed and poured herself a cup of steaming coffee. She wanted to beg, to plead with him not to leave, to stay over every night but her head throbbed and her stomach griped. She said fretfully, 'I've fortune enough for the both of us.'

Gabriel replied softly, 'I wouldn't be the man you think I am if I didn't try to make my own way first.'

'You're man enough for me as you are,' she said miserably.

*   *   *

48

'I must go,' he said. Gabriel got up and went over swiftly to where the widow sat disconsolate and yearning. He kissed her briefly. Desire for Mattie never stirred him but he felt a slight unease at witnessing such blatant need. Her obvious loneliness was like the stranglehold of some rampant weed that threatened to choke him but in cutting himself free he had to be careful. He had to restrain, not destroy her devouring appetites.

'I'll try and free myself from an engagement I have for Saturday and then I'll spend the entire weekend with you,' he promised. The way her eyes lit up at once and her head fell back, mouth puckered for another kiss, dispelled his momentary unease. He disliked scenes and reckoned there was more real kindness in sweet deception. A woman who was deceived to the bitter end was less damaged, he thought, than one who discovered the brutal truth and was driven out of her mind with mortification. The greatest art was in winding up a seduction without bitterness and he was genuinely dismayed when, as on occasion it turned out, his own performance faltered in the last act before the curtain came down on the proceedings.

At last he disengaged himself from her embrace and went upstairs to fetch his jacket. When he came down she was waiting in the dark cramped hall, a small package wrapped in silver tissue in her hands.

'This is just a little something I embroidered for you,' she said edgily.

'You shouldn't my dear,' Gabriel responded easily. 'You're far too good to me.' He opened the package she offered him and took out a good blue silk waistcoat embroidered with ivory dragons.

Mattie placed her fingers over his mouth when he tried to thank her and said, 'Now you really must let me invest in some good clothes for you. Allow me to make an appointment with a bespoke tailor. Do humour me in this Gabriel. You said yourself a good outfit would improve your chances. Don't refuse me dearest.'

He kissed her again then. How she loved the way his eyes narrowed and his smile tightened.

'You see I can refuse you nothing my bossy little woman.' He thrust his tongue into her dry mouth. 'Till Saturday, Mattie. Till Saturday farewell, sweetheart.'

She had helped him on with the waistcoat before he left but it wasn't until he was out in the street that he put his hand into the breast pocket of the waistcoat and his fingers closed on a discreet sovereign.

Of course if he married the widow he would be master of all her sovereigns, guineas, clothes, bricabrac, furniture, living-quarters, stock, shop, custom; and master even of Beth the servant and Jeremiah Cutts the impudent shop assistant. He would have a world and a settled place in the scheme of things. And Mattie loved him. He sighed. They all loved him and he felt nothing. He almost envied these women the rich sustenance of their desires. He was empty of everything, he thought bleakly.

Just then he caught his reflection in the opulent plate-glass window of a gin palace. Gabriel smiled at

50

himself. God hadn't put him on this earth with the looks of an angel and the charm of the devil just to sell sugar and bootlaces. With his gifts he might go anywhere, do anything, win anyone. He mustn't sell himself cheap to the first bidder. He could imagine prettier, younger ladies, greater riches. His imagination was infinite.

ᔕ **FOUR** ᔒ

A frosty evening and Gabriel was chilled to the bones by the time he'd made his way from Mattie's house in Blackfriars to the penny gaff that was off Leicester Square.

He rehearsed his lines to distract himself from the bitter cold.

Tonight he was engaged to play the part of a villain who drowns his wives in their own washtubs; a popular piece based on the crimes of the notorious Nathan Sprigg who was hung seven years ago in 1840 for drowning five common-law wives in nine years. Only the last wife somehow survived long enough to gurgle a soapy accusation to a neighbour who apprehended Sprigg, as he slipped on the suds, by winding the villain's arms through a mangle that stood in the scullery waiting for the dripping laundry.

The gaff was next to a tap room and the audience arrived half drunk and giddy or fractious, shoving a penny at the man with the box and pushing their way into the cramped premises that were converted from a stays manufactory. There were wooden benches, a makeshift stage and a rudimentary gallery. The actors walked about sponging free swigs of ale from the youths and maids who came to watch them. Insults were hurled if the show wasn't to the liking of the audience and sometimes an empty pot cracked a player's skull; otherwise the digruntled children satisfied themselves with throwing cabbage stalks.

A comic turn was on stage when Gabriel arrived and the audience was joining in raucously with the bawdy songs and lewd gestures.

A pinched girl, whose too brittle hair fell in shrivelled coils like the husks of dead insects, stroked Gabriel's thigh as he made his way through the crush. Another maid with teeth worn thin as fishbones pressed her piercing kiss on his hand that was already shrugging off the embrace of a third besotted admirer. Gabriel was the undoubted favourite. The room was full of girls who'd come to swoon at him.

He made for the small room set to one side of the stage where the players made their exits and their entrances. Behind the canvas door a couple of actresses were applying face powder in white and ochre to acquire ghastly complexions for their scrubadub roles as laundered corpses. The elder of the two women, who had known better days performing at the Adelphi, offered Gabriel some blue from her powder box to give his villain a raffish, unshaven appearance. Two boys were shifting a washtub, filled with flock pillows to resemble suds, on to the stage where it was set down behind a dimly lit gauze screen so that, of the murders, the audience would observe only malevolent shadows.

Gabriel removed his jacket, applying burnt cork to create fiercesome eyebrows and grease to darken his hair. Mattie's waistcoat would come in useful to seduce the eye of admirers who might throw a few pennies in his direction. He cleared his throat and drew some deep breaths. A voice pitched low and sonorous to terrify, beetling brows, a stern thrust of the chin, all these he could assume. But he could do nothing about that languorous stride caused by his limp. Still, a certain lameness had its advantages. Women pitied him and when they pitied they softened and when they softened they applauded him. And how he relished such cheers of approval, more heady than drink, more seductive than caresses.

The comic turn being over, one of the actresses went on and sang *The Ballad of Wash Monday* so the audience were quietened and in a tearful mood for Gabriel's turn.

His eyes flicked over the crowd of girls to search out the soft touches so he could fix their eye at moments of suspense or excitement. The usual lot were in attendance: milliners, dollymops, seamstresses, flower girls and costermongers' daughters who were particularly loud and sometimes pelted the stage with stale herrings as well as cabbage stalks. A cluster of his keenest followers sat together, wilting posies or straggling feathers in their bonnets. They made little squeaks of ecstasy when his gaze fell on them – girls who were mostly pale and thin and undernourished; girls with scabby flesh who wore greasy dresses. A few were clean, others bold, propositioning him brazenly. A hussy had actually offered him half a crown to go home with her once, so he did, but with little relish for the affair lacked the uncertainty of seduction.

She was here tonight, her palm sweaty with a florin.

'Feaver! Feaver!' she hooted, and that sent all Gabriel's admirers squealing and wriggling. The apprentices who partnered them or hoped to win their favours glared at their rival, who even now had vanished behind the screen to dunk wife number three in her washtub.

Gabriel was about to make away with wife number four when a small commotion at the rear of the room let in some latecomers who pushed their way on to the already overcrowded deal benches. A little group of girls, mostly drunk and giggling, fell and sprawled over the benches although the tallest of them looked ashamed at her companions' carry-on and hushed them nervously. Then some of the boys began leering at the newcomers and their girlfriends started barracking and the audience quickly forgot the play with their own histrionics.

Pleased at any rate to be spared pelting and derision, the players continued to the end of the drama. The interruptions could be ignored until the moment when they could begin to scavenge for the pennies that were flung by a few faithful supporters towards the stage.

Gabriel made his way down through the crowd, some of whom had begun again to sing bawdy songs as the band struck up a popular tune. As he passed along the benches, girls tried to touch him, or offered drink. And here was the hussy waving her florin. He ducked because he could make more in free drink if he accompanied his little group of admirers to the tap room. And he needed drink to relax so he would be ready for tonight's session at Bell's bordello.

'D'you fancy me country cousin?' an inebriate voice called as Gabriel made his way out trailed by the fillies. 'Rosie by name and rosy by nature! She says you're the most beautiful fella she ever clapped her eyes on.'

He was addressed by a slip of a girl whom he vaguely remembered.

'It's me, Sairy. Don't you recall our good times at Bell's a while back, Gabriel.'

Little Sairy reeled back into a laughing crowd. A spiky haired waif with no stockings and slipshod boots. She wore a shabby mantle over a soiled petti-coat.

'Hush your chatter, Sairy!' a tall, robust-looking girl admonished her.

'She's drunk sir. Pay no heed.' The tall girl helped Sairy to her feet.

'I'm not drunk,' Sairy protested. 'And you great lummicks can stop sneering,' she scolded the fillies who had clustered round Gabriel. 'You ain't so grand. You think you're better than me with your feathers and posies but none of you ave *had* Gabriel as many times as I had.'

She belched. 'Gabriel got me maidens out of me,' she boasted. 'Ain't that true my love?'

One of the fillies began to spit at the careening Sairy. Another started to abuse her: little ragamuffin, snotty nose cretin and the like as they pushed Gabriel towards the door.

Sairy seemed not to register the abuse and with a drunk's waywardness returned to an earlier theme.

'Lovely maiden, she is. Rosie. My cousin,' she told Gabriel who recalled Sairy now; she had been one of Bell's girls a few years back. As death he had undone her.

'You'd better get Sairy home before the cats claw her,' Gabriel warned the tall girl who was evidently Sairy's country cousin Rosie. He was about to move on and then he stopped. Rosie was almost on a level with him. He stared into eyes big as blue marbles. Her hair tumbled with buttery gold curls. She had a bright pinkish complexion and a strong chin with a dimple. This Rosie was an amazon of beauty. And Rosie stared back at him, smitten; a fresh country maid in this city cesspit. She had a clean shawl pinned over her cotton gown. Her skin glowed like honey. Her teeth were rubbed clean. The freshest woman he had come across in a month of Sundays. He said quickly:

'Let me help you. Where does Sairy live? We'd better get her home before they tear her to pieces.'

'Off Drury Lane, sir. The others won't leave so soon,' Rosie replied, nodding towards her companions, 'and I don't know that I'd manage her on my own. It's kind of you,' she went on gratefully as Gabriel picked up

Sairy, who now fell into a drunken swoon. Escaping the clutches of the squawking fillies, they made their way out of the gaff.

They supported little Sairy between them. Rosie had sturdy shoulders and powerfully muscular arms from three years' dairymaiding. She told Gabriel she had just left her village a little way out of London in Hertfordshire because she was weary of milking cows and patting butter. The city had enticed her.

'Have you found any work here yet?' Gabriel asked as they dragged the comatose Sairy through an open sewer at the entrance to a narrow passage.

'I've only been here a fortnight. Sairy says I could maybe get taken on in a cigar shop or a shop selling gloves and lace in Oxford Street,' Rosie said. 'But in the meantime I'm helping Sairy.'

Gabriel was curious. 'What kind of work does your cousin do now?' he asked her.

'Day cleaning for a few shops and businesses. It's poorly paid but better than living in where you get no freedom.'

'That's all she does?' Gabriel pressed her.

'Why yes. She told me her mother, my aunt, sold her into service some years back but when she got a bad illness they threw her out.'

'Domestic service?'

'Yes,' she said. 'But p'raps you know the house she was in, sir? Or was it only the drink made her boast about knowing you?'

Gabriel chose not to answer. Was this girl such

a country innocent? He swore he could almost smell buttercups and sweet grasses wafting on the night air. He changed the subject.

'Would you really like to work in a cigar divan?'

'Oh I should love to wear a fine dress and serve the gentlemen,' Rosie replied with an innocent voice.

'Well sometimes I hear of a position of that nature going begging,' he confided. 'Are you sure you'd like to serve gentlemen?' he asked carefully. 'They can be exacting customers you know and they may care to purchase that which you won't want to sell?'

'Well they say in my village that in London, if a gent has money enough, he can buy anything,' she answered a little breathlessly because Sairy, tiny as she was, had become a drunkard's dead weight.

'That's true,' Gabriel acknowledged sagely, 'and in London too, if you've money enough, you can even buy your way into becoming a lady or a gentleman. Do you like money Rosie?' he asked, his voice now wonderfully softened.

'Oh I love money more than anything.'

'And so do I,' Gabriel said.

Gabriel was about to ask Rosie whether she would meet him at a chop-house tomorrow at noon when Sairy indicated return to consciousness with a strangled moan.

'Oh she's going to be sick sir!' Rosie exclaimed. She grabbed her cousin around the waist as Gabriel removed his hands from Sairy's arm and stood well back as the wretched girl vomited into the gutter. 'I'm sorry, did she soil you?' Rosie worried as the spasm spent itself.

Gabriel indicated that he had escaped contamination and permitted Rosie to assist Sairy unaided the final yards back to their lodging.

'Would you care to come in?' Rosie asked Gabriel. 'I think we could manage a sup of gin. The other lodgers won't be back yet,' she added as Gabriel hesitated.

'Thank you but I can only stay a few minutes. I've another engagement tonight.'

The lodging-house was saturated with damp and sagged like a slattern whose stays had busted. Gabriel followed Rosie and Sairy up the stairs worried that bugs and lice would alight on him from the plasterless ceilings that trembled from the passage of footsteps overhead. The girls' room was on the first floor. Rosie lit a couple of smelly tallow dips and put Sairy to bed on a straw mattress that was one of three placed on the floor. There were two chairs in the room and some sacking stuffed through a broken window pane.

''Tis only for a few weeks until I can get myself in the way of making some decent wages,' Rosie apologised as Gabriel refused the gin and sat gingerly on one of the unsteady chairs.

'How many others share this rat-hole?' he asked her frankly.

'Well we're lucky this is a place that only lodges women. The landlady wants to run a respectable house and don't allow mixed accommodation. Six of us girls share this room, only two to a mattress. She's not the real landlady of course. She pays rent to the man she sublets the house from and he in turn must pay the owner or real landlord.'

'Where are your fellow lodgers now?' Gabriel asked her. Rosie drew up the other chair and sat next to him. There was no fire and no means to accommodate one in the room. The girl's hands were blue with cold. He caught her chilly hands between his own and deftly began to rub warmth back into them.

'Annie, Tessie, Molly and Madge are all at work selling boot and stay laces, oranges and lucifers,' she told him. 'They generally stay on the streets till gone ten. I'm always free at nights and may have this room to myself for an hour or so 'cause Sairy likes to go out carousing,' she went on, drawing her breath hard as Gabriel began to blow on each purple-tipped finger.

Sairy slept like the dead on the filthy mattress.

'You deserve better than this,' Gabriel said as he finished warming Rosie's hands. 'Beauty like yours should have a fine setting.'

Rosie stared at him wide-eyed.

'Might you really help me to a place in a fancy shop?' she implored him.

'I'll ask about. Can you meet me tomorrow?'

'I told you I can be alone here in the evening.'

'Not here,' he said distastefully. 'Anyway I must work at nights.' He stared at Rosie. Her large breasts were palpitating with desire. Her legs had opened slightly.

But not here, not against the wall that streamed with the nightsoil from next door's privies, and certainly not on those mattresses that teemed with fleas and crawling creatures.

He knew a better place to enjoy her.

ᔆ FIVE ᔒ

A better place! . . . There were many fine establishments along the Strand, excellent restaurants where a woman could be entertained in a private dining-room, for a price! For the sort of money Gabriel could rarely afford. But he had a currency almost as potent — his imagination.

Rosie was early and spent her time observing a woman in a cigar divan through a window, imagining herself in such a modish gown, hair coiffed, serving rich gentlemen. Gabriel was a few minutes late and she watched him approach from the Trafalgar Square end of the Strand, his light brown hair glinting gold in the wintry sunlight. Gay women turned and stared as he passed them, ignoring the richer pickings in their stovepipe hats and thick coats. Rosie's heart pounded when he got up close, smiling his thin-lipped smile. He didn't ask her how long she'd been waiting. She said:

'Is that the sort of place you're going to ask for me?' indicating the cigar divan whose assistant she had been studying.

'All in good time. These things aren't as direct as you may imagine. I thought you'd fancy a jolly luncheon first. Then we'll talk business.'

Gabriel took her by the elbow and led her across the road to a building with high smooth walls and clouded windows.

'We'll lunch here,' he said, urging her up broad whitened steps to a swanky entrance.

'But it'll cost you a fortune,' she gasped, her knees quaking as she spied the interior of the restaurant with its glittering mirrors and mahogany tables. 'And it can't be open yet for there are no other diners.' But Gabriel, paying no attention to her protestations, told her to sit down on one of the plush sofas in the lobby while he ordered their luncheon. Then he disappeared into a room off the reception area and was gone such a long time Rosie began to fancy he'd been arrested for daring to enter a gentlefolk's establishment. At last the door opened but no Gabriel appeared, instead a plump, expensively dressed woman, past middle age, who raised tiny eye glasses and stared hard at her. Rosie hid her feet, shod with clumsy boots, under her petticoats. She held her shawl tightly across her chest. The woman returned whither she had come and shortly after the door opened again and Gabriel reappeared.

'It's all arranged,' he told her. 'I explained how we'd

prefer some quiet arrangement for dining. I was right wasn't I in thinking you'd find it an ordeal to sit in the public rooms?' He spoke quickly, breathlessly, ushering her up softly carpeted stairs.

'But the cost, it'll break you,' she said, bewildered as she was led along the corridor to an unnervingly sump-tuous room. Gabriel sat her down in an upholstered chair. He stood by the fire and lit a cheroot from a supply on the mantelpiece. The blue smoke formed a garland around the chimney breast. She was about to say this will cost you an arm and a leg, then looked at his poor foot and thought better of it.

A young man with a white cloth around his waist entered and laid the table swiftly. Rosie could smell the pomade on his hair. The fellow didn't look at her or Gabriel, bustling out, then returning with champagne which he poured into two glasses. Gabriel handed her a glass and told her to drink it quickly, it would get rid of her nerves. The champagne tasted bitter but she had downed a second glass by the time luncheon was served. Meanwhile Gabriel continued to smoke his cigar, staring at her thoughtfully.

At last he extinguished his cheroot and said very softly:

'Your beauty quite unnerves me, such pink skin, golden hair, as if you stepped out of a faery tale.' Rosie, unused to soft words from her suitors, blushed and looked down at the dishes of mutton and fowl. 'Of course, your life is hardly an enchanting one, living in all that squalor,' he went on. 'I should think you'd be glad to find a berth where you could wear fine clothes and dine on food like this every day of your life, wouldn't you m'dear?'

'A shop girl couldn't afford this sort of thing,' she giggled nervously.

'A girl who provides an extra special service in her job may make a good enough living,' he said. 'It's a matter of finding a suitable position, the right stage, to show her beauty off to advantage.' He leaned across the table confidingly.

'The thing is, you should never underestimate your beauty, Rosie. Such beauty could purchase you a good life; just think of that! You could be set up in silks and satins, stepping over your plainer sisters cowering in the gutters.'

The girl will thank me in the long run, he thought, even if at first she protests. He was older than her and wiser. What he did was for the best. After a time she would come to see that. She would see he really had found her the best place she could have hoped for.

Rosie stared at him perplexed. His talk was all riddles. She supposed it must be necessary to possess good looks to obtain a position in one of the finer London shops. And perhaps the wages were much higher than she had imagined.

When she thought she couldn't manage another bite he left his place and came over to her with a dish of confectionery. He opened her mouth gently and fed her sweets. The sugar paste crumbled on her lips and Gabriel licked them clean.

'Sweets for the sweet,' he intoned as though she were an audience.

She began to ask what was to be done about getting her a place at a shop in Oxford Street but his tongue foiled her. When they finished kissing he fed her more champagne until she was so dizzy it was difficult to resist his invitation to lie down. She swore the room with its high mantel and fancy table melted away and she was magicked into a chamber with a window so high there was no possibility of looking out of it. She lay on a bed soft as dreams and Gabriel lay down with her, murmuring how fresh she was, how sweet, more delectable than stale city women.

He couldn't remember the last time a seduction had had such urgency for him. It was the girl's freshness that made her beauty so sweet, like a rare wine that first crisps before it finally blunts the senses. And he so seldom stumbled across such exquisite spotlessness. Only after he had possessed her did her charms seem to wane, Rosie's skin growing blotched with the effects of drink and ardour. And what was she but just another poor girl one step from the workhouse? In a year or so her beauty would have grown blowzy with gin or pregnancy or she would have coarsened with hard work and consider herself lucky to be given bed and board by some dolt-headed sot. Gabriel watched over Rosie as she fell into a soiled drowsiness. When the girl was older and wiser and knew the value of a silk dress she would thank him for his little bit of deception. He was confident of that. He was being cruel to be kind really and that slight queasiness in his stomach was the unaccustomed richness of the lunch, he reckoned.

The drink made her languid, falling in and out of

consciousness as Gabriel loved her until at last she sweetly sank to the fathomless deeps of sleeping.

When she woke the first thing she saw was the reflection of a woman looking down at her from the looking-glass that was set into the canopy of the four-poster bed. A mad-looking woman with heavy eyes, a dull complexion and a pugilist's mouth. She stared at the woman in the glass who wore such an unsettlingly bruised expression. Her head ached but moments seemed to pass before her grimace of pain was imitated in the elevated glass which, in claiming Rosie's image as its own, made her recognise herself in the sorry reflection.

Her breasts throbbed. Her shins were sore from the friction of his military boots. But of her lover the only traces were a slight indentation on his side of the feather bed, heat which lingered on the mangled sheets, and his scent, on her own skin, of vanilla essence.

The world had turned and seemed to have lost its corners for, when she tried to raise her sluggish body from the bed and throw her chemise on, the room spun like a hoop. She pulled the chemise clumsily over her breasts, belly and thighs. She slowly climbed out of the high bed. Her legs were unsteady. The Turkish rug seemed to levitate beneath her treacherous feet that refused to walk and so she floated out of the bedroom.

She was in a long corridor with many doors that shut on sighs, frou-frou whispers of falling petticoats and the raw exquisite shiver of flesh rubbed by silks. Then one of the doors opened and two painted women sauntered out supporting a drunken man between them.

The women laughed, 'Come along Walter,' and the man groaned how much he longed for more of the sweet gruel, the gruelly syrup that he swore was the only thing to slake the dementing thirst in him.

Rosie passed them.

Further along the softly carpeted passage Rosie met a man and woman undressing beneath hissing gas jets. The woman threw down red skirts like flares and the man's garments, dark as floods, extinguished them.

The floor slipped away. Rosie glided easily down-stairs with effortless languor.

At last she heard Gabriel's voice lift and fall like a ballad singer's. She stopped and listened at a door that was a tiny crack open. Pianissimo! The very oldest of ballads! But it sounded a cold song to her and there was no feeling to the female chorus, a refrain that sang out 'five guineas' between the verses.

Rosie stood outside the door that led off the lobby and waited for the ballad of the five guineas to fade into silence.

'A cigar divan?' The plump woman laughed easily. 'Well she'll get the chance to light many a cigar and have herself thrown on her back on enough divans to accommodate a regiment in this trade.'

Gabriel kept his voice low.

'She's a good fresh girl. I shouldn't like her to be mistreated.'

'My girls are treated like ladies so long as they behave themselves. I have some of the best bawdy houses in London where her beauty will be appreciated. Don't worry. She'll soon settle. They all do when they're made to put their minds to it.'

'Ten guineas then?' Gabriel put his hand out. The plump woman rattled her keys and unlocked a drawer in her desk.

'Five guineas,' she responded.

'We agreed she was worth ten,' Gabriel insisted.

'Oh she's worth an outlay of ten all right. Only you've had three guineas worth in bed and board already dearie and that ain't counting the champagne and the little bit of stuff to quieten her. Then there's the doctor's fee! I got to have her looked over to make sure there's no ladies' fever. If any of my gentlemen get the clap word'll get round and I'd soon go out of business.'

'Eight guineas then,' bargained Gabriel. 'She's a fine specimen.'

'Five guineas!'

'Seven!'

'Five guineas!'

'Six and I'll take a bottle of your champagne with me.'

'Five guineas!'

'With a bottle of champagne and a drum of chocolates for one of my lady friends,' Gabriel persisted.

'Done,' the madam said.

'You should have locked her door,' the woman scolded Gabriel. Rosie, in her chemise, looked blankly at them.

'You left me,' she whispered hoarsely.

'Just to settle our account, my dear.' Gabriel glared at the madam and removing his jacket wrapped it around

Rosie. 'And I've paid a little extra so you may have a nice rest all afternoon in that soft feather bed,' he went on, prodding the dazed girl out of the office.

'Five guineas was it?' Rosie asked.

'What? That's right. Five guineas it cost me.' The sum troubled her.

'Five guineas! That's a mortal amount Gabriel.'

'Don't trouble yourself about it. I told you I've settled up with the proprietress.' He half led, half dragged the somnambulant girl upstairs, along the gaslit corridor past the amorous couple who had fallen like flame-stricken moths on their backs into the ease of shadows.

When her legs began to sag and buckle he lifted Rosie in his arms and carried her, semiconscious back to the bedroom.

> 'Oh what care I for a goose-feather bed
> With the sheet turned down so bravely O . . .'

She warbled, beginning to revive the moment her head hit the pillow. Gabriel looked down at the girl.

A feather bed in a whorehouse is better any day than a straw mattress in a midden, he told himself as he poured Rosie more doped champagne. And what she loses in freedom she gains in comfort, he reassured himself, plunging between the thighs she opened freely not knowing they were already purchased.

In the drowsy aftermath, the drug still coursing through her body, Rosie announced in a thick voice that she must leave — Sairy would be home soon

71

and she must have a bite of bread and cheese waiting for her.

'Did you tell Sairy you were meeting me?'

Rosie's eyelids drooped; she made little snorting
sounds as though she spoke from her dreams and her
words were like driftwood on a fathomless ocean.

'Noooooosh,' she snuffled.

'Are you sure?'

Gabriel tweaked her bedraggled curls and a snore
lifted to a hiss.

'Yeeeeessssss! I must go,' she sighed.

'Go where?'

'Hooommmme!'

'You have no home,' Gabriel told her.

Fighting against lovely languor she tried to tell him
that wherever her cousin was that was home, wasn't
it, even though it was a broken-down hovel.

Gabriel laughed.

'Do you think that little stray cat Sairy would pad
home to you so fast from the arms of her lover?'

'Yesss,' Rosie sighed. 'You don't know her.'

'I think I do,' he said.

Rosie lifted her head a few inches from the oh so
reposeful pillow. She tried to force her eyes open. His
pale face swam before her.

Was he saying he knew her cousin?

'It was true then . . . last night . . . Sairy rant-
ing to those girls about you?' She snorted again and
Gabriel laid his hand over her mouth and nose so Rosie
almost suffocated but didn't have strength enough to
free herself.

72

He put his mouth close to her ear.

'I have to confess, sweetheart, Sairy's boasts were no mere drunken ravings.'

Gabriel removed his hand so she could breathe again easily. He began to stroke her hair that was darkening with sweat. He sat up and poured more champagne as Rosie struggled to rouse herself. 'I certainly did know Sairy and she wasn't a domestic skivvie when I knew her. Not half so wrecked in those days. Of course she was a servant of Eros at that time. Do you know what that means my dear?' He stroked her body that was now clammy with perspiration. 'It means wearing fine clothes and receiving the attentions of gentlemen, it means being looked after, it means as much gin as you like and lying abed late every morning with no hard labour to disfigure your beauty. An easy life, Rosie. I must say it hadn't struck me that way until a woman I met recently pointed out to me the hardships that face a poor working woman in the so-called respectable world. And it strikes me, judging by Sairy's appearance last night, she must regret exchanging a life of comfort for one of servitude.'

'Servant of Eros?' Rosie screwed her eyes up trying to focus on Gabriel. 'You really had her?' Rosie struggled to recall Sairy's inebriate ramblings.

'But I wasn't the first, as she claimed last night. I didn't spoil her. The girl never found out I suppose. Before she came to us her mother had Sairy chloro-formed and sold her virginity to a board of workhouse guardians.' Gabriel sighed at the perfidy of mothers. 'They were rough fellows and didn't treat her so well

I assure you. She had a good berth with us but her drunken capers became too outrageous and they led her into such a sickness of mind and body we had to be rid of her.'

'We?' Rosie puzzled. Gabriel raised Rosie's head and held the champagne glass to her dry lips.

'I always had a soft spot for little Sairy but I'm glad you didn't tell her you were meeting me this afternoon.' Gabriel spoke very gently as Rosie's eyelids shut like jalousies. 'She won't know where to find you now, will she? She won't be able to drag you down to the squalor of a slavey's life. She won't spoil your chances,' he murmured.

He left by the back entrance that looked out on a frigid February river. Fog, like a composition of lost souls, hung gloom on the streets. Hackney cabs crawled through the limbo of thick, exhausted air. Gabriel had to feel his way down the passage that fed back on to the Strand where the gaslights wore cowls of mist and the gay women, vagrants, street vendors and heavy swells were erased by the filthy vapour.

He gagged on the evening's sooty breath. A scarf of ghastly air wound itself round his windpipe. Two fat fingers of fog plugged his nostrils. His eyes filled with silt.

Stumbling back through the Strand he headed in the direction of Covent Garden, the atmosphere lifting gradually as he got further away from the river.

↶ SIX ↷

Time passed at Bell's bordello like beads on a rosary. There were the joyful as well as the sorrowful mysteries when the whores recited to each other their litanies of desire.

At noon, when the kitchen stove belched promiscuous heat and tea stewed in the massive teapot on its trivet, they rose with white faces, brown aureoles staining their eyes, throats swollen with the night's excesses; they gasped for the hot bitter brew that was served with bread sliced thin as communion wafers. Silent as Poor Clares at their refectory table, swilling tea, gnawing their crusts, each awoke to new cravings or sorry promises of never again will I suck on an opium pipe or drain liquor like Christ's blood as if it could make me live again.

Their muslin wrappers were so filmy you could see their livid veins through them, their stays so cruel they cut like hair shirts and reminded them of their afflictions as they staggered to their places at the table.

Missy always spoke first and scattered the lethargy with her energetic complaints. She sharpened the blunt bread knife like a razor on a leather strap, managing to shave the last stump of bread into flakes for soaking in the tea so the weakest whores could sup the pap to appease their starvation.

She flourished the knife like a rapier for wasn't she the daughter of a man who set to work sharpening knives. Like father like daughter, she had a cutting tongue and always an axe to grind. Even her seduction story was a brutal amputation.

Thirteen stories passed around the refectory table. Some groaned because they had heard each other's woes so many times they were no longer insupportable.

Kathleen listened eagerly. The stories the whores told each other were not the tales they'd served up when Bell had interviewed them as candidates for the bordello. They were not always tales of innocence and ravished virtue.

The cruellest tale was the dirge of Delirium Tremens Tess.

Tess was the voluptuous beauty with strawberry lips who was possessed by demons. She howled whenever there was a full moon and said she'd left her village in Dorset because she had strangled her husband when he tried to run away from her on account of her monthly madness. Even now when Tess had her courses the other whores hid knives and sharp implements and they were careful not to pass Tess in the dark corridors or on the stairs those nights when the moon waxed.

Tess wept as she told the story of her marriage. 'A good man but weak as water. I skinned his back like a rabbit when he didn't have my breakfast egg cooked as I liked it. Then he would take an hour too long collecting the eggs so I threw a bucket of water over the fellow and locked him out in the yard on a snowy night and he almost died of the cold on me and wheezed ever after. It drove me mad, I couldn't sleep at nights. Then I never let him put his thing in me and Bell couldn't believe her luck when she got a twenty-one-year-old maiden even though by that time I had to drink gin by the quart to black out the memory of his purple lips blessing me even as he choked on my stay laces. When he shuddered his last I felt remorse but now only death could love me and he was an elusive fellow. I couldn't find him in Dorset so I got a lift on a milk cart and began the long journey to this city where they say death stalks the alleyways.' Tess shook, the way a condemned building trembles when a steam train thunders past. Bell employed her as a lycanthrope because with each month her hair grew thicker and her howls chilled men's hearts.

The Snow Queen's story seduced them all. How could it not when a rare beauty whispered of ruby blood with her voice like ice melting in the mouth? Gertrude Frey had long silvery yellow hair and skin so cold and white it must have been prised from an iceberg. Her story was frozen in time because she was still petrified in it.

She loved a man much older, a rich man who was debauched. Like Kathleen she had sold water-cresses morning and night on the streets of London. But her beauty marked her out: chill beauty without a blemish. Gertrude scattered her tale like snowflakes between the pauses in her companions' chatter. The story was that she loved this man still, though it was ten years since he had seduced her as a child. He had brought her home to his Regency terrace in Regent Street and lain her down in velvets and ermine; and when she bled, bled her heart out so only a clump of ice was left, he threw her out to haemorrhage her maidenhead on the streets of Soho. When the bleeding stopped she was left so pale that Bell took her on because of her bloodless beauty. But she was a sad, obsessed creature who thought only of the past; she could not rid herself of the memory of the handsome gentleman who had seemed to love her for a moment. Now she was lost in a dream of love for a brute who had discarded her.

Missy's tale was like a whiplash and cut the other women's confessions to ribbons.

'Always maundering on about your true loves, soggy wiv sorrow that you gave your fellows a hard time or drooling wiv desire that can never be satisfied 'cause the days are dead and gone when your first love led you a merry dance that ended wiv a jig in a bawdy house,' Missy snorted.

'And you should know better, Corrie,' she said addressing Old Corruption. 'You should be older and wiser, being as how you were the first of us to set to work ere in the far off days before the Reform Bill when the member of parliament who kept you passed you off as payment to coves in his borough so if they voted for him they got permission to poke you twice a fortnight for the season so half of friggin Hampshire had you. And yet you still spout tears over the bugger and boast how you were once the paramour of a great statesman.'

Missy tossed her corkscrew curls. 'You don't see me repining. You don't see me shedding tears over some donkey who don't know a girl's fanny from a chamberpot so he plonks hiself on it any ole how.' Then Missy told them all over again to buck their spirits up, how she'd made sure the red-coated soldier who'd botched her deflowering before falling down drunk got a seeing to he'd always remember: slowly, slowly, ever so slowly, to remind him how speed dulls the sensation, she'd produced a carving knife and castoroiled him.

Bell sent Kathleen to inspect the bordello bedchambers to make sure all was in readiness for the evening performance in which the whores would play vampires lapping cochineal from the throats of yielding gentlemen. Vampires! Tonight they would drain the very lifeblood of money from the pockets of the punters!

There was to be no séance and Kathleen's task merely was to help clear the mess afterwards and cleanse the crimson spatters of fake blood from the gentlemen's shirtfronts and the Turkey carpet. Bell was most particular. The cochineal stains must be washed away and the gentlemen should be offered steaming towels so they could refresh themselves or what would their wives and mothers suppose when they returned home like victims of scarlet fever?

They must be turned out looking respectable.

Would Gabriel stay late tonight, Kathleen wondered as she had wondered every night since that first night drinking gin with him. He seemed to enjoy talking with her over a glass of wine. He liked wine better than gin and sometimes the punters left half-finished bottles in the whores' bedrooms and if Bell was in good humour she left a tipple out for her master of ceremonies.

Kathleen loved it when he sat up late into the night with her, imbibing, his lame foot raised on the fender. He never said if his lameness troubled him; he never mentioned it, just as he never exposed the tortured limb to anyone in the bordello. In the shows he staged he always managed a fully dressed role for himself and his stern boots stayed welded to his feet and calves. Highly spit-and-polished boots, they never had a mark on them.

They would talk for hours. It was odd, he said once, smiling his sharp-toothed, heartbreaking smile, he'd never got much in the way of conversation from a woman before. But then he'd never come across a woman who loved reciting verses and painting pictures with words the way Kathleen did. Women usually only wanted a man to tell them how much he loved them or else they quizzed him with endless questions that lassoed him like apron strings, he declared. Most of all he relished Kathleen's fund of stories, tales of banshees and changelings. Only when the stories stopped and when it was very late and the wine threatened to spill from her eyes, he grew chill and withdrew the warmth of his company.

But there was no wine tonight and he'd no taste for gin, he said, having supped a heavy port at a lady friend's house earlier. He craved the lightness, the fizz of champagne.

Bell, having ordered the maid to finish up cleaning, went off to count the takings. She did her reckonings alone in her bedroom where she slept with a moneybag for her companion.

'Wears sovereigns instead of pennies on her eyes as death weights, to help her sleep at nights,' Missy declared angrily because Bell never provided quite enough money to give the whores real freedom.

Kathleen began to set the kettle on the hob to make tea for herself and Gabriel. As she did so he turned aside from the mantel where he had been lighting the stub of a cheroot and lifted the kettle from her hand.

'I need lively company tonight. Let me clear it with Bell and have a late supper with me Kathleen.'

'There's only bread and a bit of bacon grease to eat in the pantry,' she replied.

'I don't mean to eat here, simpleton. Bell don't know anything about feasting. Come to a supper room in the Haymarket with me.'

'Will Bell allow it?' Kathleen asked doubtfully. 'She lets us have our freedom by day, but night-time is her time she says.'

'She won't refuse me. It's in her interest to keep me

on board her bawdy house,' he said. 'Wait there. I'll tell her it'll give you a lesson in how the best class of whores disport themselves in pleasure houses.'

Whatever Gabriel did say, Bell left them to it. Kathleen borrowed Missy's velvet mantle and another girl's silk bonnet and, heart racing like a steam engine, Kathleen Mangan walked out with Gabriel Feaver into the West End Elysium.

∽ SEVEN ∾

She couldn't, she simply couldn't sleep. Not tonight. Was it the port, heavy, ruby, syrupy stuff that tickled her stomach? What was it that kept her awake and so agitated, moving from chair to horsehair sofa even to squat on the Berlin wool footstool? She had drawn back the curtains, peered through swathes of Nottingham lace to see if there was a full moon that would account for such madness but a thin lady with a chill ruff of cloud and a curved spine beamed wanly at her. No lunar mania then! She looked up and down the street. All was quietness. Not a carriage to be seen. No lumbering hackney cabs. No late-night revellers.

Mattie went over to the hearth and kicked some glowing cinders back into the grate from which they had fallen scattering flakes of ash on the carpet. I must check at the ironmonger tomorrow, she reminded herself, and see if the fender's repaired yet. That careless Beth had scratched the polished brass, tumbling down on it with the coal bucket. The girl seemed to be falling down all over the place lately, her clothes disarrayed, her skin bruised, nails broken. Even Jeremiah, who was an agile lad, had apparently managed to scratch his face with the bacon knife. How could she keep a neat house with such oafs in attendance? Mattie liked everything perfect without a mark. If china was chipped she got rid of it. If she wasn't too bothered about cleanliness she hated untidiness or any kind of disorder. Disorder seemed to link itself with some turmoil within, a disarrangement of the feelings. She liked everything clear cut.

If only . . .

Would Gabriel name the day now, she wondered, that butterfly sensation churning her stomach. Perhaps some bread and cheese would pacify her innards. She went out into the hall and down the two steps to the kitchen. The bread was hard. She must bake a fresh batch in the morning. There was half a cheese left. She cut herself a thick wedge. And a pot of tea, no cocoa perhaps, would help to calm her. There was a naughty thrill to feasting alone at such an hour. Gone midnight! She put her supper on a pretty papier-mâché tray and was about to carry it back into the warmth of the parlour when she remembered the good apple pie Gabriel had left uneaten. A delicious heavy crust and she'd put a few cloves in with the apples to spice them up. Mattie went into the larder and fetched the

84

pie dish down from its shelf. She didn't usually have such a craving for food. It was this agitation. It must be the deadly excitement of not knowing whether tonight would be the night. She was a bundle of nerves, highly strung as a mere girl with her first swain. 'Calm down, Mattie, go easy Mattie,' she told herself.

She drew a high-backed chair up by the fireside and held the tray on her lap. The food was heavy in her stomach. The tickling sensation subsided and the cocoa, like mother's milk, made her tongue lazy and sweet.

Mattie finished her meal, stirred up the fire making it roar by holding a copy of the *Illustrated London News* over the grate and cavity of the flue. Then she sat back in her chair and moaned softly to herself:

'Oh Gabriel, Oh my beloved . . . husband? Let it be . . . husband,' she prayed.

And last night in the darkness she'd told him, 'The clothes will be ready tomorrow. Can you be there for the final fitting?'

'Naturally,' he'd replied, leaning over to deposit a dry kiss on her mouth.

And today when he'd put on the exquisitely tailored frock coat, neat trousers with a stripe, the modestly ruffled shirt and silk cravat together with a plain black waistcoat, he'd said plain black and only plain black was the thing to impress theatre managers, he'd looked a real gentleman.

He had stood there, his head tilted high, sneering with a horse-and-carriage-and-six-thousand-a-year arrogance, saying, in his rich theatrical tones:

'Gabriel Feaver offers you his eternal gratitude

ma'am.' Then he'd smiled and had come over to her, even though the tailor was still clearing away his pins and threads, and said those precious words that must have started her stomach leaping in a polka of rapture: 'They'll have to take notice of me now Mattie. I'll present myself at a few theatres in this swell rig and see if they don't give me lead in half a dozen tragedies. And there'll be a new part for you too, sweetheart. Every hero needs his leading woman.' Then he had pressed her close and gently kissed her.

Leading woman! That could only mean one thing. He was going to propose to her. But what if he didn't get a place at any theatre even though he looked a gentleman through and through? If they still didn't offer him anything what then? Would he marry her? So scrupulous he was not wanting to live off a woman's earnings!

Tonight, while he was still so hopeful, she must somehow get him to offer marriage. She simply must, she told herself, lighting a lamp and settling down to read a penny periodical, determined to wait up for him.

Naphtha lamps and candles lit up the street stalls around the Dials. Kathleen sniffed bacon knuckles and tripe and onions, pea soup and ham sandwiches.

'I could fancy a kidney pudding and baked potato,' she said. The street vendors were doing a brisk trade in boiled meat puddings, gingerbread, mince pies and little tarts filled with rhubarb or damson.

Gabriel made a grimace of distaste. 'It'd poison

my bowels to ingest that stuff,' he said fastidiously. Kathleen's mouth filled with saliva.

'I could eat a cat I'm so famished. All Bell's liquor and laudanum don't take away my appetite.' She looked so disconsolate Gabriel laughed and drew her thin arm through his. They walked companionably along the busy streets.

'You know you really mustn't develop a healthy appetite or you'll get too stout for the Resurrectionist Club,' he teased her.

'Well if I got too fat maybe that would be for the best because then Bell would sling me on the streets before some heavy swell grinds his machine in me.'

Gabriel stopped her outside a gin palace under a fusillade of gas jets that fired a hard, shadowless light.

'What nonsense is this? You're not going to spill more milksop? If you can be indecent with me I don't see it makes such a difference to earn your keep administering to other fellows.'

Kathleen looked white as leprosy in the naked light.

'It's different as night from day. It's not what I thought, I never expected . . .' Her voice was low and trembled. Gabriel was exasperated. He cut in, 'For God's sake woman. You're virtuous or you ain't. You're up to tricks or you're too squeamish to turn your hand to the job. But don't go all spoony and blame *me* for these attacks of modesty. I told you before. Our little performances mean nothing to me. It's work. Work I soon hope I'll be free of.'

Tears spilled from Kathleen's eyes and streaked

her rouge. They walked along slowly and Gabriel disengaged his arm from hers.

'If you escape, take me with you,' she implored. 'Help me get out of whoring into acting, Gabriel. I'm afraid when I think how little time there's left to me before I'm to endure the attentions of those horrible men, with their cod eyes and red lobster mouths and scaly flesh and . . . and . . . tools that waggle like fins and . . .'

Gabriel laughed despite himself as they passed a fresh fish stall.

'Hold your tongue woman. You spin words like a top. I said, didn't I? I'd look out for you. Well tonight if I can carry off the part I've in mind good fortune may lay ahead for both of us.'

'What part? I thought we were going to have supper and a drink? You didn't say anything about performing. We're not going to another bawdy house are we?' Suddenly suspicious, Kathleen dried her tears and clutched her bonnet defensively.

Gabriel seized her by the arm again and without a word of reassurance urged her down an alley into a labyrinth of courts and passages away from the illuminated streets into foetid darkness.

'I'd never have guessed this was a public house. It's so cramped and there's no sign outside.'

'The Slaughterman's Arms wasn't always like this,' the landlady informed Kathleen. And if there hadn't been a small counter and half a dozen shabby men sitting on upturned barrels drinking ale, Kathleen would have thought she'd stepped into a witch's cavern, for the woman who presided over the gloomy establishment looked swarthy as a gypsy in the light of tallow candles. Her hair was black and seemed glued to her skull by some foul-smelling grease.

'When Gabriel were a lad we had next door too and a piano and singing and recitals.' The woman had a hard bony face that seemed to have been worn away by looking at the bitter truth of things. 'Gabriel were such a pretty young fellow and the punters used to throw him coins when he read out broadsheets and ballads or, with his angel yellow hair sticking out over his shoulders, told them bawdy tales about the royal family or the fornications of the gov'ment. He were a right little actor even then.'

'Give Kathleen her beer and lemonade, Jessie, and stop jawing about the past,' Gabriel interrupted. He turned to Kathleen and whispered in her ear, 'I'm going upstairs to change my rig. Wait here for me.'

When Gabriel left them Jessie leaned confidentially over the counter, dunking her elbows in beer slops. god-forsaken hole did he dig you out of?'

'I work with Gabriel,' Kathleen said warily, not knowing how much she should reveal. Jessie batted a knowing eye at the girl. 'Didn't know as my Gabriel ever *worked* for his living anymore.'

'*Your* Gabriel?' Kathleen couldn't imagine this gypsy crone claiming blood-kin with him.

'I call him mine because it were me saved him from the workhouse when his ma went mad. I took him in

89

and one of me reg'lars who were a patterer who'd been a clerk in better days taught him the way of reading and writing in return for free ale. So Gabriel earned his keep by entertaining the customers. He were the best eddicated pot-boy in the Dials he were. And I must say he ain't forgot old Jess who provided for him neither. Gives me a shilling or two every time he comes round.'

Kathleen swallowed the warm beer.

'I wondered where Gabriel came by his learning.'

'You've got a fine ladylike voice yourself,' Jess said admiringly, adding a drop more lemonade to Kathleen's ale as she saw the girl's mouth wince at the sour draught. 'I've always admired eddication. Where did you learn to talk smart?'

'Before I went into service I was looked after by the nuns at a convent orphanage in Tipperary,' Kathleen told the woman. 'They were mortal cruel to a girl but were great ones for a bit of learning and I had to recite the mass in Latin; though I never knew a word of what I was saying it gave me a liking for the taste of words on the tongue. Latin words tasted of burnt cinnamon,' she went on thoughtfully, 'and Irish, slippery as carageenan jelly, vanished down the throat in a trice and English, like bon-bons with sugar-dust coating a hard kernel, left a lingering sweetness in the mouth.'

Jessie regarded Kathleen, a troubled look in her eyes.

'God help you, girl, you sound just like Gabriel. I think he's met his match in you. You're two of a kind.'

She put a stiff claw of hand on Kathleen's shoulder.
'Listen to an old coot, girl. I won't put you wrong.
Look after yourself. D'you hear what I'm telling
you? Don't mind anyone else. Look after yourself,'
she said.

'Here under the gas lamp! Now what do you think?'
    Kathleen simply looked at him.
    'Well?' he asked, proud as a peacock.
    I really don't have any chance with you, she
thought.
    'You look just like one of the gentlemen who used
to come to musical evenings at the house where I was
in service. I'd watch them through a crack in the
drawing-room door and see how they'd turn sheets of
music for the missus as she played on the piano. It was
the only time she was happy, surrounded by gentlemen
admirers. Her husband was a devil to her so, miserable
as I was, I often thought I wouldn't change places with
her for all her finery.'
    Gabriel leaned against the lamp post. They were
alone in a bitterly cold street. 'Never mind all that
now. Do I look the part?' he asked her impatiently.
    'You look just like a proper gentleman,' she said.
    'I kept the change of clothes at Jess's today. Didn't
want them knowing too much at Bell's,' he said.
    'Where did you get them?' Kathleen asked, admiring
the sobriety, the thickness of the tailored cloth.
    'I earned them,' he replied quietly. 'They're my
ticket to fortune,' he went on as he linked Kathleen's
arm and urged her in the direction of the Haymarket.

Kathleen felt very cold in her thin dress and velvet mantle.

'Where are we going now?' she asked him.

'To dine of course.'

'Dine where?'

'The Venus Rooms in Haymarket.'

'But that's one of the best places where the toffs meet the finest whores I've heard.'

'You heard right then, Kathleen. Tonight I'm a toff and (with a deprecating look at her borrowed garments) you're one of the finest bawds in London.'

He was up to something. Despite his little bit of help to Jess from all Kathleen had heard Gabriel didn't spend money freely. He was tight with his purse-strings and loved money as much as Bell did.

But when they got to the brilliantly lit supper rooms the shadows of fear and doubt shrivelled in Kathleen's heart. Spellbound by the gasoliers that revolved in burning globes, she was reminded of the yellow glories worn by saints in religious paintings and she accepted Gabriel's proffered arm gladly.

'That's him. He's the one. I can tell by the way you've been watching him.' Kathleen put down her dessert spoon and drank a glass of the icy champagne.

'Yes. That's Henry Markham,' Gabriel said.

'I don't like it Gabriel. What if your coves get too violent? He might be really hurt.'

'No fear of that. They're practised in the deft

deceits of stage fights and duelling.' Gabriel topped up her glass.

'I wish you hadn't told me. I wish I believed it was for real,' she said.

'So you could imagine I'm a hero,' Gabriel laughed. 'What a quaint girl you are Kathleen.' His smile darkened and he went on. 'I've planned this night for months. It's my best chance. Now I'm wearing this rig he'll suppose I'm a real gentleman.'

'But now you've got all these good clothes couldn't you just present yourself to one of the better theatre managers?' Kathleen asked nervously. 'Why can't you do things straight and above board? Why complicate matters with plots and pretence?'

'There are too many down-at-heel clerks who've managed to hold off pawning their best coats and hats long enough to try their luck at the Adelphi or Drury Lane,' Gabriel told her impatiently. 'Many's the drivelling gent who has fancied the boards will save him from the workhouse and has tried to persuade theatre managers to give him a chance on account of how he can supply his own wardrobe. Being able to provide your own rig ain't enough nowadays. A fellow needs connections.'

'The Adelphi! Drury Lane!' Kathleen looked at him as if he were crazy. 'You aim too high Gabriel. Why don't you try theatres south of the river?'

'I did a bit of work at an East End theatre once,' Gabriel said gloomily. 'Weren't nothing but a bull pit, fighting and rioting night after night. I get enough of that in the gaffs and at least they're close to my other businesses so I can fit in a good night's work and get paid twice over. God knows I need it; a fellow would starve on what gaffs pay their actors. And if it weren't for my imagination I wouldn't be able to squeeze the madams of London for a few sovereigns either. What you call pretence is my living, girl.'

'Then why work the gaffs if they pay so bad?'

'I have to keep my hand in with acting so I'll be ready for the good chance when it comes.'

'You sound so confident, so sure you'll get what you want Gabriel.'

He shrugged his shoulders. 'I always imagined I'd end up a gentleman,' he said.

Henry Markham, first man of letters in England, with his heavily oiled locks of dark hair and florid mouth, was drinking steadily. Kathleen said he was a disappointing figure, a bantam of a man, slight if energetic. He sat with two heavily painted young women.

'How did you know he'd be here?'

'He's a regular in all the haunts of the Haymarket. I made the acquaintance of some of the whores he dabbles in and got them to tell me his habits.'

'Why did the whores confide in you?'

'I paid em.'

'And when do your rough merchants arrive?'

'They'll skulk outside until the great man emerges. Then they'll have him by the alley next to the entrance.'

'And that's when you follow him and beat them off.'

'So he supposes I'm his saviour. Then I give him my card like a proper gentleman,' Gabriel's voice shook slightly as if his own audacity unnerved him.

Kathleen looked puzzled.

'But won't your address, whichever one you use, give you away?'

'You mean Bell's Bordello, or Holton's Groceries, or the Slaughterman's Arms, Seven Dials ain't prepossessing enough residences?' Gabriel smiled grimly and produced a silver card case. 'Read that then.'

Kathleen opened the card case and took out a stiff white card with a gold border.

'But this says you live at an hotel in the Strand,' she said open-mouthed.

'And so I do. From next week,' he said.

And then it had all gone according to plan. The two bawds led Henry Markham like a lamb to the slaughter. Out the famous writer had strutted with women on either arm, his large cravat bow bobbing with expectation, his dapper feet tapping to the tune of the lively orchestra, out into the dangerous night air of the promiscuous West End.

Mattie was still up waiting for him. Her hair had been washed and hung sparsely over her shoulders. She wore a new soft wool shawl over a cambric nightgown. Her feet were bare and she toasted them before a dying fire.

That plaintive voice. He shivered as it cut his ears.

'So late, so very late again Gabriel. Why must you

95

leave me alone at night, why, why when we've only three nights a week together?'

'Don't start nagging me Mattie. I've had a hard night.'

Mattie's pasty complexion turned puce.

'Don't tell me you've been acting in plays until four in the morning!' she spluttered. 'I'm not some greenhorn girl you may gull so easily.'

'I've told you before. I must have a little pleasure after a performance, a drink, a carouse if you like. I can't just come home and sleep.'

Mattie drew her feet up on the chair and tucked them under her nightgown.

'You're not drunk. You're never drunk. And you'd be intoxicated if you'd been drinking into the small hours. You've been with some woman,' she said. And after I've bought you such lovely clothes that you look so dashing in, she wanted to say but thought better of it and buried her face in her hands, hoping tears worked better than words with him.

'A light supper that's all,' he explained. 'A group of us players sit and chat about the night's show. You wouldn't deny me a little pleasure, companionship, would you Mattie?' He knelt down by her chair and lifted her face up to him kissing away the mutinous tears.

A heaving sob like a child and she wailed, 'But I want the pleasure of your company, Gabriel.'

'And you shall have it in a little while.' He paused and stared into the dim fire. 'A little while longer.'

'But why not now my dearest?'

She put her arms round his neck but he eased her back into the chair. He stood up and limped over to the window, parting the thick lace and staring down the empty street.

'Perhaps I'd better go now,' he said.

A coal fell from the fire. She jumped out of her chair and ran over to him.

'No, don't say that. You must come to bed now Gabriel.'

'It's hopeless Mattie. You see I made some enquiries tonight.' His eyes narrowed and he wouldn't look into her distraught face.

'Enquiries. What enquiries?'

'I had an interview with a theatrical agent,' he lied.

'And?'

'Well he advised me that to stand a strong chance of a leading position in a good theatre I need to supply an extensive wardrobe, not one suit of clothes merely. And then . . .'

'Yes?'

'There's the question of appearances in general.'

'Appearances?'

'Yes, I must not only look the part of a gentleman. I must act it too. Or they'll suppose I'm a sham.'

'You have beautiful manners. No one would suppose . . .' she began.

'Yes. Yes,' he interrupted her. 'It's not merely a matter of etiquette. It's things like a good address and a horse and carriage.'

Mattie peered up at him, such a tall man despite his limp, she only reached his chest.

'Perhaps he was hinting at something else, Gabriel?'

'Something else. Whatever do you mean?' His voice hardened. He stared at her, his eyes narrowing.

Mattie looked down at his bad foot.

'Nothing. I meant nothing, Gabriel.'

. . . And Markham had fallen like a ripe plum after all. The most famous playwright in England thought himself beholden to Gabriel . . .

He almost laughed as he struck out into Mattie like a prospector in a gold mine. She had removed her nightgown despite the cold, she was so desperate to hold on to him, to clutch him close to her tight little body. Panting, 'Don't leave, don't ever leave me Gabriel, you won't, you must promise!' the fear of being abandoned almost driving her into a frenzy of passion.

'I won't leave you Mattie,' he heaved.

'I love love youuuu,' she sighed.

'How much?' he pushed.

'This much,' she gaped.

. . . Dropping like full fruit. Like a damson plum . . .

Gabriel almost shouted with relief as Mattie's methodical spasms began to count

One for a horse

Two for a carriage

Three for a good address

And four for . . .

'Marriage,' Mattie hissed as though her life expired.

'Yes,' Gabriel murmured, 'but an engagement first. A respectably long engagement. Then we'll be married.'

↶ EIGHT ↷

Gabriel lay awake a long time before it grew light. A few birds called brisk sharp songs. A cart trundled along the rutted road. Mattie breathed heavily in her sleep, dreaming of bridal veils and the spiced fruit cake she'd bake for their wedding breakfast. His throat was dry with intoxication, not drink; it was as if his imagination had thrown its paints on the canvas of reality, his dreams had materialised and he was delirious on too easy success. A tight spasm of pleasure in his guts at how easily the writer had fallen. Recalling Markham's stunned expression when he had drawn his hand from his face and seen blood on it, Gabriel almost laughed at his own impudence. Lunging at the attackers, striking a well-timed fist and with a theatrical flourish he had executed a spin that closed the rogues' hard heads together like nutcrackers.

At Gabriel's signal the bawds had taken voluptu-ous flight and it was but another moment's work to pursue the fluttering petticoats in the name of chivalry, allowing the villains time to escape. He could then restore Markham to the honeyed balm of the women's arms and produce the victim's wallet with a discreet gesture.

On the whole as fine a drama as he'd performed. And the supporting players were splendid foils to his virtuosity. From nowhere he'd summoned a carriage, helping Markham and his women into the cocoon of expensive leather upholstery. The bawds, whispering shivery phrases of comfort to the shocked writer, had winked at Gabriel.

A triumph! For hadn't Henry Markham in the light of a lucifer match struck by Gabriel accepted his card and read aloud, 'Gabriel Feaver, Esquire, Green's Hotel, Strand.' And hadn't he said, with the maudlin sincerity of a man half in his cups, offering his card in return, 'I'm forever in your debt, sir.'

Mattie stirred. Gabriel stayed very still hoping she wouldn't waken and expect him to make love to her. He was weary of loveless lovemaking. He was sick of all women except the one he'd never met but often imagined. The endless permutations of love exercised his ingenuity. With Mattie, just as with bawds, any ecstasy was purely functional. He was used to acting a state of amorous excitement and could turn on hot passion as he chose. Whenever she began looking at him with a face unscrupulous as her weighing scales he assuaged her suspicions with an ardent performance, though he was careful not to practise the repertoire of whorehouses at Holton's Groceries. Mattie must think of him as the prospective gentleman he surely was, not a denizen of low life. This despite the fact that he knew how to make her lose grip on her own sense of decency — hadn't she herself said that her husband would turn in his grave if he knew about the sport that went on in his old bed. A cold man from what Mattie had told Gabriel. Much older than her and after seven years' marriage there had been no issue. So if Gabriel's plans had failed and there had been no possibility of advancement, he would still have come in for old Holton's shop and bank account, lock, stock and barrel. If his plans had failed! Already that was a hypothetical past. He was on course to success. He was going far on the gratitude of Markham.

Mattie's arm fell across his face and struck a sharp blow on his nose. He shifted her arm back across her breast. A sour early morning smell spilled from her mouth. He looked at her distastefully. Her unattractiveness made deception oddly harder. Her money lay as heavily in his pockets as her food loaded his belly. Much as he loved money he needed to spend Mattie's gold quickly to lighten the burden of guilt. Out of sight, out of mind. Dog eat dog. The devil helps those who help themselves. If he were a rich man he could afford a conscience. But conscience would make a pauper of him. And would he ever have enough gold in his purse to buy honour, the hallmark of the true gentleman? But things *are* so when they *seem* so he argued with himself. Just as in a play. Looking the part was the first step to breathing life into the role. All actors knew that. If people looked at him and saw a gentleman then a gentleman he was. And yet! . . . All this simulation made a puppet out of a man. He felt sometimes as though he was made out of straw: dry, chafing straw, coarse strands pricking the throat, needles in his throat choking him, mouth stuffed with straw, gagging on the thrusting stems of soiled straw that had been torn from a mattress, straw smelling like rotten fish . . . best not to think of that! He gagged even as he remembered . . .

His loins dry as straw but his heart pumped pure gold as he thought: Markham, Markam, Markham . . . And then he slept again.

'I told her. Straight out I said, "You must think we're soft in the head. We put up wiv starvation 'cause we understand it's necessary owing to what you might call the otherworldly nature of our job." But why should we put up wiv starvation wages too when she's raking in a fortune? And only Sunday night off, to get a bit of relief and escape from pleasuring dirty pigs, wiv our drops of satin and laudanum or sucking on our opium pipes.' Missy thrust her arms akimbo on her narrow hips. Her green eyes were bilious with indignation, breasts heaving beneath a tight, boned bodice. She went on.

'I ain't afraid to speak me mind so she reckons I don't know me place. I ain't afraid like some I could mention,' her eyes skimming the circle of her seated confidantes, 'to speak up for me rights, for the money that's due to me . . .'

'Due to all of us,' interrupted Old Corruption, clacking her ringlets righteously.

'And I told her how I know she's making a killing out of our performances. We're worth double what she pays us.'

'But we ave more freedom than most whores in bawdy ouses,' a whore with a swathe of ruby curls gurgled from a horsehair sofa where she lay in a state of semi-undress, cradling her gin bottle.

Missy made a rude gesture with her fingers, almost knocking over an oil lamp.

'All the freedom you want, Susannah Fossit, is the freedom to drown yourself in a bottle, pickle yourself like an onion, souse yerself like a, like a . . .'

'Herring,' offered Kathleen.

'Erring,' Missy agreed. She pointed a finger accusingly at the company of women. 'All of you got to support me in this. If you don't you'll all be the losers. Don't say I aven't warned you. If you show you're afraid to speak up in case your feet skitter down these whorehouse stairs on to the cold streets faster than you can slip catgut on a cove's doodle, then she'll know she can use you up until she's no further use for you and you'll face the workhouse in your old age if you have no slavings.'

'Savings,' Corrie corrected her.

'What I say is what I mean, Corrie. She expects us to work hard for hardly no payment, just like, just like a . . .'

'Husband,' Kathleen said softly. 'Perhaps the best thing would be to ask Gabriel to appeal to Bell for us? Well?' she asked.

A heavy silence thrust through the room. Whores in unbuttoned bodices, whores in scarlet satin stays, whores in drink-stained chemises and lace-edged drawers, whores in full evening dress; gowns with low décolletage and narrow arms and horsehair-padded petticoats. The women spluttered over their drink, choked on their doses of laudanum, throttled on their opium smoke, and stared in astonishment at Kathleen.

A bloated whore, who was kept on board to replicate the swollen corpses of drowned suicides, put a dropsical hand on Kathleen's arm.

'Best not ask him anything of the sort, dearie.'

'Why not?' Kathleen asked. Missy guffawed. She held up two crossed fingers.

'Mr Feaver and his madam are like that. You may be sure he won't annoy Bell by taking our part in anything.'

'And you may be sure, Missy, your plans to confront her won't come to anything. In all the years I've been here I've seen the toughest of bawds outmatched by that old buzzard. No one but Gabriel Feaver's been able to worm money out her.'

'And that's only because there's something she'd like to worm out of *him*,' Tess laughed coarsely.

'Well I dunno that I want to hexactly confront Bell. It'd cause a rum do and that's for sure,' Susannah said.

106

'A rum do,' agreed Old Corruption, 'but I say even if we don't get much money at least Bell lets us work when the first bloom of youth has gone which is more than they do in other establishments.'

'I still think approaching Bell through Gabriel might be our best chance of increasing wages, Missy,' Kathleen said.

Missy hawked up some phlegm from her throat and spat into the fireplace.

'Just 'cause you think Gabriel takes a shine to you, don't think you can charm him into being on our side. Mr Feaver won't put himself out for women who can't advance his ambition.'

But I will ask Gabriel about it, Kathleen thought, hoping that she wouldn't stay in the bawdy house much longer herself. Bell would be sure to ask her to become a full participant in the performances any day now. She simply must press Gabriel about finding her work in gaffs. But even if she could make a quick escape the thought that some of the other whores who had become her good friends might face a future of penury troubled Kathleen at heart. Even the prickly Missy, with her tantrums and splintery voice always raising objections to everything and everyone, had found a place in her affections, lending her clothes and scent, always generous with her own portions of gin or laudanum if another had run short. During these weeks the whores had become Kathleen's family and she was curious to discover whether Gabriel, who'd known some of the girls for years, had any concern for them.

Jack's Coffee House, the Strand, Kathleen memorised.
She was sure she wouldn't disgrace him in this rig-out.
What a surprise it had been to see the gown laid out
on the horsehair sofa waiting for her; after a tiring
session being possessed by the voices of a choir of fallen
angels Kathleen had been looking forward to cold gin
on her parched throat. The other whores were at work
whoring and Gabriel had left immediately after the
séance part of the session. Kathleen was alone. A note
was pinned to the bodice of the sweet blue silk. She read:

> *For Kathleen who brought me luck, I hope this
> gown wins you good fortune. Meet me tomorrow
> luncheon at Jack's Coffee House in the Strand.
> Don't fail me!*
> *Gabriel.*

Blue silk, blue as her eyes. The shirred sleeves gripped
her shoulders as masterfully as any dream lover: bone
insertions to the bodice guarding her heart that felt as
though it would burst with anticipation. When she
moved across the creaking floors the seductive pull
of the swaying skirts was as irresistible as being
drawn between voluptuous sheets. A chaste rim of
lace prickled the shivering skin on her throat. And
for the first time Kathleen shut her eyes and imagined
the prospect of being beautiful.

With Susannah's new black cloak and another
whore's black satin bonnet she might even be a
lady. Smug glossy ringlets that had been tortured
into submission with hot irons spilled to her shoulders

108

and her feet looked respectable crammed into Missy's dainty elastic-sided boots.

Kathleen minced along the Strand.

The first thing Gabriel said when he saw her was: 'No gloves! The whole effect is spoiled if the accessories aren't right you know.' They were hidden from view in an oaken booth. Cigar smoke choked the air. A low murmur of discreet voices.

'How can I ever thank you for the dress,' Kathleen said. Gabriel shrugged.

'Not wholly my doing you know. Bell was going to order you a black merino. She provides all her girls with a decent wardrobe. It makes a favourable impression with the punters. I simply made a contribution so something better could be afforded.'

'Why?' Kathleen asked him. There was a pause as the waiter attended them. Gabriel ordered coffee, ham, bread and cakes. 'And how could you afford it?' she pressed him.

He grinned.

'I had a windfall from an admirer,' he said. 'And the gown isn't spandy new, you know! Though it's had little wear as you can see.' He leaned towards her. 'I really believe you brought me luck the other night when I snared Markham. You're my lucky mascot Kathleen.'

'The gown will come in useful when I apply for acting work,' Kathleen said. 'Have you heard of anything I might try for?'

'Well there is something I had in mind which involves acting of sorts. If we can pull it off it'll mean a lot more money than you could make in the gaffs.'

'We?'

'I've a fancy our fortunes are linked, Kathleen. We are a match of a sort having a way with words and play-acting. You've the voice and I have the imagination to construct the most fantastical scripts.' Kathleen looked puzzled. He went on. 'The kind of money I plan to earn can't be made on the stage even if I get to be a leading man. Anyway I always like to have a few sidelines. You can never be sure when one thing or another will let you down.'

The cakes and coffee arrived and Kathleen fell to them ravenously. Pink icing sweetening her tongue, hot coffee warming her stomach, she feasted greedily.

Gabriel ate not at all, merely drinking the coffee. When she had finished her third cake, Kathleen said: 'But I thought you had it in mind to earn your fortune through contracting a splendid marriage.'

Gabriel laughed.

'All in good time,' he said. 'A fellow must first put himself in the way of getting a place in respectable society. Rich widows or young heiresses can't be found in the vicinity of Seven Dials or Haymarket whorehouses.' He leaned over the table and spoke in a low voice. 'What I plan is for us to devise a most respectable form of chicanery. I intend we should astonish London society with your talents.'

'Talents?' she queried suspiciously.

'As a medium, a vessel for communication with spirit voices. Together we could conduct séances of uncanny accomplishment, Kathleen.'

Ignoring her look of surprise he went on. 'As your manager and protector I will of course share in your fame and though we shan't be so vulgar as to charge for our sessions I shall enlist conscriptions from eager patrons. And that's where Markham comes in. He's known to have an enthusiasm for the super-natural . . .'

'But I thought you were going to cultivate his acquaintance in the hopes of him putting in a word for you with the management at Drury Lane?' Kathleen interrupted.

'And so he will,' Gabriel grinned triumphantly, 'when I've hooked him on the bait of Arabella Lockhart.'

'Arabella Lockhart! Who on earth is she?'

'Who is she? Why, only Henry Markham's own true dead love, a sweet virgin who died of a consumption twelve months since, Kathleen.'

Gabriel helped her on with the cloak and the courtesy made her heart leap with reckless hope. An icy wind cut down the Strand. Kathleen drew Susannah's cloak around her tightly. They walked through the throng of clerks, street hawkers and demi-monde. All London seemed to be pursuing its business along the crowded thoroughfare. Waiting for an inter-ruption in the flow of traffic to cross over the Strand they loitered at the corner of Villiers Street. A clutch of whores were busy selling themselves to a party of swells. Kathleen was watching the transaction with interest when she felt a pull on her arm.

'Excuse me Miss, I want a word with your friend.'

Kathleen was about to jest that her companion was already suited thank you but thought better of it when she saw at once Gabriel knew the woman.

'How are you Gabriel?' the woman said.

'Rosie is it?' Gabriel flushed and looked around to check if a minder was trailing the girl. Sure enough a grim-looking woman and a pox-scarred ruffian were staring at her just a few feet away at the entrance to an alley.

'Why did you do this to me?'

Gabriel, ignoring the question, said affably:

'I'm delighted to see you look so prosperous my dear. What shade of rouge is that? I must say it suits your complexion and that crimson dress is really splendid. It quite shows off your form.'

'I don't care about dresses and paints. I only want my freedom back,' Rosie said. 'Why did you do it Gabriel?'

'Why? Why, for five guineas,' he said smiling narrowly.

'You sold me for five guineas?'

'Hardly sold,' he protested, turning away so Kathleen couldn't see his expression. Aware of the minders still watching them, he casually put his arm round Rosie's waist. 'You know, I went to a great deal of trouble to see you set up in one of the better establishments where they would give you nice clothes and introduce you to gentlemen,' he said, sounding astonished at her discontent. 'Why, with your looks you could probably persuade one of the punters to set you up in style. St John's Wood, I shouldn't wonder, if you were clever and used your beauty to get some cove to pay twenty pounds to release you.'

Rosie looked nervously in the direction of the alley.

'To be sold into another form of slavery with just one gaoler instead of a regiment?'

Gabriel spoke to her more firmly. 'You may think you had liberty before but I assure you poverty is merely another kind of cage, as you'd surely have discovered, and as Sairy doubtless knows whenever she raises her head from a gin bottle.'

At the mention of her cousin's name Rosie's eyes reddened with tears.

'My poor cousin Sairy won't know what's become of me. Every day I look up and down the Strand hoping she'll find me and see some way to getting me home again. My poor little Sairy.'

'Yes, *poor* little Sairy,' Gabriel emphasised. 'Sairy would only think you've done well for yourself to be tricked out in silk dresses.' Then, noting the fierce scrutiny of the ruffian who trailed Rosie, he added, 'Look I'll have a word with your madam and see if she can't find her way to showing your beauty to its best advantage at one of the more splendid nighthouses she has in the Haymarket,' he promised. 'And if you're seen to be content in such a berth you'll be given more freedom.'

But Rosie wasn't persuaded by his assurances. Turning to Kathleen, as Gabriel caught hold of his companion's arm and tried to urge her across the road, she said, 'You've got a kind face Miss. I hope he serves you better. Don't trust him, don't trust the devil . . .' She fell silent suddenly as the pox-marked ruffian, seeing how things were turning out, scampered over to snatch back his victim.

I can't ask him to intercede with Bell, now, Kathleen thought. I know the answer. He won't help Missy. He won't help any of us if there's no profit for him in it. Kathleen's heart was heavy with longing and dread. It tugged her heartstrings to see him limp, it broke her heart to see his eyes clear as a June sky when he looked at her and it had made her heart ache to hear his voice slide smooth as a stream over pebbles, saying 'five guineas'.

ᴄ NINE ᴄ

Bell poured Gabriel a glass of flat champagne and told him to sit down and give his leg a rest. He sat sullenly on the leather chair next to her desk where she was counting sovereigns.

Gabriel looked out of the window at a lopped tree that was coated with soot. It waved black stumps at him.

'I won't take less than seven guineas for the new scripts,' he said.

'Seven!' she widened her rheumy eyes in astonishment. 'Do you want to beggar me, Gabriel?'

'I don't think you'll end up in the workhouse yet a while,' Gabriel said. 'And you'll still see a huge profit out of the business,' he added.

'You forget my expenses, Gabriel. The girls, running

this place, costumes, props and everything.'

'You and I know you're raking in a fortune, Bell. Don't waste my time. I've got the skills you need. Without me you couldn't manage the job. It's me who has the wit to devise your little charades. I want seven guineas this time and make no mistake.'

Bell sighed.

'Very well, but you'd better come up with some new . . . excitements. We don't want to start losing custom.' Gabriel replied, 'Don't I always,' and when the madam nodded agreement, they clinked their glasses together on striking the bargain.

'Well?' Bell quizzed him when they had both fin- ished drinking and Gabriel still sat in his chair looking thoughtful. 'A penny for your thoughts, Gabriel!'

'I need some time off. A particularly intriguing job has come my way,' he said. 'But you've no cause to worry. I'll fit in the bit of writing we just spoke of.'

Bell's mouth twitched. She fiddled with her cot- ton mittens.

'I hope you're not about to leave us entirely, Gabriel.'

He stood up and leaned over her desk.

'Don't fret yourself, I know you couldn't run this place on the same terms without me. But I expect to take a less active part in your business in the not so distant future.' Bell bit her lip.

'Is this a ruse for more tin? Is it more of my takings you're after?'

Gabriel ran a light finger over her sunken mouth.

'I'll look about for a lively lad we can train up to

work with the girls,' he said. 'I'm getting too old for these frolics, you know, and, besides, I mean to get on in life. I don't want the old ways dragging me down, Bell. I want to be established before I'm thirty so I need to spread my business interests,' he went on, 'and that means assuming a purely backstage role here. And . . .' he stabbed the madam with a sharp glance. 'I'm worth half of everything you make you know,' he added.

Bell trembled.

'Do you want to beggar me?' she said, her voice rising to a squeak.

'No I don't. I feel no malice toward you and that's why I won't leave you in the lurch, but things have to change. I want a third share in the profits from now on,' he said, 'or I take my imagination elsewhere,' he threatened her.

Bell looked at him a long time like a frightened rabbit.

'Wherever should we be without your imagination, Gabriel?'

Kathleen pulled rose silk stockings over her knees and fastened them with pink ribboned garters. She admired them in the piece of mirror she'd taken down from the window sill and placed over the mantel but the boiled potato whiteness of her skin where her thighs barely swelled over the stocking tops displeased her. A life of starvation had denied any pearly translucence to her alabaster flesh. She stretched the hose further up her thighs until they disappeared under her cambric drawers. Rose satin stays to match the stockings laced

117

her so tight that her waist was a mere fourteen inches and she looked as though an amorous grasp would snap her in half.

Kathleen tottered in boots two sizes too small. Her arms were gripped in the vice of excruciatingly narrow sleeves designed to discourage exertion but it gave her satisfaction great as her discomfort to know she looked like a lady. It had taken three pots of grease to restrain her hair and the horsehair petticoat pricked her. When she walked her breath came in short feathery gasps that were charming signals of dependence. She crammed her long fingers into kid leather gloves apparently designed for a five-year-old. Her fingers buckled and she couldn't pick up her bonnet so she had to remove them to complete dressing. Now surely Gabriel couldn't fault her!

But what if she failed him?

Kathleen saw Gabriel's grey eyes narrow to slits behind a mask of darkness.

She tried to draw a deep breath but the stay laces squeezed her rib-cage. No rouge. No carmine. She widened her eyes with a stare of innocence. She put on the exquisite Indian shawl Gabriel had apparently borrowed from someone, she didn't ask from whom, and the poke bonnet that shadowed her blushes. A little eau de Cologne on her neck and wrist pulses. A beadwork bag she had to wield carefully as half the bugles were missing. She must persuade Henry Markham, somehow she must convince him she was clairvoyant, an ethereal creature, a passive vessel for pure souls, a meek lamb of sacrifice who could be possessed by spectres. She must submit to Gabriel's will and become the blessed temple, the living shrine to Arabella Lockhart.

Gabriel had told her not to breathe a word to anyone about their plans. For the moment she would only need to disappear from the brothel in the afternoons and when they saw her done up so fine the other whores would assume she was carrying on a little private whoring with a proper gentleman. This Saturday afternoon, if she pleased Gabriel, maybe he'd arrange for her to be out of Bell's within no time, before her turn to . . . Kathleen picked up a little ivory fan, put on the gloves again and tiptoed down the stairs past shut bedroom doors, down into the bare hall.

Gabriel was waiting for her at the set of rooms in Bedford Street. A respectable house run by an ex-whore Gabriel knew from years ago. There was fine lace draped across the windows; a black painted door, spiky railings and whitened steps. Kathleen raised the heavy brass knocker and rapped. A woman admitted her discreetly and led her up to the first floor where Gabriel lounged on a chaise longue.

'You look splendid Kathleen,' he said agreeably. He helped her with the shawl and bonnet. When she smoothed out her blue silk skirt with nervous movements, he actually kissed her lightly on the forehead and said, 'None would suspect you were a whore you look such a delicate creature,' so she blushed and trembled and thought she would walk through the gates of hell itself for him.

'When will Markham arrive?' she asked Gabriel as he poured Madeira from a decanter into two glasses.

'Drink this, slowly mind, it ain't to be swigged like gin,' he said. 'I expect our guest shortly after two . . . Have you learned the script I gave you?' She nodded and looked out through the windows.

'It'll make it harder to act up with all this daylight,' she said.

'We don't want it to look like a bordello when Markham gets here but before we begin the séance I'll draw the blinds,' he promised her.

'Does Markham suspect . . . ?' Kathleen began to ask, the Madeira warming her spirits.

'That his dead love is winging her way even now towards Bedford Street to commune with him?' Gabriel put down his glass. 'He suspects nothing. When I played cards with him last night I acted dumb about matters to do with Miss Arabella Lockhart. I merely informed him about a pretty young woman who'd entertained the best society in Dublin on her pure intercourse with the shades of those who had departed to a higher form of existence.' He bent forward and stroked Kathleen's cheek. 'A modest lady whose growing fame led her to flee her adoring followers and seek peace and anon-ymity in London, a peace she means to retain by holding only the most discreet, the most private audiences with a cherished few. And Markham understands that such discretion is to be extended even to your name and he and all the others who'll soon flock to your salon will know you only as Celestine,' he murmured, 'celestial Celestine who can revive the dead for them.'

Kathleen's stomach swooped as Markham was shown in by the landlady who stayed to make up the circle. In the daylight she could see how the candle Markham burned at both ends flared too fiercely, devouring his volatile energies. His complexion flushed and paled in rapid succession, his eye glittered and filmed with a too ready emotion and his looks went everywhere.

When Gabriel made the introductions Kathleen averted her gaze modestly but to her surprise Markham raised her chin with a sudden intimacy, and remarked on the otherworldly nature of her expression. A slight man. Kathleen was astonished how his febrile personality seemed to set the room ablaze with agitation. The very air seemed unsettled and the lace panels at the windows stirred flirtatiously as a woman's petticoats.

'Feaver tells me you have quite a following in Ireland, Celestine,' Markham said informally, clasping her hand with a grasp tight as strung nerves. When he bent over her she smelled a heavy sweet fragrance of musk and Havana smoke and oleaginous Macassar. 'You musn't worry you know. We shan't allow any rabble to harass you here. Your talents must be preserved in amber.' He flashed her a loose smile with a mouth that had kissed too many women. His dark ringlets brushed her shoulder and a thrill of revulsion shivered down her spine so she was momentarily distracted, forgetting to begin her peroration. Gabriel coughed deliberately to rouse her.

'We must all link hands in a circle,' he said,

gathering the hard fingers of the landlady within his own. Kathleen stared at Gabriel.

'There's too much light,' she said. ''Twill make the spirits nervous.' Gabriel drew the blinds, then they all joined hands again in the semi-gloom, seated together around a small card table. Markham's hand was light and cool in Kathleen's; she felt his vapid pulse thrum her fingers. His rich scent helped ease her into dreamy languor. She began to chant a little verse about being brushed by the wings of angels. Her listeners bent their heads as in solemn veneration.

'. . . Spilling grace into my soul,
On thrilling wings of holy rapture . . .'

Her voice very low now, barely audible, like the murmur of summer flies in a shuttered room. Her words trailed, faded into whispers then silence and she might almost have slept for her eyes closed and her breathing grew faint, ever fainter . . .

The atmosphere became close and oppressive as if thunder clouds gathered around the ornately carved acanthus leaves on the ceiling.

Gabriel said, 'Celestine you must instruct the spirits to communicate with us by rapping the table.' Kathleen's throat gurgled.

'What's she saying?' the landlady asked in a loud voice, enthralled as Kathleen's head flung back and her throbbing white throat was exposed, her slender white neck thickening suddenly. Gabriel hushed the woman.

122

'We mustn't frighten the spirits away. Quietly, quietly,' he urged.

'Ask her something,' Markham said, the ghost of a smile pouting his disturbingly red mouth.

'Does anyone wish to address us?' Gabriel spoke looking directly at the almost comatose Kathleen. 'Rap once for yes, twice for a negation,' he instructed the unseen listeners. A moment's hesitation . . . then a loud ghastly rap that echoed around the drawing-room.

'Have you come to us from the great beyond?' the landlady asked, thin nasal voice as matter-of-fact as if she were ordering a haunch of mutton. A brief light rap responded positively to her question.

'A female spirit?' Gabriel asked and was answered in the affirmative.

'Good or evil?' queried Markham who sat back in his chair casually crossing his legs, slackening his grip on Kathleen's hand.

'It can only answer a yes or a no sir,' the landlady reminded him. But she had barely finished speaking when the table rose huffily as if the spirit were greatly offended by the question. It hovered for a moment before jerking back on to terra firma and Markham, much amused, said: 'That's a fine trick ain't it?'

Gabriel frowned at him.

'I think perhaps levity will disrupt the proceedings.' He stared at the sprawling figure of the medium. 'Can you speak to us through Celestine?' he asked the spectral interlocutor. There was a long pause and Gabriel repeated his question; still another pause before Kathleen began to rotate her head very slowly and a light girlish treble lisped from her throat: 'Who calls me? Who is it will not let me sleep? I've crossed eternity to come to you, who is it dares not let me slumber?'

Gabriel silenced the landlady, who made as if to speak, by raising his finger.

'A friend who wishes you to rest in peace ever after,' he responded. The table shook violently.

'I cannot rest in peace now you've called me,' the spirit wailed.

Then the spirit voice set up a piteous weeping in Kathleen's throat and Gabriel allowed the being a few moments to spend its grief before again probing.

'What is your name?'

'There are no names nor giving of names where I come from,' the spirit's sobs died to a whimper.

'Why do you weep, poor spirit?' the landlady asked it.

A chilling rasp of breath, then the spirit said in a small voice, 'Because I am locked out from the heart of love. Faithless love,' the spirit moaned.

'From God's love?' Gabriel helped her.

'From a man's perfidious affection,' the spirit retorted tearfully. 'Locked out. He has locked his heart against my memory. Only twelve months and I am forgotten by his philandering heart.'

'Whose heart?' Gabriel pressed.

'Locked out, the locked heart, locked heart, Lockhart . . .' the spirit voice dissolved to a shiver of air that swept round the table, a cold breath that must have chilled Markham's heart for he grew suddenly ashen and his lips seemed to shrink and pale as though the lifeblood drained from him. He stiffened in his chair, frozen with shock, clenching Kathleen's hand painfully.

'Arabella?' he whispered.

Then the spirit sighed heavily, 'Hhhhhhhheeen-ryyyyyy!'

'Oh God it can't . . . you cannot . . . the devil confound it . . . Arabella!' Markham jumped up from his seat, the coiled tension Kathleen had sensed earlier beneath the man's oily composure unleashed like the crack of a whip. Violently overturning his chair, almost upsetting the table, he grabbed the listless figure of the medium.

The writer, perhaps expecting merely a little harmless diversion, appeared unprepared for this rout of uncanny emotion.

The spirit's sigh guttered.

Markham's flaccid lips were coated with spittle as the words poured in a torrent from his mouth: 'Bella, my love, my lover, don't torment me. How could I forget you? I swear the others mean nothing, nothing. My love, come back to me . . .' Then Markham covered the pliant medium's throat with wet kisses, scratching her face in his frenzy, kneading her breast, pinching her waist with his urgency, almost suffocating the woman trying to suck the spirit of his beloved from her promiscuous throat.

'For God's sake leave her be, Markham,' Gabriel shouted, a satisfied glint in his eye as he dragged the writer away from Kathleen and told him to compose himself and didn't he realise it was dangerous to tamper with the spirits in such a crazy, a carnal way and did he want to *trap* the poor soul in the manner of earthbound spirits who wander in a desolate limbo for time out of reckoning?

'This is devil's work, sir,' the landlady added reprovingly, putting her arm around Markham and sitting him down on the chaise longue and pouring out brandy for him.

Kathleen, dazed, slumped over the table: 'I feel sick, I want to be ill,' she complained. 'I feel as if I shall be sick,' and then she started to retch violently.

Markham dashed aside the landlady's ministrations and brought a draught of the brandy over to the medium and when she had drunk the entire glass he knelt at her feet, trembling, pressing her hand that shook with a palsy matching his own.

'I feel as if skeins of ether are unreeling from my skin,' Kathleen said, pawing her face, her arms. 'The spirit stitched herself into my flesh and now her departure unravels me. Leave me be, sir. Your touch is like hot coals. My flesh is raw,' she groaned.

'Markham, get up man! Whatever demons pursue you are gone now.' Gabriel strode over to the windows and lifted the blinds so shrewd light could shrivel the shadows.

'Forgive me, ma'am,' Markham began to recover his composure though his face was livid, 'but that was no demon, only the purest soul that ever took human form, whose sweetness I thought never to encounter on earth again.' His voice broke with a sob. Kathleen stroked his gleaming ringlets softly. 'I'm grieved if her eternal soul discomfited you ma'am,' he said. 'I would not have you suffer pain on account of my follies.'

'There is often such pain,' Kathleen explained kindly, 'but I suffer it gladly to join again those hearts whom death has sundered.' She assumed a pious expression.

'You're a saint ma'am. A saint, dear, kind Celestine.' Markham bent and kissed the hem of her petticoat.

'But how can I ask you to endure such torments again?' He threw her a look of blatant appeal.

Kathleen smiled at him with a smile she remembered from a painted statue of the madonna.

'Next time it will be easier,' she promised him. 'If you can persuade her that she is not forgotten, her possession will be a joyous experience.'

'Joy, oh joy,' Markham mumbled. 'Already my sweet Bella's perfume anoints your body. I can scent her even here.' As he buried his head in Kathleen's breast and his breath came hot and fast, she pulled away carefully.

'I must conserve my strength until the next session, sir.'

'Saint Celestine, I could swear your breasts swelled with bountiful grace when Arabella Lockhart entered you,' Gabriel laughed triumphantly. 'A miraculous visitation! Together we're invincible Kathleen.' He snatched her by the waist and executed a brief polka around the drawing-room but she stumbled over his languorous foot and they halted, suddenly thrust together. Gabriel disengaged himself then leaned against the mantel and fingered in his waistcoat pocket for a sovereign.

'A little something to be going on with,' he rewarded her.

Kathleen's dark ringlets had begun to fray. Her hair tumbled over her narrow shoulders. She stood very straight, very still, looking up at him.

'I don't want your money,' she told him.

'You don't want payment?' Gabriel flashed her a piratical grin. 'Then what do you want, me lover?'

Kathleen held out her hand. She looked at the chaise longue and said the blinds must be drawn again.

Holding out her hand saying:

'I want you to love me, Gabriel. I want you to love me without an audience.'

↶ TEN ↷

'More money!' Mattie's face was green with apprehension. Where had he been all week? Why hadn't he turned up the two nights she'd expected him? She'd had half a mind to make her way over to that hotel her money paid for and discover whether some floozie had detained him.

Gabriel's face was stiff with resentment.

'You shouldn't have agreed to the project at all if you were going to be half-hearted.'

'Half-hearted!' Mattie spluttered. 'I don't call three hundred pounds half measures on any count. And I don't see any sign of a horse and carriage yet,' she frothed, peering out of the window.

'Should you like me to draw up accounts for you? It can be arranged,' he said grandly. 'The hotel is devilish expensive and of course entertaining gentlemen who may help my career has proved a heavy drain on my purse.'

'Was it entertaining gentlemen kept you from my bed twice this week?' Mattie said with sarcasm. Gabriel bit his lip with annoyance. It was all he could do not to box the woman's ears.

'The servant will overhear you,' he said sternly.

'No she won't. There's none here to spy on us,' she said looking vexed. He noticed then there was a ruffled, disordered air about her.

'Are you unwell?' he asked.

She threw him a look of irritation.

'It never rains but it pours,' she said, sinking down suddenly on her small sofa. A strand of hair fell greasily over her face. Her black silk was stained. Mattie looked up at him, her eyes puffed with self-pity. 'A woman on her own is taken advantage of by everyone,' she sulked.

Stiffer than ever now he said coldly: 'If you believe I'm bilking you let's finish the thing at once. I can relieve you of your promise to marry me.' He bent down to pick up his beaver hat. 'I will of course return what is owing to you as soon as I can make other arrangements.'

But as he made as if to limp away, she threw her net of woe over him, sobbing: 'Don't desert me! I can't bear it, you all fail me.'

'Fail you!' Gabriel watched her shoulders heave as a glut of tears streamed down her face. Mattie's fury melted into grief.

'I'm sorry,' she wept. 'Such a day I've had and after sleepless nights wondering whatever kept you . . . coming on them . . . like that . . . the impudence.' She sniffed and rubbed her nose on her sleeve.

Gabriel put his hat down. He went over to Mattie and sat her on his knee, coaxing her, quietly, firmly as though she were a bewildered child.

'And the creature's shouting, the coarse hullabaloo . . . it could have frightened away custom.' She coughed more tears from her throat where she had swallowed them.

'What creature, what hullabaloo as you put it? What on earth are you in a fix about, Mattie?'

Mattie's complexion flushed to a liverish hue. She coughed again and searched feverishly in her reticule for a handkerchief.

'That brazen hussy Beth. A bold slut. I caught them,' she whispered in Gabriel's ear, 'in the larder. Their shenanigans spoiled the blancmanges.'

'You saw Beth doing something indecent?'

'I went out this morning but returned because I'd forgotten my sal volatile and I'm liable to dreadful headaches when I pay visits because they never serve the tea quick enough and if I don't have refreshments right away I'm like a wrung dishrag. Well the sal volatile was at the bottom of my reticule after all. I discovered it as soon as I'd stepped into the hall and as I made to go out again I heard an unholy racket coming from the back of the house. They were in the larder together.' Mattie's face was aflame.

'They? Was Jeremiah Cutts in the larder with Beth?' Gabriel helped her.

'Mister impudence himself, with his trousers . . . and her petticoats thrown up . . .' Mattie blushed furiously. 'And her hollering fit to rouse the dead. You never heard anything like and the shop unattended so anyone could have come in and helped themselves to whatever they pleased . . . it was awful.' Mattie buried her shamed face in Gabriel's coat lapels. 'I ordered them both off the premises at once, treating my house, my business like . . . like . . . a bawdy house,' she said in a voice hollow with affront.

Gabriel stroked Mattie's greasy hair, smiling narrowly.

'I daresay the girl was kicking up a fuss from outrage not degeneracy,' he said. 'I've noted how Jer was always teasing her.'

'I won't speak of it,' Mattie said obstinately. 'She must have invited blame. Always blowzy in her low-cut bodices. I've turned the pair of them out and now I've not a soul to help me in the house or the shop and anyone I engage will have to be trained up and I'll have to get used to them all over,' she wailed.

'Poor Mattie,' he patted her head mechanically.

She was quiet for a moment, crouching in his arms, listening to the tick of the phlegmatic grandfather clock in the hallway.

Then she whispered: 'How weak a woman is, how easily the world uses her. That sort of thing wouldn't happen where there was a master in residence.' Gabriel shifted her uneasily on his lap. 'How much longer must you live at an hotel Gabriel? I need you here with me all the time,' she said.

He spent the night with Mattie and was careful to make love to her more solicitously than usual. It was only five minutes from Holton's Groceries to the stew where Gabriel knew he'd be sure to find Jeremiah unless the lad had found work already. Bell would think he'd gone mad, bringing such a rampant sapling into her garden of spotted roses. But he guessed the very abundance of wanton blooms would soon prune Jer's rambling. And when Bell thought about it she'd be sure to see the potential, as Gabriel did, of Jer's raven-black hair and ivory skin, the bluish tones his lips assumed when they weren't puckering up to tease some damsel. And the boy's sinewy, underfed body would please the madam. Gabriel was less sure, though, about the lad's shrewd cockney wits that made him seize the main chance but were deficient in those imaginative powers so necessary to appreciate the consequences of his actions. Still, whatever was lacking in the lad's mental faculties was certainly recompensed by his resemblance to a revenant.

With Jer in his place, reciting the gloomy words, doing the dreadful deeds, Gabriel would have more time to help Kathleen succeed with Henry Markham.

Mattie's bank draft crackled in Gabriel's pocket. He returned to his hotel by way of Seven Dials, calling in on Jess and giving her a larger than usual present. Now that things were taking him into another world, he thought he'd be able to give the haunts of his childhood a wider berth than of late.

Another world. How often he had dreamed of it. Like an ache in his heart. How often since he had first read the old romances he had thought himself into that world, full of the optimism in which the foundling hero, at the last moment, is discovered to be no knave but a fine-bred gentleman. Gabriel remembered opening a large story book the patterer had given him and trying to climb between the covers, clawing through the dreamily tinted illustrations with the vain hope of inserting himself into the tale.

To have a story, not mere life; romance, not drudgery and humiliation. To conceive himself, not be the sorry by-blow of a drunken conception. Even as he slithered on the filthy dung heap of the Dials where he had too many times limped through the stagnant sewers, Gabriel anticipated the cool marble halls of his future.

At the hotel there was a message waiting for him. Better than he had dared hope. His spirits soared. It was an invitation for Gabriel Feaver and the incomparable Celestine to be Henry Markham's house guests at his country residence, Rees Hall, in the county of —shire.

A couple of shillings in his slippery hand had soon persuaded Jer, whose eyes popped when Gabriel unfolded the nature of his business.

'And don't even think about letting your former

mistress know any of this. I have the acquaintance
of any number of slavering brutes who'd enjoy nothing
more than to watch your carcass swell with Thames
sewage or sizzle in a brick-kiln, or be flayed at
one of the anatomical schools, young sir,' Gabriel
told the boy lightly. But Bell, as he had expected,
proved less impressionable until Gabriel forced her to
agree that the youth's emaciated form would prove
a profitable diversion, slaking the appetites of the
punters who had supped too long on Gabriel's own
shrouded cadaver.

'And mind your manners with my young ladies,'
Bell told the youth, noting the wandering light in
his eye. 'None of your costermonger pawing the ripe
fruit that is on display for those has the money
to buy, not for the like of penniless ne'er-do-wells
such as you.' Turning to Gabriel, she said, 'I'll
take him 'cause he looks deathly enough but he'd
better behave like a gent and mind everything I tell
him. But it's you that'll ave to learn him the trade
Gabriel.'

Gabriel waved for the boy to wait outside. When the
door was closed behind Jer, Gabriel said, 'I've sprung
the lad on you, Bell, because I fear I won't be able to
perform over the next few weeks after all. I have to
go away.'

'Not perform?' Bell protested. 'Do you propose to
get this scallywag up to scratch for me before you
leave then?'

'I'll do my best with the boy.'

'But what about the new scripts? There's a good

135

price been agreed for them, remember,' she reminded him ruefully.

'I'll get back with some new scenes written up for you, as I promised,' Gabriel said thoughtfully.

'Where are you going?'

'That's my affair,' he said shortly. 'Don't fret. I've got you the boy. I won't let you down. I'll begin showing him the ropes this afternoon,' he said. 'There is one other thing though.'

'What's that?'

'I'm sorry but I'm going to steal your star performer from you Bell. I really need Kathleen.'

Bell's mouth set in a thin line.

'And before she's even earned her keep properly,' she grumbled.

Mattie waited. And waited. She had woken to a cool bed, her heart missing a beat when she felt the plump indifference of the pillow where his head should have rested next to her. She got out of bed at once and put on her wrap. The house was very still, the stillness made her shudder. There was no warmth from the kitchen stove because there was no one to light it. The cast-iron pot was glutinous with last night's uneaten stew. She heaved at the unappetising odour. Her breasts itched and ached beneath her cambric nightgown and it was a weary business lighting the stove when she felt so wretched. Only six in the morning but the dawns were already growing spring bright. Her head throbbed. She left the blinds alone, preferring to brew her tea in the easeful darkness. She sliced currant bread and buttered it thickly, sitting down between the tedious rituals of boiling water, fetching cup and saucer and a little plate, scooping tea from the caddy, scalding the teapot and then pouring the hot water on to the Indian leaf, waiting for the beverage to draw, and then, sweet bliss, drinking hot breakfast tea.

Today when she poured herself a second cup she fancied there was an edge to the brew, then the butter tasted a smidgeon rancid and made her queasy. She drank the tea quickly and it curdled in the poisoned well of her stomach. When she finished breakfast she must have stood up too quickly because the room span and the floor leaped up to her astonished vision. She leaned heavily on the table, scratching her breasts that itched more insistently, shivering when her nails snagged the molten nipples. She went into the scullery and pumped cold water over a cloth, discarding her wrap, lifting up the nightgown she pressed the wet rag to her inflamed breasts. Such an itch, it was dementing. A new symptom; there was usually mere soreness when her curse was imminent. If only she had an assistant, what with heartache and headache she felt all done in. She could barely stand let alone fetch and carry, weigh and measure, wrap and tie parcels of foodstuffs for her customers. And then to have to smile that — pleased to see you — call again — any time I can be of service — rictus of calculation was more than she could bear this morning. This bright spring morning of brazen indifference when the birds sang joyously to their mates, the intrusive sun put feelers into amorous bedrooms and the fragrant, daffodilly air scented the tender embraces of awakening lovers. This insouciant morning when Mattie waited, breakfasted and sickened alone in a hollow of despair.

Where the devil was Gabriel?

Rees Hall

Only I discern—
Infinite passion, and the pain
Of finite hearts that yearn.

Robert Browning, *Two in the Campagna*

⌒ ELEVEN ⌒

'Valley of roses, they call this place,' Markham said. 'In summer a drowsy scent thickens the air. A man could grow drunk on the heady exhalations of these blooms. A man could swoon inhaling their scorching perfumes, my dear Celestine.' He cut a tight bud from its thorny stem and gave it to Kathleen.

Beyond them, Rees Hall, Markham's country residence, seemed almost to drown in a bower of trees and bushes and artfully wild plantation.

The horses were led away. Gabriel watched the carriage roll smoothly over the gravelled drive. Then he turned as Markham offered his arm to Kathleen and Gabriel was left to walk side by side with Markham's sister between the thicket of briars that tore at his sleeve; and as he wondered why in God's name Markham didn't have the thorny bushes hacked away the girl said suddenly, 'My brother's a romantic. He thinks the pains of beauty are worth suffering. There's a certain recklessness in him that delights in nature's contempt for restraint.'

'Such rampant beauties soon strangle everything in their path,' Gabriel responded with some asperity when he saw that his jacket sleeve was ripped.

'I'm sorry,' the girl grew flustered and offered the services of her maid to repair the garment. Her delicate voice was a little cracked as though she were afraid of him and at once a slight defensiveness slipped away from Gabriel.

It was a new idea to Gabriel, that disorder, like fastidiousness, could be cultivated. He was surprised by the muted, worn interior of Rees Hall with its distressed furnishings where he'd expected lots of scrolled gilt and shiny surfaces. This decaying family seat was at odds with what he knew of the writer's dandified city persona. Gabriel looked down at Markham's tiny sister who only reached his elbow. Virginia, her name was. She seemed of a piece with the house in any case, dressed simply, girlishly in a plain frock without any ornament. The absence of the reflective surfaces of wealth made him for a moment uneasy but when Markham led them to take refreshment in the conservatory the unease fell away as the charm of massed flowers in crumbling stone and terracotta, the exquisitely prepared food that was casually handed to them and the excellent wine aroused convivial feelings.

Markham's effortless conversation flowed over the silences of his sister.

Their host promised to show them the gardens after they had rested but when Gabriel came downstairs again he found the girl alone with his carefully repaired jacket.

'Henry's still shut away, writing,' she explained, blushing very crimson, 'and Miss Celestine has sent down word that she is too exhausted to join us. If you like I'll show you the grounds,' she went on in her tight little voice. Gabriel was surprised at her lack of composure. He'd always supposed real ladies were like those effigies you found in old churches: white stone carved with the chilly lines of hauteur. But of course Virginia Markham was the merest child; just out of the schoolroom he supposed and unused to society.

There was a walled garden with violet blue flowers and low spreading trees. Patches of grass darkened under cool green branches. They walked down an avenue of biscuit coloured stones and the girl was surprised when Gabriel could identify few of the plants and flowers.

'Oh I'm a city man, born and bred,' he said, feeling the first tremor of alarm at the audacity of his pretensions.

The city. Where her brother fled from the tediums of his writing. She told Gabriel that Henry had promised to take her there next year and of how she longed for and yet dreaded the stir of society.

'Do the women of London wear elaborate clothes and have artificial complexions, as my mother always

143

said they did?' she appealed to him as they stood under a tree, the wide flat leaves swaying over them. Her voice very low, her nervous voice that barely reached him.

'Artificial?' He was still thrown by his unguarded display of ignorance on botanical matters. Had he fallen into the error of becoming overconfident? There was more to a convincing performance than simply looking the part. He had better make use of Markham's library and see if the information in books could supply any deficiencies in his conversational repertoire. His thoughts teeming with plans and misgivings that forked like the heavily swaying branches he had only half attended to the girl's words.

Did London women paint their faces, it seemed she was asking him. Well, on that subject, at least, he was proficient. A drooping branch had caught itself in her long ringlets. Dutifully he unwound the pale hair that was knotted with twigs. He had to move closer to her. He looked at her scared-white complexion, the faery-tale red-as-the-rose-in-summer mouth with its serpentine curve, the princess-in-her-tower long smooth hair falling limply over his artful fingers as he pried the snarls loose. He looked at Virginia Markham and he thought of rich men's wives in their sleek carriages that bowled through Oxford Street, women in harshly coloured silk, their coy hints of rouge and rice powder, applied lightly and almost rubbed away again to mark them out from more questionable women who undeniably painted. City women with their sluggish, powdered complexions. City women who wore paint as slyly as their virtue.

'City women would do well to learn country simplicity. I'm afraid you'd find London women underbred,
Miss Markham.'

He bent over her, freeing the last strand of pale
hair. As her mouth opened slightly, the coolness of her
breath was indistinguishable from the sweet country
air. He straightened his back and inhaled the scents of
the garden. He felt almost intoxicated, his sooty lungs
washed clean. His brain was reeling and he suspected
that nothing would ever be the same again.

They had reached some kind of summer house,
a fanciful affair of yellowing stone with a cupola
and crumbling steps. He followed her up to the
raised platform that was filthy with leaves and bird
droppings, stones and earth. Small unripened apples
were strewn there. Virginia Markham was a mere
child, after all, he decided when she gave a whoop
of delight and began to gather the windfalls. He sat
down on a circular stone bench in the somewhat gloomy
interior. The girl sat next to him, biting into one of the
apples she hoarded in her lap, holding out a layer of
muslin, offering a share of the grimy feast to him.

The fruit possessed a vicious bittersweet sting and
the flesh was hard, impenetrable in his mouth. Discreetly, he spat it out again into a handkerchief.

'Not ripe enough!' He felt like warning the girl
she risked stomach ache but refrained in case that
sort of comment might be considered too coarse for a
gentleman to utter to a lady and he wondered whether
Markham kept any books on etiquette in his collection.
But Virginia's enthusiasm for the crab fruit swiftly

waned in any case and she left lightly gnawed apples on the bench, skipping away towards a copse, saying she'd show him their stream before returning to the house.

The stream was one of those streams in a faery tale running like quicksilver down to a woodsman's cottage. The girl opened the cottage door and he followed her into the cramped single room where there was a table but no chairs, only some sort of palliasse on the floor. A rudimentary shelf held candles, tinder-box, pewter plates and drinking vessels. He watched her tiny form as she reached up for a couple of the tankards. The girl's limp hair had already lost the discipline of ringlets and hung straight and lank to her narrow waist. In the dark room, with her ghostly muslin, she looked as if she'd slip like water through his fingers.

Virginia Markham flitted about like a winged creature and all at once she was outside again where he found her crouching over the stream filling the tankards.

'Sweeter than any wine,' she promised him and it was: a peculiar green coldness that hinted of sap and blossoming leaves. He swallowed the long cold draught of water, then watched her as she sipped daintily from the incongruous working man's tankard. The sweet water and the over-arching trees, the stir of small animals and the surprisingly heavy thump of birds as they alighted on the roof of the woodsman's cottage, the greenish light, the barely materialised girl, but above all the chill rush of water down his dry throat cast a spell over him: as if I've been set down in a story, he thought and when darkness fell suddenly it was as if someone had folded stiff board covers over the plot and shut him up safely inside the faery tale.

Later, when Kathleen and Gabriel were for a moment alone in a room with high ceilings and fraying tapes-tries, Kathleen said: 'It isn't what I expected.'

'What isn't?'

'This house, it's so . . . faded,' she said. 'I expected something more . . .'

'Opulent?' he suggested. Kathleen ran a tapering finger over a dusty table.

'Something finer, more glittering surfaces, I suppose.' She shrugged her shoulders. 'It doesn't fit with what I've observed of Henry Markham but at least I'm not so afraid now. All this mouldy furniture doesn't make me feel that I'm a charlatan, that I have no right to be here.'

'You feel that?' Gabriel mused. 'It's odd but what I always thought exquisite, all those rich, those sumptuous furnishings in the gentlemen's nighthouses in the Strand and the Haymarket, I begin to see now is showy, vulgar, not really gentlemanlike at all.' He looked around the room in wonder. 'The charm of what you call this mouldy stuff leads me to think that refinement might be a matter of time, not just money,' he said. Refinement, he thought, his mouth twisting into a slight smile. As if she read his thoughts Kathleen changed the subject suddenly.

'Doesn't she remind you of someone?'

'Does who remind me?' Gabriel was looking a little shaken Kathleen thought, his voice unsteady.

Perhaps there were tremulous undercurrents beneath that usually unruffled surface.

'The little Miss Markham of course.'

'She looks like no one,' he said.

'But you must have noticed.' Kathleen was incredulous. 'Why she's the very spit. That pale yellow hair. The miniature form.'

'The form of a faery,' Gabriel interrupted.

'The very spit of the Resurrectionist Club's own spoilt faery,' Kathleen responded. 'Gabriel you must admit, lady or no, she's the image of Missy. They might be sisters.'

He looked at Kathleen with pity. What could a waif from beyond the pale know about the refinements of ladies? No, he thought, not like sisters at all, scarcely the same species even. His expression must have stung Kathleen. She looked suddenly spiteful, backing away from him like a cat withdrawing to spitting distance.

'I suppose you're going to utter some banality, such as whores and duchesses are all sisters under the skin,' he said.

'I was just thinking all men are fools,' she snapped.

'Fools?'

'All men are fools because they hate real women. I see that now,' she added slowly.

Real women, did she say? He laughed shortly. Whores, she meant, he supposed.

'All men hate real women because they cannot imagine them,' she said.

'Well I had imagination enough to bring us to this,' he boasted, throwing open tall French windows. 'Could you ever have imagined Markham's valley of roses, Kathleen?' He called her out to the terrace. 'Just breathe this night air. Only inhale the scent of the flowers.' His eyes were dilated with an excitement Kathleen had never seen there before. 'It's like the place folk go to in the old tales,' he told Kathleen, 'where they forget all about their real lives and stay for a hundred years with the goblins and faeries imagining themselves away for a night only.'

'But then they return and no one knows the lost people and they recognise nobody and they are in another century,' Kathleen said.

'A chilling prospect!' Gabriel conceded.

A large moth landed on his hand and he brushed it away carelessly.

'But the frightening thing is,' Kathleen went on, 'after their sojourn with the faeries they are unfit for reality, they're unfit for the real world,' she said. 'And they can never, never find again the road that leads back to enchantment.'

Gabriel turned back into the drawing-room. 'Ah what is real, dearest *Celestine*?' he said sardonically.

Days at Rees Hall were languid with ease. Breakfasts set out in tarnished dishes on sideboards, long windows opening on to terraces planted with flowers and slender trees; walks, intriguing rambles through winding paths that descended intimately to bowers, to hopelessly impenetrable woods, slippery undergrowth and gelid pools where the frogspawn shivered and small fish turned lazily in the sluggish depths.

Markham was mostly shut away writing; his inattention to his guests during the day at first disconcerted Gabriel but at least it left him free to devise scenarios for the séances, to rehearse Kathleen who was plagued with fits of anxiety. But his accomplice was lazy as a whore in the morning and soon became accustomed to lie abed, her breakfast tray delivered with a novel for her diversion. Kathleen loved stretching like a kitten, feeling the plump ease of her feather bed billowing beneath her skinny body. She liked sipping her coffee from the repose of antique lacetrimmed pillows, savouring the delicious food with a mouth still slack with dreams and rolling sensuously in the cambric nightgown Gabriel had bought for her along with a small but respectable wardrobe of ladylike clothes.

Kathleen agreed with Gabriel that the days were a haze of enchantment. But the nights! The nights pressed heavy and scorching as a flat iron.

It had all gone better than expected. Markham seemed entranced with the little medium. Taking Kathleen's thin blackmittened hand in his own that was dusty with Havana leaf he would lead her into the drawingroom after dinner. Kathleen, her disciplined ringlets glossy with pomade, was demure and unusually silent until the time came for her spectral trances. Then, the folding doors closed firmly on Markham's susceptible younger sister, she would perform; perform consummately after all as if it were second nature for her to dwell with the angels.

That first séance they had sat holding hands, just

150

the three of them, Markham's sister banished to her virginal bed. Just Markham, Kathleen and Gabriel. They sat very close at a small table, sweating hands clenched hard with excitement or tension. It was a hot night and a servant had flung open the glass doors that led from the dining-room on to the conservatory. A few candles had been lit out there between the ferns, potted palms and flower-filled vases. Tapering smoke drifted through, pulling a dull light after it. In semi-darkness Gabriel's eyes gleamed at her. Markham so close, his ringlets brushing her throat; Kathleen couldn't bear to look at him in case he saw through the deception. Her stomach felt hollow. Fear prickled the nape of her neck. Her arms were covered with goose pimples. Markham's thigh pressed against her silken skirts, his breath smothered her. Or was it the night, the airless night that made her chest tighten? She waited for the cue from Gabriel.

'Celestine shut your eyes now, think yourself in a dream,' he instructed as Markham drew his breath eagerly.

'In a dream,' she repeated.

She sat stiffly on her high-backed chair, conscious of Gabriel's limp hand in her own and shrinking inwardly as Markham's grip crushed her other hand. Gabriel began to recite a poem about a woman calling from the grave to her faithless, still living lover.

Markham never flinched, his breath only growing more fervid as Gabriel's poem described the earthbound ecstasy of the sundered-by-death lovers. Kathleen had the poem by heart and already in her mind's eye could see the white, writhing limbs, the disordered hair, the red swollen lips of the doomed couple; the man had light brown hair and mean eyes, the woman was the spit of Kathleen Mangan. When Gabriel came to the part where the wretched lover tore through clay to embrace the remarkably preserved corpse of his beloved, her eyes flew open.

Now! She told herself.

'As I come, as I come now,' she panted. Markham's hand curved tightly round her fingers. 'Through clay, through filth . . . black night . . . the suffocating darkness . . . Oh my beloved.' Her voice was very thin, her mouth thick with spittle.

Kathleen felt the writer's hot breath on her cheek. He seemed aroused and yet not out of control as he had been at the séance in Bedford Street. This time he was prepared . . . for something.

'Arabella?' he said.

'Not yet Markham,' Gabriel ordered. 'Continue, Celestine!' Her own grip asserting itself, squirming against Markham's ringed fingers, mangling Gabriel's knucklebones.

'I can't find you for the darkness,' the spirit wailed.

'Must I light the lamps?' Markham said sounding just a little too casual.

'Light a lamp in your soul,' the voice instructed. 'Lighten all its darkest places.'

'Spirit do you have a message for us?' Gabriel broke through, nudging Kathleen's elbow.

'My words are for the ears of he alone who deserts me.' The voice now was small and drier and muted.

'For Markham?' asked Gabriel.

'For him alone else I cannot break through the darkness.'

'I must leave you it seems,' Gabriel murmured in Markham's ear. 'Will you be all right man? Take your lead from Celestine. If there's any disturbance call me back at once.' Then, as Markham raised no objection, he withdrew quietly and Kathleen's right hand fell with a thud on the table.

Gabriel left her alone to deal with Markham as he had said he would. Her lungs drew in deep breaths of simmering air. The sticks of whalebone in her bodice jabbed her. She felt the waves of nausea rising in her stomach. Her throat heaved on the spectral words, the voice strangulated, toneless as an automaton.

'Alone at last, across the endless acres of the beyond . . .'

'Perhaps we *should* light a lamp,' Markham whispered. Kathleen pretended she couldn't hear him and indeed his voice seemed almost the ghost of itself, like a wisp of ether, although his flesh became somehow more gravid, as though his blood thickened and his body swelled beside her.

'Bella, come back to me!' Markham's plea to Kathleen's keen ears was resonant less of awe than urgency.

'I am here dearest, my desires beat like angel wings,' his dead love cooed at Markham. There was a sudden gust of reviving air as a window flung itself open.

'I'm yours only, only yours,' he said rising excitement in his voice, his thigh pressing hard against Kathleen. 'The others, I tell you, were the merest nothings, the confusions of my bereavement.' The spirit sighed like a lover. 'Possess me!' Markham demanded. 'A sign. Can spirits make themselves felt as flesh and blood are able?'

'Only as flesh and blood,' the spirit moaned.

'I don't understand you,' Markham called out to the darkness. 'Come to me, for pity's sake let me feel you as a living woman again.'

'I'm a dead woman,' the spirit sounded desolate.

'Your spirit lives on. Live on in me, dearest heart.' He was insistent. 'How may I keep chaste if you deny me?'

'I deny you nothing. Flesh does not deny, blood does not chill. Here . . . here,' as Kathleen's petticoats rustled, as her petticoats rose stealthily and Markham's thigh pressed against lacy garters, '. . . the kingdom of the dead through the portals of the living . . .' The voice trailed away into darkness.

Someone or something lit a dim lamp by the open window. Kathleen's hand slid from Markham's fingers. In the meagre light he could see the flush on her cheeks. He could hear her stertorous breathing. Her ruby lips parted slightly. A sudden perfume exhaled from her body, that scent of mignonette and lavender, the fragrance favoured by his own Arabella. The medium sprawled now in her chair, seemingly unconscious of anything.

*   *   *

'What on earth are you doing here?' He held a candle to her misery white face.

'I'm so cold,' her teeth chattered.

'Curse you woman. You're not going all lily-livered on me?' His anger made her draw back, baffled.

'It's not as easy as you think,' she said, unaware that his coldness sprang from a small knot of panic, a dis-avowed fear that lay beneath his husk of confidence.

'I thought the whole thing went very smoothly until this moment.' Gabriel poured some brandy into a small tumbler from a silver flask at the bedside and gave her the drink.

'You heard it all?'

'Every shivering word. Now drink the brandy, it'll put some *real* spirit into you!'

'Don't mock me,' she said.

'If I didn't mock you I should be tempted to beat you for all this dithering foolishness but remembering your first-rate performance earlier I'm inclined to make you bravely drunk instead.'

'It was a good show, wasn't it Gabriel?'

'Bloodcurdling, but it was over too quickly,' he growled. Kathleen put the emptied tumbler down.

'How so? Didn't I go through the entire performance right to the bitter end as you bid me?'

'The bitter end,' he echoed her, sitting down on the bed sullenly. 'But the performance isn't over yet, Kathleen. You didn't make it to the final act tonight.'

'But I did everything, everything you told me,' she said in a bewildered voice. 'I pretended to be a medium possessed by the spirit of Markham's dead love. And he seemed to believe me,' believed too well, she thought. Remembering his scent of Havana and oleaginous Macassar she shuddered.

Gabriel stood up again, frowning at her.

'Tell me, what are the qualities a first-rate medium must demonstrate?'

'Qualities?'

'How can she convince an audience?' he asked impatiently. Kathleen thought for a moment.

'Why, to go into a trance and give herself up to spirit possession, I suppose.'

'Give herself up, exactly. A medium's passivity makes devilment possible.'

'Devilment?' She was confused.

'A woman entered by spirits knows nothing of what happens to her body, does she?' He put his fingers under her chin, drawing her gaze towards his own, watching her as he spoke slowly. 'A woman in a trance is an empty space that desire may fill. Such a woman may be ravished by, or herself ravish, demons and will remember nothing of the matter. She will smooth down her petticoats when the trance is past and continue to be a virtuous woman with blame from no man.' His strong fingers curved round her throat. 'Markham will hardly think less of you. Our host is a genial man, Kathleen. His liberality is unbounded. Only this afternoon he asked if I would care to read through the play he's nearly finished writing and I told him I'd always had a fancy to be an actor myself. "Oh you must act out some of my characters for me

156

then," he said. I agreed, lightly enough of course, I don't want him to suspect . . . but I think my talents will entertain him.'

Gabriel spoke to her firmly, his voice over-loud. Perhaps he needed to convince himself as much as his accomplice. There had been a shaky moment or two earlier, when Gabriel had nearly failed to laugh at a jest Markham had framed in Latin. It must have been some kind of joke because Markham had chortled at his own wit and luckily Gabriel had quickly picked up the cue and guffawed until his sides ached.

Kathleen tried to twist her neck away from his bruising fingers. 'You entertain him Kathleen. I've seen how he watches you. But one or two paltry scenes are not enough; that man requires a whole night's diversion.'

'What are you saying?' she gasped.

'Don't you want success for us both, Kathleen?'

'Success?'

Not success, only love, she thought.

'I want success for both of us,' he insisted. 'But success means hard, even unpleasant work. It doesn't come with the waving of a wand like in the faery tales, Kathleen.'

Not like a faery tale.

'Our venture won't be all plain sailing,' he went on. 'Perhaps our performance should have been grounded on more thorough research,' he waved aside an imaginary insect. 'Still if we keep our heads and polish our act we should summon enough bravado to see us through. And just because,' he admonished her, 'I spirited you away from the bordello doesn't mean I'll be able to save you from every little unpleasantness.'

Not save me.

'You'll have to develop stamina, Kathleen, if you want success. We're a good partnership, aren't we?' he continued not waiting for her answer. 'I'm working for both of us, you know. I can be an actor and your manager. As I told you, Kath, I can manage you profitably. You could become an outstanding medium. You could be a phenomenon. Rich and famous too! Imagine it! But talent is only half the battle. You must have stamina,' he reiterated. 'An hour's transports, loosening your garters, aren't enough. You must extend your repertoire or you'll surely bore Markham.'

'But I did as you told me,' she repeated dully.

'Do I have to spell it out? Have you no imagination, Kathleen?' His grip tightened on her throat. He smiled to himself because he had remembered just in time, just when his confidence was about to betray him, that knowledge isn't everything. You don't need hard facts to convince anyone of anything when you can cast a spell. You seduce the audience before they can perceive the trickery behind your performance. Seduction's the thing! He looked himself again, charming and resolute as he said: 'When you wake each morning you must pretend shock, the trance was so numbing, how could you know such love as Arabella possessed for Markham was stronger than eternity? You must be perplexed, unable to account for the last night's excesses when you awaken each morning to find yourself sprawling, without a stitch of clothing, utterly abandoned, ravished by passion in bed with Markham.'

'In his bed,' she repeated.

'In his loving arms,' Gabriel said, pressing his hand at the back of her neck, drawing her mouth towards him.

᧤ TWELVE ᧥

Virginia Markham admired her ivory satin pumps tied with velvet ribbon. She ran her hands through her drooping ringlets; such fine, slippery hair it never *would* hold rags or curl-papers. She sat stiffly in her dress that she had laced too tight in defiance of her maid's warnings. She kicked out her thin ankles enjoying the pearly sheen of her feet beneath starch-white petticoats. The swing edged gently to and fro, to and fro. Her pinched waist and whalebone-crushed ribs made her suck in the morning air with little whoops of hysteria. The grass was still sappy with morning dew and she was careful not to trail her feet, thrusting them out before her, her tiny hands gripping the rope handles that were fastened high up to one of the topmost branches.

The broad green leaves shivered and rustled over her. Swaying backwards and forwards with gentle, reflective movements.

What was that pitter-patter as if an army of spiders wearing velvet boots were marching over her stomach? Why had she pumiced her barely-out-of-the-schoolroom inky fingers, after writing letters, until they sloughed the stained skin and curled pink as shelled prawns into her rosy mouth where she gnawed the soft nails that tasted bitter because she had begun to apply aloes to foil the childish habit? Why did her stomach shrink before the breakfast, dinner and tea table? And worst of all why did her voice fail and her body tremble whenever she saw her brother's houseguest, that man, that . . . Gabriel? The lump in her throat, the constriction of her breath made her words detonate like gunpowder whenever she spoke to him. Her own voice mortified her. A cracked useless voice. Words failed her.

Why?

And why did this man frighten her?

She swayed to and fro, to and fro, nerves bubbling like a witch's cauldron. Up into the caressing air, down, down to the swooping green sward. Faster, her ankles kicking out, her breath steaming. Rocking harder, advance and retreat, about to press upwards once more when that sudden jolt from behind cast her out into infinity, the blue morning air dizzy with exultation, her feet dabbling the suds of clouds before dipping again, her stomach dropping alarmingly, her breath fighting. And when she thought there was no

162

hope, she must fall ever further into the bowels of the earth, again the swing was pushed with a violence that catapulted her high where the air was hard and shot her to pieces like a slain pigeon.

Down she fell. Down. Down. Her heart flew out of her. The swing shuddered. The earth stopped. The man laughed. The world span.

'You!' she said. 'You?' Was it the way his eyes fastened on her, drinking her in, as if she were the only light in a world of darkness, that made her so fearful?

The hectic swing had so braced her, the punching air so filled her throat with oxygen that her voice was smooth and clear again. She forced herself to laugh: 'I've never flown so high,' she said.

'Did I frighten you?'

'A little,' she confessed.

His eyes were pale in the sharp sunlight.

'Sometimes we need to be pushed, we need terror sharpening our responses if we are to feel truly alive,' he said.

She bent her head shyly. Terror? His breath caressed her neck. A knot of fear squeezed her stomach. This man standing so close to her. In the schoolroom she had merely read of men, youths in stories, warriors or kings in the histories her governess had read to her. Her widowed mother had been a recluse and when she died and Henry had come to live with his sister he said she must begin to know the real world.

'You know so little of society I shall have to introduce you to it slowly or you will take fright and go back to your cage forever,' he had explained kindly enough though he had seemed at a loss to know what to do with her. The first time a party of his houseguests had descended on Rees Hall she had developed a strategic illness and so avoided their company. Now this man and his odd companion with her wild hair and staring eyes, a woman who looked like a wraith, had changed the very atmosphere at Rees Hall. This man, this terror, weakened her knees and choked her with palpitating dread. What was this terror? Was the terror life? Real life at last? I never knew what life was before, she thought. But she said nothing and her voice shivered to pieces in her throat like broken glass again.

He wanted to touch her. Untouched, he thought, she looks as if life itself had been afraid to lay hands on her. Virgin flesh, he thought, with a shiver of anticipation. Her touch-me-not air beguiled him. Whenever he approached she withdrew as in some stately dance from another time, another milieu. He knew only one set of steps, the familiar pavan of seduction, but his partner danced to another tune and gave him the slip, disappearing into the shadowy recesses of her brother's house. When he advanced she retreated.

The girl fled from him.

And at first he enjoyed her blushes that were called up too easily, was diverted by her cracked voice and the way she trembled whenever he was close to her. Then he discovered he forgot his own fears in the spell of mastery his mere presence cast over her. The girl was obviously entranced by him; her response had all the humiliating loss of control that spelled first love and Markham, like most writers lost in contemplation of his own obsessions, noticed nothing. There were no female chaperones, her governess being lately dismissed, so it seemed the coast was clear for dalliance. Well-bred lady or no, what seventeen-year-old could resist a lover more than a decade older than her?

The way her gaze averted itself from his, her painful sense of shame that she should fall victim to the treacherous vagaries of her body, the way she evidently sought to avoid his company, to hide herself away, was a startling novelty. For hadn't women *always* pursued him? Even where they feigned reluctance he could see the hoyden light in their eyes that flashed a certain signal indicating lust. If they had sometimes held back it was only a tactic to arouse him or a shrewd hope that if they held out long enough they'd gain a wedding ring.

But this exquisite creature, a child still, ran away from him.

Like no woman he'd ever known. But at seventeen scarcely a woman nor yet like the centuries-old infants who walked London streets and whored for their supper. Virginia was like no one.

Virginia!

Her pale hair tapered in long ringlets.

Her throat was narrow as the flame of a church candle.

Her feet had the waxen heels of the madonna who crushed Satan.

Her white hands chaste as if they dealt only prayers and benedictions.

Her complexion pure as the conception of angels.

A mere girl, Markham's beloved sister, kept safe from the world like a nun in a cloister. Gazes now, emerald green eyes recognising only Gabriel.

Recognition. Yes I know you, he had thought. That the world had such a creature in it, his first thought, like a dream when he saw her beneath the canopy of briars. He had always known. Wasn't her hair bright as sovereigns? Weren't her eyes green as jealousy? Didn't her mouth draw shut like a purse hoarding desires beyond avarice? The little heiress, the incarnation of beauty and wealth he'd always imagined. A faery princess. Beauty and wealth were a spell. A spell could make a princess love a cowherd. And didn't faery princesses always have to marry the poor youths who battled demons to win them?

'The house isn't mine, you know,' Markham had remarked casually to Gabriel. 'It's part of the inher-itance my sister will come into when she's of age. Virginia is my half-sister of course, the child of my late father's second marriage. Her mother died not so long ago. As Rees Hall belonged to her mother's family, naturally it passes to Virginia.'

'Naturally,' Gabriel had murmured.

She jumped down from the swing and ran now, scurrying like an animal let out of a dark cupboard, running she knew not where in confusion. He ran after her. His wretched limp slowed him but he bore down mercilessly. When he caught her at last, the feel of her

166

shivering body startled him. 'A woman has no right to be so beautiful! So wary!' he whispered to Virginia. To tempt a man this way! What defence could any man have against the exquisite enchantment of pursuit? What chance had he who had been pursued by too many women? Her fear enchanted him. He looked at her thirstily and fearfully she smiled up at him. All her life the looking-glass had said: beauty, enchantress; and now Gabriel stepped like a genie out of the cold glass and in uttering the same words warmed her.

She only gasped when he held her in the thicket of roses.

'Say what you want,' he urged her. 'Say it,' he demanded. Her mouth opened. But she said nothing. He kissed her and his breath filled her throat. 'Tell me what you want of me,' he insisted. 'I don't want you to blame me, after . . .'

After what, she didn't dare ask him.

'Speak to me won't you,' he wondered at her silence and it wasn't until he had kissed her repeatedly that she found her voice, so tiny, so strangled.

'I'm afraid to speak to you,' she managed to say.

He looked down at her tremulous mouth, afraid of language.

'Afraid to speak!' His heart leapt in his throat. She knew then, she knew words could be knives that cut out the heart of everything. Better a mouth filled with straw than speech. 'But not afraid to love, surely,' he murmured. And there, in the scratchy briars that tore at their clothes, amidst the very thorns that collaborated in her deflowering, without any words he stripped her fear away.

Like no woman he'd ever known; a woman who knew there were words that could spoil everything. He bent back the overgrown briar that caught Virginia on its thorny stem, the brutal spikes snaring her bodice; but scarcely was she torn free, as he pulled her towards him, than the briar snapped and the thorns sprang at their mouths as they fastened on a kiss, entering cruelly, so they fell together in pain and rapture that was mute with glory.

ᴄ THIRTEEN ᴄ

Thrown back: milky pale covers; mussed sheets, sweetly moist. The sweeter scent from her hair lying over his face. Enfolding her body like angel wings: arms, naked limbs shielding her. Drowsy heat of a sultry spring morning, alien and lovely like a flower forced in heat to bloom to soon; too hot, this April sun opening her limbs, so hot, unfurling, as she dreamed, her mouth open and wet so he slaked his strange thirst. Creamy skin slick with ardour; pressing her beneath him until violet bruises gleamed on her breasts, thighs; veins in her neck knotted, straining to murmur sentiments learned long ago in old verses, the meaning scarcely registered till now on this hottest of spring dawns as he thrust himself recklessly like a shipwrecked mariner, down, down. Fathoms deep she lies and he must prise her open.

He'd never known such thirst, bittersweet as addic-tion.

Sucking her like the rind of exquisite fruits that melted as he feasted, sucking deeper, grinding his teeth, tearing the very pith for the faint tang of remembered juices, quenched and parched in relentless succession. For even as he sated himself with this sweetest of loves he drank the wormwood agonies of yet more raging thirst.

A thirst that must be slaked, that must be appeased this hot morning when he burned to fever pitch.

But even as she swallowed him between thighs and lips, consuming his very thirst, he was stricken with a drought so terrible it seemed his throat was stabbed with burning needles dry as straw, chafing sticks of straw gagging him so he no longer savoured Virginia's sweetness.

He sighed, exhausted at last. The lovely girl smiled weakly at him.

'Virginia!' he whispered. 'Virginia, Virginia, Virginia!'

His hair was damp, his heart beat furiously and he lay in her arms that were cool and moist as a dawn flower.

'My sweetest of sweethearts,' she murmured. The muslins at the long windows hung still as shrouds in the dead heat. The dawn air was thick and light as cotton fluff. Every breath suffocated him. His skin burned to her cool touch.

'Such dementing heat,' he groaned. 'I've known no

April like it, a season hot as hell,' but as he turned in her embrace and her yellow ringlets fell over him she whispered: 'Hot as our love even,' running her light hands across his brow, his throat. 'You're burning Gabriel, your skin is molten!'

Love hot he pressed down on her again, burrowing into her coolness; small slight body beneath his, cool as a waterlily. Her narrow hips, slender shortish legs, thin arms, merely sprouting breasts and that long yellow hair limp as washed muslin and her voice high and light as a changeling's, a faery child.

Was this love's fever then? This enchantment of languorous heat and burning thirsts? Was this creature, with her silken sheets and delicate grace, flesh and blood like other women?

A briary scent spilled into the room. When the roses were in full bloom, he could imagine the rich perfumes casting a spell vertiginous as love to craze a man's senses. Now the scent was virgin, the merest sweetening of the air as though someone burned incense in a distant chamber. Her skin had a rosy fragrance too, though white it was, white as the waxiest of white roses. White roses for love dead and forsaken. But here the roses were scorching red for love triumphant. In summer immolating red blooms would celebrate their passion. In summer, when summer came and after Markham had found a suitable position for Gabriel, these lovers would steal away into the bliss of clandestine marriage. But she was puzzled why their love should remain hidden, for Gabriel was a gentleman wasn't he? And though she was young, her brother wasn't an ogre, would gladly see her settled; Gabriel's lack of fortune wasn't really a problem, he was such a through and through gentleman and what a pity it was he was orphaned for she would love to embrace the mother who'd given birth to him.

'Hush!' he said. They both stiffened with fear. A door slammed shut somewhere in the echoing silence.

'Only a servant,' she soothed him.

'If I should be discovered here all would be lost,' he said. The chance of theatrical introductions gone. 'Your brother would have you locked up. I'd never be allowed near you.'

She shivered and clutched him nervously.

'I'd die sooner than give you up,' she vowed.

'Don't say die, you're young, you know nothing of the indignities of death.' He kissed her mouth solemnly. 'Promise me not to speak of dying,' he said.

She began to whisper endearments, her voice very low, halting, listening for unobserved watchers, fiends of hell who would envy and so destroy their heaven. Her voice low and yet so light, frothy as a dandelion seed, drifting on the air, lulling him, shivering on his flesh, seductive sweet words of love stroking him. My love, lover, kiss me hold me words; here, no here, here, her voice trembling, broken into feathery breaths that were barely words at all. Love had its own language, strange and exquisitely modulated: humming, urging; drawn-out gasps or sighs that tasted delicious in his mouth, words he could savour and inhale where he could not hear, the ardent utterances leaking from the very pores of her skin, damply scented rustle of her hair, gentle sweep of her eyelashes, tinkle of her pearly teeth, lapping of her tongue, slapping waves of her blood; all her love speaking to him.

Even now he could barely believe the woman he'd only ever dreamed of, the woman of his dreams, lay in his arms at last although from almost the first moment he'd planned her seduction. Her seduction seduced him. It was all he could do to keep his mind steady and focus on the business with Markham.

Seduction: there were so many paths leading to the garden of enchantment. How often he had led women there but himself hung back behind the gates watching them drown in the pools of desire. Paths narrowed as you approached those gates. Sometimes the women themselves hung back, fearful at the last moment lest they should never find their way out again, knowing Gabriel might shut the tall gates irrevocably on all that dreadful wonder. To be alone, marooned in the rampant garden! Like dream turned into nightmare.

Seduction: he could seduce with a look, a mere squint of his eyes, the slothfulness of his limp might do the trick. How could anyone account for it? Of course he could play gentle, bold, fierce, tender when he'd a mind to. Then there were his piano-playing fingers, light and practised and nimble, his confidence tricks learned in brothels, a certain cool ardour that could coax yet remain aloof making him even more desirable. He could threaten too! 'If you won't surrender I can have some other woman.' But after a time such crude manipulations had palled on him and the women too easily fell, bruised, wormy, the juices sour in his mouth. They were a disappointment and his thirst never slaked. He'd grown thirstier. Seducing women no longer seduced the seducer. He was thirsty for his own seduction.

Sometimes he sensed his power over women sprang from this: the humiliating need that scorned what it fastened on. Women responded to the *wanting* he had disguised as prowess. And he thought how Kathleen had once told him, her eyes popping with fright, that on a cold wet night, as she had gone upstairs at Bell's place and had just reached the half-landing, how she had heard him follow her up the stairs — although by then he was, in fact, with Mattie, eating thick soup mopped up with oatcake. Kathleen swore she turned round and for a brief moment had a vision of Gabriel a few feet below her, a rope fastened to his ankle; she had seen him choking on long grass, or hay or straw or something prickly and inedible; a piteous, struggling Gabriel, spewing chaff, writhing in paroxysms.

Sweet fever of love. He would never feel cool again.

Kathleen lay on her feather bed on this sultriest of April mornings but with a writer not a novel beside her. Markham had followed her into her room last night in the trance of séance, as she had known he would. He had been so ready for his ghostly seductress, so adept in his part as the ravished mortal, so fearless in the medium's spectrally charged embrace, indeed so erotically aroused (as much aroused as any of Bell's punters with their perverse pleasures), that

Kathleen could almost have sworn he had rehearsed his role as keenly as she and Gabriel had. And yet his satisfaction had been too exquisite, his sighs at the height of delirium, that called on Bella the sweetest, the most innocent, too rapturous to be faked, so that she was sure Markham was convinced he actually lay with his lost love, wracked in the grip of a *real*, not a make-believe passion!

How late was it now? Was Gabriel with the girl, with the exquisite Virginia Markham, she agonised. Markham turned in his sleep. His dreams were restless and he thrashed and twisted all through his slumbers. A slight man but his body felt heavy on hers. Markham's arm was flung across her throat. He muttered in his sleep, murderous words, sensational exclamations, exotic names and thrilling whispers so that she supposed his sleeping mind was rehearsing his own melodramas.

Perhaps a leading part for Gabriel? Or did she only imagine that Markham's left leg, which sprawled over her awkwardly, was inert? It seemed the heaviest part of him, a dead weight, numb, so he didn't respond to her pinches and the foot hung limply out of the bedclothes in an ungainly fashion, the foot of a lame man.

Kathleen felt uneasy. When the girl had laughed off her scratches no one thought anything of it: a piece of carelessness to get entangled with thickets of briars. But then she noticed how Gabriel let his coffee grow cold before he drank it, how he refused rum and brandy and his wine had to be watered and when he spoke his thin lips were tighter than usual.

So when they found time alone to rehearse more of the stimulating stunts that Gabriel devised for her to delight Markham, Kathleen had said, 'Show me how to kiss him as though a devil sucked his soul out, Gabriel!' And before he could pull back she had thrust her tongue in his mouth and discovered the still bleeding wounds there.

Kathleen distrusted this valley of roses, was wary of the malignant thorns piercing a right of way through shady foliage that dripped with morning mists and humid dew across the interminable acres of Markham's gardens. Choking pollens hung on the air and as she breathed the lint-thick atmosphere she thought that to live here was to experience suffocation. If she could be transported back to London, feather bed intact (after first tipping out Markham), she'd breathe more easily.

And yet, how the ease of everything and the delicious flavours of the food seduced her: the taste of thinly sliced ham and freshly laid eggs for breakfast, melting butter on the crispest toast, and the coffee! The coffee was ambrosial. The very feel of tenderly threaded lawns and cambric soft as clouds was cosseting. She wanted nothing more than to lie in the bliss of comfort, she told herself; she wanted nothing more, she repeated sternly, gobbling slice after slice of dripping toast, swigging cup after cup of stimulating coffee. To want more was to descend to the perilous paths of addiction. To want more was to drive herself mad over Gabriel.

176

Gabriel. Arch. Angel. Gabriel.

When Markham's scented ringlets smeared her mouth she felt the beating wings of her imagined lover smothering the air. The strange coupling of desire and revulsion disturbed her. Markham's too eager thrusts from which she instinctively withdrew were yet met by the sudden quickening of her own body that leapt to the bait, remembering Gabriel.

Markham moaned something unintelligible. Kathleen recoiled, edging away from him. Any moment now he would awaken, any moment he would murmur, 'Arabella . . . dearest . . .' and the whole rigmarole would begin again. Turning even now, his mouth pressing her flesh, turning, sucking like quicksand.

'I can't believe the time has passed so quickly,' Markham's eyes slid away from Gabriel's keen glance. The ladies had withdrawn from the dinner table. The inevitable port which Gabriel disliked. A sweetly cloying drink. His mouth felt thick with sediment. The ruby liquid burned his sore tongue.

'We've enjoyed your hospitality Markham,' Gabriel said smoothly.

The writer's mouth was a little swollen with drink. His mouth had a feckless looseness to it. Kathleen was right, Gabriel decided. Markham was an unfathomable fellow. His host looked shifty in the light of the candle flames. And hadn't he responded to their little games too readily? Hadn't he succumbed more easily than Gabriel could have hoped or imagined? If he guessed the truth and yet ignored it, choosing to believe in the myth of love reaching beyond the grave, it must be because he followed his base desires before his reason. 'I suspect the fellow's a charlatan of the sharpest kind,' Kathleen had protested, 'the kind that believes in his own fakery.'

'I hope Celestine's gifts haven't disappointed you,' Gabriel added after a pause. Markham looked away from him. The man had lost weight, Gabriel thought. His febrile movements now had a jerkiness, his dissipated mien had become slightly feverish; he seemed to have lost grip on himself amidst all these occult exertions.

'Celestine is all and more than you promised,' he said quietly, pouring himself another measure of port. 'To tell you the truth, Feaver, I rather dread your departure.'

'But won't you be returning to London yourself?'

'No, I must stay here and put the finishing touches to my play.' He swallowed his entire drink and went on: 'You've been an immense help. Your dramatisation of certain scenes made me realise the revisions that were needed. That's a rare gift you have.'

'Well, as I think I mentioned before, it's long been a whim of mine to tread the boards but I really know nothing of the theatrical world.'

Markham smiled apologetically.

'We fellows who pen plays are obliged to consort with a sort of demi-monde set. But in recent years, even if actresses may still be frowned on in polite society, the likes of Macready and others have done much to raise the esteem in which thespians are held.'

178

Gabriel measured his words slowly.

'I was never one to tremble before the codes of propriety. I really have a fancy to try my chances but I hardly know how to . . .'

'I could help to effect introductions; you really have a fine talent, you know,' Markham interrupted. 'If you could see your way to putting off your return to London for another few weeks, I could arrange for you to audition for a part in this play of mine.'

Gabriel took a deep breath:

'That's very good of you,' he said. 'There are a few matters I must see to in London over the next few days however, but if you don't object I could return as soon as my business is effected.'

'Celestine wouldn't mind staying on here a while, would she?' Markham asked carefully, pouring yet another glass of port. 'She wouldn't mind staying on even if you're not here?'

Markham was flushed with drink and excitement. A writer's ultimate fantasy to live out his delusions: every night a comatose woman abandoning herself to his dreams; every morning Gabriel fleshing out his creations. Excitement enveloped him. He had to prolong the delirium.

⸏ FOURTEEN ⸏

The city threw a shadow over Gabriel, summer beginning with a heat that the open sewers made sultry and venomous. He held Virginia's handkerchief, a gossamer fragment, over his nose and mouth as the carriage rolled through Oxford Street.

Virginia! Already his fastidious heart ached for her refinements. 'A few days! I'll be back with you within a few days,' he had vowed and even then he'd surprised himself and wondered whether the paltry money was worth losing hours of precious love for. Virginia kept to her room; theirs had been a private leavetaking. Markham was busy writing so only Kathleen waved him farewell. As he climbed into the carriage she had run suddenly down the flight of steps that led from the entrance of the house and leaned in through the window.

'What is it?' he had asked her.

Kathleen was a bundle of nerves.

'Don't go back to Bell's!' she begged him.

'But there's business to see to, money to be earned.'

'I have a feeling . . .'

'Keep your feelings to yourself,' he said abruptly.

'A sense that things will go bad for you,' she insisted.

'Women's fancies! I'll be back in no time, no time at all. Keep Markham amused while I'm gone won't you?'

'And who's to amuse his sister?' she asked sullenly but already the carriage was drawing him away from her.

The heat of London oppressed Gabriel. A poisonous atmosphere kept the wealthy from the streets and only whores, costermongers, beggars and a colony of fever-dazed Irish spilled out of the broken-down courts into the thoroughfares through which he had to pass before he found himself at Bell's place.

Heat made the black paint blister and bubble on the front door. The shutters were closed against the dangerous sun and there was a listless air to the bordello. He let himself in, calling out for Bell when he couldn't find the madam in her office. He called again and then Missy trailed in from the scullery where she'd been washing.

'Where's Bell?'

Missy looked pleased and worried all at once.

'We ain't seen hide nor hair of her since Friday night. There's been no business done neither. But there's a letter for you on her desk. That rapscallion you brought ere, young Cutts, ain't been seen since then neither. The girls don't know what to do. We were going to open your letter if Bell still didn't turn up after a bit. It's a right mystery. We wondered if some cove was after the ole skinflint.'

Gabriel tore open the sealed letter.

Well you've landed me in it this time Gabriel! What madness was in you to leave me with this jackanapes this Jeremiah Cutts larrikin? Your madness and my bad judgement! The fellow soon worked on my weak spot which some may think is yourself but you and I know is my pocket! Well he persuaded me that more money might be made if I extended my business. He argued I should open the house to a different sort of cove: to those whom life has hardened until their hearts have turned to stone bearing only the imprint of their desires like fossils. Men who have stripped life of dreams in their desperate quarrying for material gain: factory owners, railway kings, bankers and those devils who frame laws to imprison us.

'And how will you get these fine fellows into my humble abode?' I demanded of the impudent rogue.

'Why but by holding up a mirror to their power that has lain the world to waste and ruin. By offering them an image of the real world, flayed to the very core, so it reflects their terrible

gaze that has made stone out of everything,' he answered.

'I'm not sure I understand,' I told the bold fellow so then he spelled it out in the language of my heart.

'You can make more tin if you stop all that fuss and nonsense about using imagination,' he said.

Fool that I was I trusted him. Imbecile that I am I was taken in by the simplicity of his notion. 'I am as canny as that there Gabriel,' he insisted. So I paid him to do the business, paid him well enough, a goodly sum. Well how was I to know? I am not one to turn down the opportunity for business. All that good money paid out! He suggested we carry out the proceedings on a Sunday night when the girls were resting and would know nothing of the venture. He said he could set it all up. To think how he pocketed the sovereigns I gave him! My money, wasted! How did that fool of a lad think I'd never notice? God have mercy on us! The very first time, the very first and I was caught like a foolish virgin! I daren't write the terrible truth here but if you go down to the basement you will see the dire outcome of Jeremiah Cutts' devilment. After I discovered what he'd done I got a pair of garters and twisted them round his neck until I half strangled the villain. But he'd already hidden the money I'd paid him and before I could summon help to keep hold of him he'd scarpered. Now you must make amends for the misfortune you've brought down on me Gabriel. You must *pay men, the sort of men you know well how to find, to do the necessary. I think it would be best to take the thing to Portugal Street where they are not likely to ask questions. Till then I stay at the address you'll find in the strongbox under the floorboards in my office. There is enough money there to pay for everything. Take three guineas for yourself. All business is cancelled until this affair is sorted. I'll return when I hear from you that the job is done.*

Bell.

'Damnation,' he growled. He had a shrewd idea what was facing him in the basement: Portugal Street indeed! And only three guineas for the grim business.

'Well?' Missy demanded.

He looked at the girl with some irritation. 'Where are the other women?' Missy shrugged her bare shoulders. Dressed only in stays and a torn shift, her disordered ringlets spilling over her sleepy face, she looked what she was, a cheap harlot. How had Kathleen ever seen the likeness to such a wanton in his angel?

'Susannah Fossit has been blind drunk day and night since Bell went. Corrie's stuffing herself silly wiv the remains of bread and drippin, some of the girls made off to do a bit of private whoring, Tess knocked Gertie's front teeth out in a row over some silk stockings, Dropsical Dillie hasn't been able to pass water and is swelling like an ot air balloon, a few of them have been laid out wiv too much opium and I've

185

been searching high an low for any money Bell might have left behind her when she scarpered.'

'Oh you know Bell's bound to have taken all her tin with her,' he said quickly, ushering Missy out of the office.

Damn that idiot Jeremiah Cutts; he hadn't thought the lad so ambitious. What the devil had the young rogue thought he was playing at?

There was just enough money in the strongbox. Not a penny more than was needed. A pity that by now Mattie's purse would be closed to him. Mattie! He felt distaste when he thought of her plaintive voice, her cramped parlour where he had had to act husbandly. Still, he hadn't done so badly out of the affair, what with the clothes and a large portion of her savings. A pity about that varmint of a shop boy. If he ever caught hold of Jer he'd . . . but there wasn't time for that now. A new world beckoned him. Kathleen's talents were first rate but he'd have to learn how to manage them profitably. Then there was his own act with Markham. So far so good and he was hopeful for the auditions the writer had promised him. But now there were complications and not just at the bordello. His plans were unfolding as distinct possibilities and now love, love changed everything.

A feverous London heat pressed against the bordello windows. Gabriel removed his frock coat, the one Mattie had paid for. All over the house women were reclining on beds, women semi-dressed, languorous with heat, doped with laudanum, restive with gin, hair tumbling, clothes askew, cheap scent perfuming their silty skin, arms thrust out in the oppressive heat, thighs agape . . . all over the house, compliant women . . . he wanted none of them.

He poured himself a glass of flat champagne from a bottle he found in a drawer in Bell's desk. Virginia, his heart beat, Virginia, his blood pulsed, Virginia, his throat ached: whatever am I to do about you?

An exquisite creature, but her youth, her passion made her blind to the ways of the world. If he married Virginia, *when* he married her, Markham would surely seek to know more about Gabriel Feaver. He could fake a personal history he supposed. Anything could be faked; family trees, even crests designed, distressed clerks, destitute gentlewomen roped in to attend wedding ceremonies as genteel relations. A whole life of fakery might be too much of a strain though and, even if he could persuade Markham of his gentlemanly status, that would hardly guarantee the writer's agreement to a marriage between Gabriel and Virginia. It was one thing to fake a history, but to conjure an estate, a fortune, was barely possible. Markham would see Gabriel in the light of an adventurer. Wherever he looked Gabriel saw complications. No, the only thing for it was an elopement after Markham had effected the right introductions. Even if the writer then turned on him and managed to damage his prospects in the theatre, he would have Virginia's inheritance to look forward to. As she had said, they could live on the expectations. But she was such a child, she probably had no understanding of financial matters. He would somehow have to gain more detailed information about her prospects. He wanted love and money both. Reputation too! He wanted everything. Love was urgent, love pressed him but common sense cautioned delay. Timing was all. If he could only resist the madness of love a little while longer he might gain everything.

Gabriel swallowed brandy from a small flask he had carried with him on the journey. That episode in the basement was a ghastly business. Nausea rose in his stomach. He decided to stay at Green's Hotel in the Strand until affairs at Bell's were sorted out. How quickly he'd got used to fine living at Rees Hall. A fastidious man. Nature intended him to be a gentleman! He could no longer bear the prospect of cheap lodging-houses.

After making arrangements with a couple of men, brutes of fellows but reliable, to deal with the problem in the basement, and bribing Missy with a few shillings to clean up afterwards, warning her not to think, question or speak about the nature of her duties, Gabriel made his way to the Strand. His thoughts twisted with matters of expediency and love, he was taken by surprise at the hotel when a clerk behind the tall mahogany reception booth said: 'A letter for you, sir. We had no address to forward it on to.'

The note was penned in Mattie's cramped hand.

Devil — your child boils within me. Demonspawn. I looked everywhere. Then at a gaff back of Leicester Square, a stew of vice, I discovered all. From sluts and bawds the truth spilled — lava hot truth spilling from their loose mouths — Liar! Whoremonger!

The everlasting lake of fire will not cleanse your sins from you.

Molten seed turning inside me. Every morning the hot vomit pushes up out of my mouth.

I want to tear this child, this horror out of me. I want you here, now, to ask you WHY? To drive my nails through your hard heart. I want the money you stole from me. I go here and there and everywhere and learn everything and find nothing. My curse on you! A curse on all your loves! You have ruined me! Where are you? I can barely walk, the hot sickness burns my stomach. I stagger the streets and do not find you. If any of God's mercy reddens your stone of a heart, come back, return what you owe to this ruin of a woman that once was Mattie Holton.

Gabriel's mouth screwed up distastefully. Holton's Groceries. He was well out of that. Better not stay at Green's after all. He didn't relish the prospect of meeting up with Mattie Holton again. Better find another place.

The heat rose like fever. The air shimmered like delusion. A close, crepey air. All the whores were tetchy and snapped shut their fans with exasperation at the soiled, cluttered mess in the bordello. The sheets were unwashed, discarded shifts sprawled on the floor, peeled stockings like sloughed snakeskins lay inert

where careless limbs had shed them. Chamberpots, unemp-
tied, overflowed and leaked through the floorboards. The
little maid had fled with Bell and none of the women
had the heart for housework. Let one of the others
see to it, each cried when she lazily pulled the rags
from her hair in the morning or laced herself loosely
because no gentlemen were calling. Sometimes one or
other of the whores would sprinkle Hungary water
or Cologne on her bedlinen, scatter crushed lavender in
the hall because heat saturated the walls exhaling its
stale used-up breath, the breath of the city, throughout
the bordello. Someone had closed the shutters on the
heat but still it seeped in through the pores of the
crumbling brickwork. Whores shrugged their fans open
again hopelessly. To and fro, backwards and forwards
the ostrich feather, the ivory, the thin silk fans batted,
batted uselessly because they could not shift the sweltering
heatwave.

Fans falling shut again as night fell and opium-fed
dreams thickened the heat that was viscid as treacle
filling the women's mouths, slowing their throbbing
hearts, calming their pulses at last to clammy delirium.
Dead to the world, most of them, as Missy, armed with
buckets of water and strong carbolic, clanked down to
the basement.

In Bell's study Gabriel finished the flat champagne.
The ledgers were illuminating. When Bell got back
he'd make sure he renegotiated a higher percentage.
He lifted the ledgers and put them back under the
floorboards with the emptied strongbox. Perhaps it was

gases from the earthen floor beneath the bordello that escaped when he loosened the boards, perhaps it was that which accounted for the strange odour beginning to fill the house. Or maybe he only imagined it.

༄ FIFTEEN ༄

Gabriel had been too weary, after all, to begin searching for accommodation in the suffocating heat. He'd bedded down at the bordello. Bell had the best room in the place and he needed only to change the sheets. He would be comfortable enough in her berth until she returned and he could journey back to Virginia. The women were glad to have him stay over. He could better deal with the coves who came wheedling at the door. In this heat none of them had the heart to undertake the responsibility of Bell's business.

He penned a note to Bell informing her that the Portugal Street business had been dealt with and she could return. He assured her that he'd managed to keep her secret from the whores. He appreciated she wouldn't want any of them blabbing.

Heat made Gabriel sluggish. A clammy odour snuffed what was left of oxygen and his lungs withered in the airless atmosphere.

'What is that damn smell?' Tess demanded of Gertie, who had turned green and complained of feeling bilious.

'Missy says it's the smell of drains,' Gertie whispered sibilantly.

'Not drains,' spat Tess, 'but love, p'raps.'

'Love?' Dropsical Dillie's smile swelled with surprise. 'How can love smell like corruption?'

'Because it's a poison that rots the heart,' Tess replied, swatting cockroaches with a meat cleaver.

'The odour lurches around the house but I'd swear it comes from Missy,' Susannah slurred.

'She smells bad, right enough,' Corrie conceded.

'Suffocate the rotting whore for she's surely got a dose of ladies' fever,' Tess dropped her cleaver with a clatter, splitting a cockroach open.

'Suffocate yourself,' Corrie growled. 'She ain't got a dose of anything *carnal* though she's sick, mortal sick,' Corrie looked perplexed. 'But it ain't no ladies' fever. It's something much more gawdforsaken. Something to do with what yous were up to the other night. What the devil was it Gabriel?'

When he chose not to answer her she went on. 'And the smell don't just live in Missy in any case. The smell has other abodes. Last night I thought the smell seemed to rise up from the basement so I went down the stairs,' she paused and sucked on her teeth dramatically, 'And

194

what do yous think I discovered there?' The other whores sat bolt upright and forgot their suffocation, eyes riveted on Old Corruption.

'What did you find?' they chorused. Corrie's false ringlets clacked and little clouds of brown dust powdered her bare shoulders.

'I stood outside the nailed door and I struck a lucifer . . .'

'And then?' the women breathed.

'And then the flame hissed and flared as it always does but then the fire faltered and no light came.'

'No light,' the whores trilled.

'No light,' Corrie continued, 'from the combustible head of my lucifer. The air were so bad it choked the flame and extinguished it.'

The whores sat round Gabriel in a circle, like flames themselves, shuddering and lurid. Slouching against the mantel, a little drunk, which he put down to the heat as he had merely sipped wine this evening, he said thickly: 'As you know that room is sealed up most of the time and a colony of rats burrowed beneath the floorboards there. It's plaguey rats that make the house reek with this festering miasma.' His narrow eyes swept round the suspicious circle. 'That's the reason Bell left in a hurry. She's got a mortal fear of the creatures. She told Jer to get rid of em but it seems he was a lily-livered boy after all and refused to lift the floorboards and throw down arsenic into their nesting place. "I don't pay shirkers," Bell told him but it was no good and, when she insisted, the coward scarpered.' The whores looked doubtful. He went on.

195

'I arranged for men to poison the pests and what you smell now are the vapours of decaying vermin.'

'There's vermin and then there's vermin,' Corrie said heavily.

'Won't this ratty air poison all of us then?' Gertie fretted, her ivory skin blotched as with a mildew.

'I suspect the miasma is most contagious, at its most potent close to the source of the nest in the sealed room,' Gabriel explained.

'I was accustomed to live with rats on the farm, rats big as dogs. They never harmed me,' Tess asserted.

'These are city rats stewed in sewer effluence,' Gabriel said.

'Stuff and nonsense!' Susannah hiccuped. 'We've all spent long years in rat-infested lodging-houses. Ain't never heard tell of ratty air before.'

'There's rats and rats,' Corrie said darkly.

'Precisely,' Gabriel said. 'Rats and rats. What with all this overwrought weather making the sewers fester, the rats have ingested the toxins and breathe the foulness out again compounded with their own filthy breath. The heat and the city filth account for the pestilence.'

The whores fell silent, each one thinking of the terible smell that seemed to have wormed itself inside Missy.

'Well, I'm going to my bed,' Gabriel put down his emptied glass. 'Make the most of tonight girls. I expect Bell will be back shortly before I leave tomorrow morning.'

'There's rats and then there's rats,' Corrie repeated

when Gabriel had left them.

The journey back to Rees Hall was uncomfortable, interminable in the dead heat. He must have drunk too much last night at the bordello; his head ached badly and his mouth was furred and cinder dry. In the jolting carriage Gabriel slept fitfully, his stomach growing queasy with uneasy dreams.

. . . The woman had turned and swayed. She laughed. A horrible laugh like a donkey coughing.

A coarse sacking bag hung round his neck.

'Eat your dinner Gabriel.' His neck was stiff. His neck ached because he held his head still as a waxwork dummy.

'I declare child your neck'll soon be queer as your leg is.'

The brown jug slipped from her hand. The gin splashed him. That vexed her. He watched her face swell with anger. The woman's neck was wattled like porridge, her cheeks were purple, lips red as sores spat curses at him.

'I'll break yer face yer little bastard. If yer adn't been so stubborn puttin yer evil eye on me hand so it shook the six pennorth of best satin out of me grasp I'd ave been set up for work down the Slaughterman's tonight. Now how will I get rid of this busting headache?'

A tear ran down his cheek. She grinned suddenly and then said in a voice that boomed with dreadful threats like a hell fire preacher giving a sermon to sinners: 'I'll learn yer to turn yer nose up at the

197

good scraps of food I forced meself to climb rubbish heaps for, almost cutting me hands open on the jags of earthenware and glass that had to be sorted through before the rinds of bacon and crusts of bread could be found. Thinks yerself too high and mighty for the leavings of others does yer? Thinks yer should be sat up nice at a table like a dainty whore. I'll fuckin daintywhore yer!' The woman's voice grew frantic. His fear riled her.

'Don't hit me ma,' he sobbed. 'I'm sooorrree ma,' he wailed. Then, 'No and don't make me, no, I'm sorry, never again, never, never, never,' . . . a litany like a prayer that went unanswered.

The woman snatched the bag from his neck, scattering the rotten food, then scuttled like a cockroach across to the little curtained recess.

'Ma, don't, please don't! Mama! Mama!'

The sound of the straw mattress being ripped with her raw hands and the chaff spilling like guts.

He gagged.

'I'll learn yer.'

Her ham fist blew his mouth open.

'Ave to be fed like a bleedin baby will yer?'

The straw tasted of rotten herrings. The straw was tenacious and worked down his throat that heaved to spew it up again. Long piercing stems, strangling creepers that choked him, spearing the words, the frantic screaming words that bubbled upwards like gas from a drowned man.

'Devilll mammmmmaaaa. DevillllllIIIIIhhhhaaaaa teeee yyyyooooouuuu!'

*   *   *

198

The carriage wheels rumbled over small stones. Someone threw up the window blind and called, 'Are you all right, Gabriel?' He screwed his eyes up at the sudden access of sunlight. The infernal heat. How long had he been sleeping? Was the journey over then?

'Kathleen is it?' The sharp sun had thrown a halo of gold over her earth-brown hair. She climbed in beside him and the carriage rolled on again. 'I walk to the edge of the estate every day,' she said, 'hoping I'll be the first to greet you. Are you all right?' she asked again. 'You looked flushed, half dazed.'

'I'm too hot, too weary and the journey was too long,' he grumbled.

'Did you get your business done?'

'It all went wrong. Perhaps your premonitions were right, Kathleen and I should never have gone to London.' How could he have left all this for paltry guineas, he thought looking out at the lush greenness of everything.

'Well I wish I could've gone to London with you. I don't like the country,' she said. 'In London you feel you can achieve anything but here . . .'

'Here?' he said vaguely.

'There's so much of everything but it's like a prison. There's no freedom to be yourself.'

'You were yourself at Bell's, I suppose?' He tried to rouse himself from lethargy by provoking Kathleen.

'Well in a way I was.'

'Aren't you singing to a different tune all of a sudden? You begged me to get you out of the bordello,' he said wearily.

'I thought you offered me freedom,' she responded. 'Bell's was a prison of course but at least I had companions in servitude. Here I'm solitary.'

'I'm back with you now aren't I and haven't you had Markham dancing attendance?'

'Oh Markham!' she said. 'He's my gaoler. I have to do whatever he wants of me. The truth is I can't bear the sight or touch of him.'

Gabriel sighed. All this heat and now altercation.

'It won't be for much longer,' he promised. 'And Markham will probably help set you up with a big present so make sure you go on pleasing him for a little longer.'

As you please his sister, she thought, not saying anything until he asked, his voice cracked, raw with emotion: 'How is Virginia?'

She shrugged her shoulders, tossed her hair that hung loose and freshly washed, springing down to her waist with a violent energy.

'How is Virginia?' she mimicked his tone of voice perfectly. His own voice sounded weak and doltish in her mocking throat.

'Why shouldn't I ask after her?'

'Why should you ask? What right have you to take an interest in a lady? Stick to whores Gabriel. They understand you better.'

He stared at his accomplice in surprise. What had happened to soft-voiced adoration? And, as though sensing his fury, she moved away from him. Hadn't she shown patience when he'd kept her dangling, trusting in the future he'd construct for them? But now with this burning agony in his eyes, this flush on his cheek, this discomposure, she was nudged aside, the future imperilled.

'Ungrateful minx!' he murmured. 'After all I've done for you. Why should I stick with low street women with all my gifts? Why shouldn't I try for something better?'

'You set your sights on Virginia Markham then?' She had to hear the brutal truth from his own lips.

'What's it to you? I never promised you love, did I?'

'No, but you promised me a future,' she said, 'and now you'll risk everything because passion will make you careless. You'll throw it all away, and for what? I'll tell you what: for pure lust dressed up as romance, just as we whores dressed up as death, a mere fantasy. You'll lose everything because your imagination has run away with you, Gabriel.'

How had she ever allowed Gabriel to persuade her into the whoring she had finally set herself against? And whoring was what it was after all. Out of the frying pan at Bell's into the fire at Markham's. Although she supposed that scandalising herself with one man was better than pandering to a whole regiment in the bordello. How could she have agreed to it, she wondered, knowing the answer: poverty and desire had led her to this place; knowing how she'd pursue the famine trail of desire through all the circles of damnation that Gabriel penetrated.

Kathleen had at first set herself to catch the lovers.

Whenever a flight of startled birds soared from a shaking bush and she flung herself at the bower like an angel with a flaming sword, she found only the lair of small animals. She had torn her flesh to shreds hunting the devious pair between the jabbing briars. In a rustic lodge she waited all day, convinced that this was their trysting place. But only a bemused gamekeeper found her and when she trailed the telltale signs of trampled grasses and flattened weeds into the tortuous woods she simply lost herself.

But, defeated in her pursuit of the spectacle of love, Kathleen had become adept in fastening on the signs that indicated its clandestine presence. A perfumy, vaporous blend of woodsmoke, wild flowers and excitement in the corridors that lingered until late morn led her through the secret passages of the endless house. A haphazard, dishevelled manner of dressing spoke volumes when the lovers emerged at the breakfast table. Their sweet abstinence from food: Gabriel and Virginia fasted single-mindedly as though food were a distraction, mealtimes burdensome: platefuls of barely toyed with delicacies cluttering the dinner table. Then the sighs, wordless, aching murmurs of breath that troubled the silence in the drawing-room. Pallor, of course, when it was not defeated by sudden hectic blushes, and the palsy of the girl's limbs grown suddenly weak from amorous entanglement. Kathleen's tortured eyes saw everything but the one thing eternally absent, preternaturally present, that her imagination pictured too luridly.

*   *   *

That night the heat thickened and the soupy air swarmed with small flying creatures. Kathleen's stays crucified her. She longed to go about half naked in a shift, reclining in sluttish freedom; but until the candles were snuffed and the oil lamps extinguished, she must play her part as decorous houseguest. And even when release from constricting whalebone came at bedtime she would be bound, hand and foot, by Markham's passion. His perspiring flesh would glue itself to the pores of her skin, rapacious mouth inhaling her last breath between the humid sheets. Another insupportable night! She almost wished she could fall into the swoon of a *real* trance and lie insensate.

They dined as usual with the conservatory doors open. All the windows were flung open too and first delicate gnats then swollen flies, greedy as locusts, settled over the table. Kathleen and Virginia languidly swatted them with their fans, making barely a disturbance amongst the hungry swarm. Then the gentlemen, glad of the excuse, lit their cigars and acrid smoke dispelled the invasion.

With the fug of cigar smoke, the piquant scorch of melting wax candles and too much heat, the air wavered. Kathleen, hot and irritable, her staybones like knives, drank more wine than she intended. The gentlemen also imbibed heavily, and with so much desire in the room the food was largely left untasted.

Virginia sipped water and toyed with her meal. Gabriel tried not to look at the girl, Kathleen noticed, his eyes fastening on Celestine instead; or on his host whenever Markham engaged him in conversation; or more frequently on the flowers that crowded the room; or else wandering to fasten on a cloud of gnats hovering in strategic withdrawal by the tall doors that led to the conservatory. It grew darker, then moths came and careered into the candles. Virginia, with a glance at her brother, made her excuses and Kathleen sensed how Gabriel's desires got up from the table too, and pursued the tiny creature up the great echoing stairs of Rees Hall.

They drank more wine. Kathleen saw with surprise that Gabriel, long hardened to drink, looked drunk tonight, his thin lips swollen; he also had a certain rakish looseness about the mouth that she associated with Markham. His skin was drained, yellowish, beads of perspiration cooling the high flush she'd noticed earlier. Gabriel's hands trembled like a victim of falling sickness.

Kathleen felt uncomfortable. Sweat dripped between her breasts.

'There are too many moths,' she protested, trying to control her terror of the swooping, crumble-to-dust fragility of their wings. Markham picked up a little sconce and snuffed all the burning flames. One lamp, turned low, barely illumined the room and the moths became disheartened, only a few remaining to circle the dim glow from the oil lamp that Markham set down on a sideboard at the far end of the room.

Gabriel seemed reluctant to begin the séance tonight and poured yet more wine into his swiftly drained glass.

'This damnable heat,' he protested when Markham asked if all was well with him.

'Take your jacket off dear fellow.' And Markham shed his own as well as his silk waistcoat with its florid embroidery, in order to make his guest feel at ease. 'No formality between friends,' he insisted.

Silence fell. Markham seemed to wait for something. Why is he waiting, Kathleen thought dully, heat and drink making her stupid. Then she remembered. She wasn't Kathleen, she was Celestine and the man waited for Gabriel to conduct her performance. Empty yourself of everything, let everything fall away until you are the empty space desire can fill. Hear nothing. See nothing. Say nothing. Monkey business . . . she told herself.

But Gabriel didn't begin, he went on drinking, his body trembling, making no attempt to break the sluggish silence. At last Markham coughed and said: 'Would you care for a brandy, Feaver?' his hand reaching reluctantly for the decanter, 'or, if you're ready, perhaps we could gather round the card table.'

'Oh not tonight, Markham,' Gabriel protested with a hazy smile. 'Really the long journey in all that heat exhausted me. If you don't object I'll retire now. I'm sure Celestine doesn't need my assistance to put on her little show.' Gabriel's voice was slurred. He pushed his chair back from the table, swaying as he stood. Then to his host's dismay he blundered ungraciously from the room, knocking against chairs, tables, torchères in the semi-darkness, his arms spread like wings as if he fought to soar free of their company or as if, like a moth, burning light impelled him.

Markham watched his departure with displeasure

and astonishment. 'We . . . ell,' his moist lips pursed. 'If you've had enough to eat and drink my dear, I rather think . . .' He looked at her expectantly but it was Kathleen not Celestine who answered him.

'Oh not tonight, sir!' she snapped. 'The heat has given me a headache.' Then to her host's annoyance she too pushed back her chair and quickly, haughtily, left him.

Tall church candles burned in Virginia's room illuminating every detail. There was the high-backed chair, there the armoire, there was the wax doll strung with some of the girl's simple pearl jewellery. Gabriel's feet were caught up in some soft nebulous stuff. He stooped to retrieve the yards of muslin and scented his beloved's fragrance from the gown she had tossed aside carelessly. And here was the girl herself, limp hair scattered over the pillows. She was here waiting for him.

They made love wordlessly. He must have drunk too much wine because he couldn't taste her familiar sweetness. His tongue felt thick and swollen, blundering in her mouth, crushing her breath. He spread himself over her heavily.

Virginia lay unprotesting, feeling his heat, his dead weight, tasting a certain London bitterness on his skin. The trip perhaps had made him moody, irritable, for his caresses were bleak, stripped of tender words or coaxing murmurs. He loved her silently, briefly and when he pulled away she saw that his face was blotchy with shadows. She thought he fell at once into sleep but he suddenly spoke to

206

her, his voice muffled, his mouth turned towards the pillow.

'What a fuss about a few stains, Missy!'

She sat up startled, reaching for the lucifers on her bedside table.

'What? What are you talking about Gabriel?'

He raised his head and looked at her blankly in the light of a hastily relit candle. His eyes were shrivelled like dead stars. Then he sank back on to the pillows as if quite drained, wrung out with exhaustion, muttering something in a thick voice, something incoherent she couldn't quite catch though she thought one of the words was − rats? − maybe. She put her hand on his brow and felt the dangerous heat there. His voice was hoarse.

'Who would've thought the creature had so much poison in her?' he raved. There was a pause, then he went on. 'All the perfumes of Araby, all the perfumes. Out damn spot . . . damned pestilence,' he mumbled. 'Use perfumes of Araby . . .' Then his voice broke off and he fell precipitously into sleep.

Trying to brush away the clammy moth wings. The creatures were curiously heavy, flapping their wings, dragging themselves over his face. He shut his fist and trapped a particularly fat juicy fellow. 'Now I've crushed you, you won't trouble me,' he said, relaxing his grip, but the sullen creature refused to die and began crawling over his face again, its damp wings settling upon his mouth. Against his will Gabriel parted his lips. The moth squirted something cold into his mouth. He swallowed and the cool liquid slid down his parched throat.

'More! More!' he croaked despite his repugnance. Again the moth released its fluids and once more he sipped the tasteless . . . 'Water!' he groaned. 'More water,' he pleaded, opening his eyes. Was it morning?

Virginia put down the damp cloth she had been wiping over his face and withdrew the glass of water from his lips.

'Are you awake?' she whispered. He nodded, unsure if this was another dream, part of the interminable night.

'Is it morning?' he asked her.

'Just after dawn,' she replied.

His head throbbed. He wanted to be sick.

'Must get back to my own room before the servants are up,' he muttered thickly but when he tried to stand the room revolved like a diorama and the floor rose and fell like the sea. He staggered, almost falling back into Virginia's arms.

'You've some sort of fever. We should call in a doctor,' she said, her eyes shadowy from watching over his delirium.

'No damn quack!' he said, trying to shake off the infernal ache in his head, trying to think clearly. No doctors with their questions and perspicacity. 'It's a low fever that's all. London's teeming with heat-sickness. A day or two will see me right again.' Raising his eyes, seeing how frightened she was. Had she spent the whole night listening to his raving? 'Forgive me Ginnie. I'm a careless brute to have put you through such a night. If I'd any idea I was going down with fever I'd have stayed in my own room. I thought I was only drunk last night,' he said. 'Well,' he managed to laugh despite the splitting headache, 'I'm trembling like a toper anyway. No, you stay here.' As the girl tried to help him back to his room, he pushed her away weakly saying, 'I only hope you don't take the sickness. Better not kiss me, Ginnie.'

He poured water into the ewer and splashed his face and swollen neck. Feeling nausea thicken in his stomach he drank a glass of water, then climbed quickly into his own bed. He lay down, burning hot then feeling contradictory cold shivers chill his bones. Must think clearly, clear the head before the delusions grip hold again. Try to avoid doctors. Markham might insist. He must get the maid to tell Kathleen first. Kathleen could cover for him. Only call a doctor if he got worse, if he took the fever really badly. But he wouldn't allow himself to get dangerously ill, not now when he had to be strong, not at this moment when destiny was ready for him.

When the maid brought tea he gave her hoarse instructions. Within moments Kathleen came, wild hair flying, nightgown still on, barefoot she flew down flights of stairs, ran along corridors and burst into his room as if a swarm of wasps pursued her.

'Holy Jesus!' she swore. 'You're burning up. Let's get those heavy covers off you,' but he seemed barely conscious of her, his fever again painting his senses with the lurid confusions of delirium. She stripped away the bedclothes, denuding him of his nightshirt that she soaked in water using it to cool his sizzling flesh. She bathed him gently, patting the cloth over his body, drawing it over his limbs, seeing for the first time his misshapen foot that she bent over and kissed like the Magdalene. She didn't stop bathing him until at last a delicious coolness ran over his body and she drew the thin sheet up over him to cover his nakedness. For a while he seemed to sleep sweetly and when he woke it was with a sudden anxiety.

'My boots, my boots.' He lifted himself up and looked around the room anxiously.

'Lie down, you've been dreaming,' she said.

'They're in Ginnie's room. If a maid should discover them! . . .' He pulled away the sheet and made as if to clamber out of the bed.

'Your boots?' Kathleen stood very still, her hand frozen where it had gripped the jug of water she was about to pour for him.

Sickness stripped caution away.

'I left them in Virginia's room,' he said.

'You took your boots off in Virginia's room?'

'They mustn't be found there.' The worry of discovery seemed to make his thoughts grow coolly lucid. Even now he was winding the sheet around the lower part of his body, allowing it to trail so his feet were shrouded. He picked up his discarded clothes.

'You took your boots off before getting into bed with the girl?' she asked him stupidly.

'The servants mustn't find them,' he said, ignoring the import of her words.

'You exposed your bad foot to the girl?' A sensation not unlike dread squeezed Kathleen's stomach. Not pure lust, after all, she thought hopelessly.

'What? You make it sound as though I per-formed some kind of obscene gesture,' he laughed unconvincingly.

'Get back into bed. I'll get the boots,' she said dully. 'The girl will be at breakfast shortly. With luck I can slip into her room before the servants are about.' Gabriel lay back gratefully on the easeful bed.

'You're an angel, Kath. You must tell Markham I've got a summer chill,' he said, trying to collect his thoughts. 'I don't want him to know about the fever. You can see to me Kathleen. Say a doctor isn't necessary and that I'd rather not be bothered by servants.'

'You don't want to panic Markham, is that it, Gabriel?'

He looked at Kathleen with his meanest expression.

'I don't want him to find out from a doctor that I've the sort of fever that can be caught in the lowest of London cesspits, Kathleen.'

'Did you come across sickness in London?'

'No, sickness came across me, I think.' He allowed Kathleen to smooth the sheet over him. He began to feel cooler, thinking more clearly. Thinking of Missy who hadn't been able to stop shuddering, thinking of Corrie and her extinguished flames, thinking of an odour like desolation, thinking of Jer Cutts and his recklessness, thinking of Bell and her avarice and his own careless greed, Gabriel began to reconsider everything.

⚬ SIXTEEN ⚬

The girl was artless, pouncing jealously on Kathleen.
'Let one of the maids see to that,' Virginia said,
reaching out a hand, lightly stroking the fresh nightshirt Kathleen had fetched from the linen cupboard.
'Or a manservant,' she coloured.

'I'm happy to care for a friend,' Kathleen said. It's
not your place, the girl's tormented eyes told her but
she merely swallowed hard and said: 'Perhaps he would
feel easier being tended to by a servant. Less obligated
you know.'

'It's the obligations of friendship that make me a
more suitable nurse. No servant can care for him as I
can. Besides he will have no one else.'

'No one?'

'Not even an apothecary,' Kathleen shrugged her

shoulders, trying to make light of the illness as Gabriel had instructed her. 'Still, it's only a summer cold.' But some devil in her couldn't resist embellishment. 'He had a terrible illness as a child,' she lied, 'I forget the name of it, some long Latin word, left him with that crippled foot, you know, and whenever he takes a chill he has fits of fever and trembling. It's a regular thing with him, nothing to worry about.'

'But perhaps we should send for one of his family. He's not spoken of them. Does he have female relations who could look after him?' The girl was palely determined. She resented that air of intimacy Kathleen assumed with Gabriel. When he was well again she must find out how her lover had fallen in with this woman.

'I know nothing about any family,' Kathleen said abruptly, beginning to push past the girl on the stairs. 'If he wants anyone be sure I'll let your brother know about it,' she pressed the nightshirt close to her bodice, running lightly up the stairs away from suspicion and envy.

The girl, self-control diminished from lack of sleep, called after her.

'If his condition worsens we *will* call a doctor. We *will* send for his family. Be sure of that. We won't burden you with the responsibility, Miss Celestine.'

But he didn't get worse. He seemed to get better all at once: drinking glass after glass of the barley water, sipping bowl after bowl of the thin soup that Kathleen brought up to him. Virginia had vases arranged with freshly cut flowers and these filled the room that faced north and was pleasantly shady with its own ivy-clad balcony looking over a pool of cool green water.

'You look as if you were born to this,' Kathleen smiled, stroking his matted hair away from his forehead and covering him with a fresh sheet but he pushed her hand away impatiently. 'Not born to it, no. Born to bare boards. Born to curses not caresses, Kathleen.'

She'd not heard him speak of his past before. The illness must have made him relent a little. He who was always relentless.

'Jess mentioned something about your mother the day you took me to the Slaughterman's Arms,' she said carefully as he scowled at her.

'I never think of that devil as kin to me.'

'Even a blood-tie with the devil himself would be better than having no kin at all.' Kathleen sighed the excluded sigh of the orphan. 'Why do you call your mother a devil? Is it because she wasn't . . . because, as Jess said, she went mad.'

Gabriel looked gloomy. 'Mad is what people say when someone is so bad, their badness bludgeons you. As she bludgeoned me,' he said, looking away from Kathleen out of the shady, ivy-strewn window.

'Bludgeoned you?'

'Bludgeoned me with words,' he repeated. 'Battered me sometimes but more often vilified me, which is worse to a child forbidden to utter a word, a child who is forced to listen day in and day out to one ceaseless voice that seems to fill the universe with its malevolence.'

'You were forbidden to speak?'

'I was struck dumb with terror in her presence, in any case,' he laughed painfully.

'Well it's a wonder you grew up to have a way with words, if you were cowed into silence,' Kathleen marvelled. Gabriel flushed as if the fever again rode him.

'As children often do, when alone I imagined companions who always listened to me. I spoke endless monologues to them, which I suppose was a sort of actorly training.'

Kathleen nodded. She too knew about loneliness.

'But why did your mother abuse you?'

'Because it was easy for her. A child is the perfect victim, having no power or authority. My father told me, before he drank himself to death, how she raged at me from the very first moment after the cruel pains of childbirth! I have his words by heart, burned into me. "You were born straight as a die," he told me, "but before the cord was even cut she elbowed the midwife aside and dangling you by one foot she twisted the ankle the way you wring wet sheets until she heard the bones snap and you screamed your way into the world in a way that we all knew meant you suffered therefore you existed."'

'Holy Jesus!'

'Holy Mary, Mother of God,' he mocked Kathleen's sentiment. 'Of course, I have only have a drunkard's word on the matter but later treatment indicated it was a likely story.'

'Later treatment?'

But his eyes narrowed and his lips tightened because the past was not really a story. The romance was only now begun. Shut out dreary history. He'd narrate no more on the matter of his childhood. A momentary weakness because of his illness. He mustn't let Kathleen's nursing seduce him from that long silence. He was a man, after all, not a milksop infant clamouring for affection. Kathleen would be getting above herself, thinking she could mother him. He stretched weakly on the comfortable bed.

'I feel much better,' he told her. 'I think I'll be well enough to get up tomorrow. I don't want Markham to feel rebuffed. I was uncivil the other night.'

'Don't worry about Markham,' she said bitterly. 'His lusts will soon overcome any resentment.' She stood up, her long silk skirts trailing, comely now, not so skinny what with the country air and the good food she'd been eating; in the sweet blue silk she could take her place alongside any lady. She walked over to the balcony and idly began to tear strips from the ivy leaves.

'Shall we go home soon, Gabriel?' she called over to him.

'Back to London you mean? Soon, very soon,' he promised her. He sat up, 'I expect Markham to arrange some auditions for me.'

'And what of me? Is anything arranged for me?' She turned and fastened her piercing blue eyes on him. To his surprise Gabriel couldn't hold her gaze. Must be this damn sickness, he thought as his own eyes slid shiftily away from her.

'I won't forget you, Kathleen,' he said.

'Forget me?' The blue eyes chilly as sapphires.

217

He smiled weakly, his eyelids lowered as he sank back on the plumped pillows.

'This illness, it's like a warning not to over-reach myself. Everything going wrong at the bordello, the complications . . .' his voice trailed. 'I begin to think spreading my interests only causes difficulties. Perhaps success needs single-mindedness. Maybe I should cut loose altogether from the Resurrectionist Club, from all the stews of London.'

'And me?' she glared at him icily.

He flushed suddenly, feeling unmanly, a little foolish.

'I don't think Virginia could bear me to form a partnership, even a professional arrangement, with another woman . . . now.'

Her blue eyes were cold stars cut from infinity.

'What are you telling me? What do you mean by speaking to me of what *Virginia* can't bear?' But he carefully ignored her rage and said, 'I'm sure we can get Markham to act as your patron. He's eating out of your lap now. Even if he tires of you, you know he's generous. You could get enough money out of him to set yourself up as a medium. You're a woman of talent, Kathleen. You really don't need me to manage you.'

'Don't need you?'

'But we'll have to set about Markham sharpish,' he went on. 'He might turn against both of us after . . . I might even forfeit my chance of the stage . . .' his voice trailed away again.

'After what, Gabriel?'

He put up a hand to shade his eyes that resignation

was already weakening. He swallowed hard. All these lies were like an impenetrable undergrowth. Perhaps some sword of truth was needed, after all, to hack his way clear again.

'After his sister runs away with me, Kathleen.'

The girl must have gone into a sulk because Kathleen had insisted on nursing Gabriel. She didn't come down for dinner. Markham and Kathleen dined alone. Quickly her host dispensed with the servants.

'You're sure Feaver is on the mend?'

'Just a chill. His skin runs cool as a stream now,' she said, crumbling a delicate pastry with her fork.

'Well I only hope Virginia isn't going to fall ill. She wouldn't even take a tray up in her room.'

'The heat, I suppose,' Kathleen said.

Markham smiled at her. He passed a darting tongue over his lower lip. He sipped some champagne. Smiling at her waiting for something. 'This heat is the very devil,' she said. He got up from his seat, came over and poured more champagne for her. Kathleen drank. Her seventh glass this evening!

'A pity that your visit draws to a close,' he murmured into her ear, his mouth almost nibbling at her ringlets but he went back to his own place again. 'Shall you set yourself up as a public medium as you did in Dublin? I seem to remember Feaver saying you wanted to escape all that.'

She confessed in a small voice that the prospect of the teeming crowds, the heckling audiences, the burly brutes who always wanted to frisk her to make sure she hid no tricks under her petticoats, was more than she could bear.

Swallowing more champagne, she told her heart not to burn, her brain not to fizz; heart and brain both must stay cold, calm, very cold, chill as Gertie's frozen romance, cold as death; neither heart nor brain must dwell on the treachery of Gabriel.

'If I could only find a protector, a patron,' she said dully, 'I might be spared such humiliations.'

Markham looked at her speculatively.

'And if you had such a patron, Celestine, what sort of . . . return might he expect on his . . . investment?'

'If I found such a patron,' Kathleen replied, her voice slurred now: 'I could lead him to that place of rapture where heaven and hell meet. Where the soul itself swoons with fleshly delight. Such a patron would find his reward in that exquisite place where devils ride angels.'

Markham shrugged off his dark jacket and his bright waistcoat. His lips very wet, spitting a cheroot from his mouth.

'I could devote myself to your cause as ardently as any besotted papist,' he said thickly. 'Would you, could you, let me be your protector, Celestine?'

Alas for too much champagne. What else could account for it? The drink went to her head. All Markham's fault. Like any cheap seducer he saw to it that his prey was stunned before he closed in on her.

She had begun smoothly enough, going through the familiar grooves of his prompts, her swoon, only this

time her head actually was reeling and her voice was
slurred, but then Markham scarcely heard her for he
had the words by heart himself and didn't need to
hear them from her own lips. He knew his part. She
supposed when they were in the niche he would set
up for her in London she would have to extend her
repertoire. She would have to study her craft. She
wouldn't be able to rely on Gabriel nor, finally, on
Markham who'd tire sometime. But if what Gabriel
said was right, the writer would set her up, intoduce
her to others who'd want her to bring back the dead
for them.

Bring back the dead. She must concentrate. Tonight
everything was slipping away. Her voices were slipping
down her throat easily as champagne. There was no
holding them. The room was slipping away too. She
held on to the table, then Markham's hands closed over
hers. He was sitting beside her now, his chair drawn
up close. He was touching her. Havana. Oleaginous
Macassar. Wetness. Heat. The dizzy champagne skelter
of everything. The table turned like a carousel.

She threw back her neck, feeling her throat swell.
She couldn't swallow. Something lodged in her throat
like a stone. A cold hard stone. The voices were
lost to her.

'Speak to me, lost spirit,' Markham urged her.
He went on speaking but then his voice slipped
away too . . .

She was in a long corridor following a distant light
or a sound or an instinct, she couldn't be sure which.
She thought Markham followed her but for all that

she was alone. The heat had withdrawn to another part of the house so she was cold now but as if made of ice or stone herself she did not shiver. She was fearless because she had no knowledge of anything. Something else had the knowledge and led her. She followed it blindly.

The corridor dipped and twisted before leading on to stairs that were wide and shallow so women with trailing skirts could glide up them easily. She floated up the stairs and Markham creaked steadily behind her. On the landing she paused and picked up an oil lamp from where it had been set down to illumine a painting. The flame scarcely flickered. The next flight gave on to a gallery with a rosewood balustrade that soared into curved arches and fretted scrollwork like a rood screen. She pursued her course along the balcony that was still as a cloister, gliding beneath the fluted stone ceiling that pleated in folds as sinuous as the tented silken swags that fall over houris in a harem.

Her softly shod feet made no sound on the polished floorboards. Markham's leaden boots paced warily and the creaking might have been the scamper of vermin.

Once she half thought Markham called her name anxiously. She thought she heard him whisper, 'Not here, surely!' But she knew if she glanced back the way would be lost for eternity. Onward she plunged like a Christian soldier. Onward into the valley of . . . love.

Oh love!

She walked on towards an alcove where the fluted stone shivered into a fall of silk hangings. The silken

swags fluttered as a draught swept in through the door
Kathleen opened.

The bed was like a bed in a dream and had endless
transparent silk muslins flying away from its four
posters that supported a satin canopy, flying away
from the indiscretion of the stripped feather mattress,
parting lasciviously to reveal . . .

Markham closed up on Kathleen. His breath on her
neck, she turned and whispered: 'I told you I can draw
down angels. I can show you where heaven and hell
meet. I can show you where devils ride angels.'

Turning back to whisper to Markham. Turning
back broke the spell. Look away and lose the enchantment. Kathleen turned away and woke from her
trance. Kathleen looked back and her words roused
Markham. The draught swept in through the door
she had opened.

The draught swept in and shivered the busy flesh
of the writhing lovers. The draught cut through their
transports. Virginia cried aloud, a sharp uncanny cry.
Gabriel looked up and saw the stern witnesses. Drawing his lame foot under the girl's neck, Gabriel couldn't
imagine what to do, he was so horribly conscious of
being naked.

Covent Garden Spirit-Power Circle

Porphyria's love: she guessed not how
Her darling one wish would be heard.

Robert Browning, *Porphyria's Lover*

ᴄ SEVENTEEN ᴄ

'He's gone and got it then,' Old Corruption said grimly, admitting Kathleen and a bag of bones she barely recognised as Gabriel. 'Another case of fever.'

'He's not sick, only drunk,' Kathleen said shortly.

'Drunk is sick wiv him. Never in all my life seen Gabriel drunk before,' Missy said.

They helped Kathleen support Gabriel. He was in a stupor and when they put his arms around their shoulders they could smell brandy on his breath.

'Put him in Bell's room,' Corrie panted.

'Bell's? Won't she have something to say about that?' Kathleen slid her arm round Gabriel's waist and curved her knee behind his lame leg, propelling him forward.

'Ain't *here* to make a fuss about anyone lying in her

bed,' Corrie said. Then conversation ceased as Gabriel was hauled up the stairs and the women puffed and grunted.

Corrie opened a bedroom door. The three women half carried, half dragged the drunken man over to the bed that was stripped of bedclothes.

'She won't care for muddy boots on her bed,' Kathleen was breathless.

'Who?' Corrie asked vaguely, dizzy from her exertions.

'Bell, of course.' Kathleen said. Missy's hand pressed Kathleen's arm lightly.

'Bell ain't never coming back,' Missy smiled thinly. Corrie sighed heavily.

'Bell were the first one carried off by fever. She came back too soon. The . . . rats may have cleared off but their venom remained,' Corrie shuddered. 'Even now although Missy made sure the passage leading to that room has been sealed with bricks and mortar I ain't certain the air here still ain't contaminated.' She looked sourly at the unconscious Gabriel. 'Rats always slink back to the nest when they think the fuss has died down again. There'll always be rats as sure as life is life and death is death,' she said.

'Bell died of fever!' Kathleen frowned. 'Gabriel took it too, though he's recovered now. What name do they give this fever?'

'Well the doctor said it was Irish fever,' Corrie said bleakly. 'The very fever you find amongst those creatures who've fled the potato blight in your homeland, Kathleen.'

'Irish fever was what the doctor called it and he cancelled his subscription to the Resurrectionist Club, on Bell's deathbed.' Missy's smile was so skeletal it looked like the rictus of a famine victim.

'And not only Bell's gone, the fever carried off Dillie and Tess and Susannah, then some of the others took fright and left the bordello,' Missy told her.

'How do you account for this, this . . . disease afflicting the house?' Kathleen asked the two women.

Missy gave her a haunted look and abruptly left the room. Kathleen's eyes followed the girl, noticing for the first time that Missy's corkscrew ringlets had unflexed and her hair hung straight and limp as muslin.

'What have I said?' Kathleen appealed to Corrie. Corrie sat down on the end of the bed and shook her hair, shorn of its clay ringlets, over her sagging throat. She pleated her hands in the skirts of her black gown.

'Missy was the first of us to go down with the illness. She were delirious and kept raving about slime smearing her, clawing at herself and cursing Gabriel but now she's well again she keeps mum and says she don't know how or where she catched the sickness.' Corrie eyed Kathleen shrewdly. 'But maybe there's others who can account for it.'

'What others?'

'Well, Bell's dead and gone of course and young Cutts has vanished but you may be sure your Mister Feaver knows something of the source of the contagion and I do believe an unholy smell rising up from the bowels of this place was at the root of everything.'

229

Kathleen lifted Gabriel's twisted ankle that had fallen over the edge of the bed and carefully placed it on the flock mattress. She must have a wash and something to eat and drink and then she could take in all these devastating changes.

'What happened to Missy's hair?' she asked absently. 'Was it the fever that knocked the curl out of it?'

'I don't believe it were the fever made her hair straight. I think that were fright,' Corrie said.

First things first. Kathleen took off her soiled travelling clothes, washed, and put on one of the exquisite frocks she had stolen from Virginia Markham. After all, as it turned out, the girl would have no further use for finery and Markham would be too distraught to notice or even care if the servants reported the theft to him, she told herself. She remembered how she had ransacked Virginia's possessions before they fled, rifling through afternoon gowns, walking dresses, riding habits, costly lace, an Indian shawl, a set of unworn chemises, stays, drawers and petticoats, slightly too small silken slippers, neat boots, velvet, beaver and satin bonnets, kid gloves, net mittens, a reticule, one really splendid cloak, a mantle, yards of ribbon, some chaste pearls, a jet locket carved with M for Markham that might have been made for a Mangan, and a couple of ostrich feather and ivory fans still in sealed boxes.

Kathleen stared into the broken slab of mirror on the attic window sill admiring herself. Her wild hair was ever thicker and had a lustre, a shine that owed nothing to Macassar oil. She had gained weight at Rees Hall. Her breasts were voluptuous. Kathleen looked stately as though weight had given her gravitas. She was now taller and rounder than poor little Miss Markham had ever been and the purloined gowns nipped Kathleen's waist and the too short skirts revealed her silk-stockinged ankles. But even if the gown fitted ill, she looked exquisite in it, the snowy whiteness of her skin shimmering beneath the frosted glaze of stiffened muslin, the swooning fall of lace at her breasts barely veiling their ripening swell. But she sighed over her reflection. What use were the gowns to her if she had no lover to admire her in them? Then the thought that Gabriel would look at the silks and muslins and sigh too, because the wrong woman wore them, grieved her.

With Bell gone what would happen to the bordello? With his heart broken, his dreams thwarted, what would become of Gabriel? He was in no state to decide anything. Kathleen turned away from the spotted looking-glass. She squeezed her eyes shut, trying to work herself into a trance. She wasn't at all like Gabriel whose imagination was always plotting. She had to stop thinking. She had to fall into a dream, a dream where everything was easy and she could float, without responsibility, drifting downstream, past Gabriel rowing energetically, borne effortlessly on a current towards many-towered Camelot.

Eyes shut, fingers smoothing the folds of her stolen muslin, delicate hands plucking at the tucks, prising open the discreet pocket, drawing out a piece of white silk netting with gilded tassels, nails snagging the delicate strands, restless fingers plying the drawstring, she eased the net purse open.

The coins were cool and weighty in her palm. It wasn't only her increased size that gave Kathleen gravitas, these sovereigns had something to do with it. She spent them through her fingers like a rosary. Twenty golden pieces. And more in a wooden box in her trunk. Nearly fifty in all. Paid up on the nail Markham had, looking at her with those magpie eyes, pouting his wet lips, mouthing something she couldn't quite hear, but his low tone suggested the coarseness of an obscenity.

'You're most generous,' she'd said calmly as he took hold of her hand and pressed the heavy purse into her dry palm.

'I pay my debts,' Markham had said.

'There's no charge for my . . . services.'

He had looked at her shrewdly.

'In this world artists are in need of patrons. My patronage ends here but I expect you'll find a replacement. Desire is endless, always craving new forms. I'm sure your imagination will go on to reap dividends, Celestine.'

'My . . . imagination?' she had faltered. But he was already turning away, leaving her alone in the room. At the door he stopped and said in a strangled voice, 'But always remember too much imagination is a dangerous thing my dear; it blurs the truth.' Then it had seemed like a dream that he half turned and said, 'The woman I loved was not the woman I imagined,'

232

before shutting the door quietly behind him. That was the last Kathleen Mangan saw of Henry Markham.

A door opened and stirred Kathleen from her trance.

'He's dead to the world, the bugger,' Missy said. 'What's he been sluggin down his throat?'

'Anything, everything,' Kathleen shrugged. Missy sank weakly at the foot of the unmade bed.

'You look done in yourself. Have you really recovered from fever?'

'As recovered as I'll ever be,' Missy stretched out, arms under her head. 'There's some things you never get over.'

Kathleen was curious. She felt there was more to this fever than met the eye. Missy's hair straggled over her breasts like unravelled threads. She's more like Virginia than ever. It's quite uncanny, Kathleen thought.

'How did you really lose your curls, was it some sort of fright like Corrie said?'

'Curiosity killed the cat?' Missy retorted, but her eyes gleamed, taking in Kathleen's spotless muslin that would fit Missy better. 'Full of mysteries yourself aren't you? How d'you come by that rig and why's his nibs so stocious?'

So Kathleen told Missy everything about their time at Rees Hall and how Gabriel's falling in love had spoiled everything.

'Still, this Markham geezer can't lock his sister up forever, can he?' Missy interrupted. 'The girl's got her own money you say, that Mister Feaver can soon get

233

his greedy hands on. And I ain't known anyone get the better of our Gabriel. In his time's he's fleeced an army of fine gentlemen.'

'You must let me finish my tale, Missy.' Kathleen's mouth slackened into a gloomy smile.

'There's one fine gentlemen that has bided his time and finally outwitted Gabriel.'

'Enery Markham?' Missy said.

Kathleen shook her head slowly.

'Not Markham, not he.'

'Who then?' Missy insisted.

'Death,' Kathleen said.

'Virginia Markham died?'

'She took the fever from Gabriel within twenty-four hours of our leaving Rees Hall. Within three days she was dead.'

'Blimey!' Miss gasped. 'How did you find out if you'd left the house?'

'Well, of course Gabriel had been shattered by his exposure but he wasn't defeated and we put up at an inn at the village close to Markham's estate. I was able to make contact with one of the servants at the hall and Gabriel pressed me to get the woman to deliver his letters. They came back unopened and the servant, perhaps feeling sympathy, or maybe wanting a few more of the sovereigns I was obliged to pay her, supplied me with every detail of the girl's pitiful condition.'

'If he were so much in love, it's a wonder he didn't break down the doors sealed against him when he heard his beloved were in mortal danger.'

'But he didn't hear,' Kathleen's eyelids lowered over her clear blue eyes. Her mouth tightened. 'I saw to it. He never even knew the girl ailed until the day after she died.'

'Watcha telling me?'

'I told you, 'twas me had the contact with the servant. I simply informed Gabriel the girl wasn't able to speak with anyone except her brother, not even her maid, until Markham believed we were well out of the way. I said that if we hung on a while it might eventually be possible for the maid to smuggle a message from Virginia out to him.'

'Why did you tell him that when the girl were at death's door?'

Kathleen paused a moment. She sat upright, back wonderfully straight, and Missy noticed how voluptuous the skinny Irish girl had grown. Kathleen reached out a dimpled alabaster arm for a bone-handled hairbrush, beginning to stroke her loosened hair rhythmically. The waist-length hair flared out in long strands that whirled and curved like tentacles.

'Well, why did you lie to him?' Missy pressed her.

Kathleen paused in her brushstrokes.

'Gabriel isn't the only one with ambition, Missy,' she said.

Black drop in ale was served at the Slaughterman's Arms. When Jess wasn't looking Gabriel got her bleary-eyed barmaid to slip some of the stuff in his tankard. There was a treacly taste to the brew but he swallowed it quickly and when Jess was taken up with evicting a fighting-drunk punter he persuaded the trollop to mix a double measure of the opiate in his ale again.

Rough coves in their dusty rags, swilling beer while gathered around up-turned barrels, began to shrivel to a fastidious distance, floating back to shadowy corners where they hung like moths, or pallid grey shades, flapping limply at the corner of Gabriel's vision. He drank alone. He drank steadily. If it had been a quieter night Jess might have noticed something but she was sozzled herself; she had to get drunk to keep up with her Saturday night customers who were often riotous and, after wrestling with a drunkard who vomited over her already beer-stained bodice, Jess had gone upstairs for a wash. When she came down Gabriel was gone, fortified with three more doses of black drop in his tankard.

He drank as he made his way through Seven Dials. The black drop eased his torment. The rutted streets ran smooth as water. He swam through the cool stream of lanes and thoroughfares, effortlessly, as though he didn't have to drag one useless foot after him. The city was like a sluttish lover tonight, breathing her ardourless amours in his keen ears. He heard everything: a mad laugh, the fall of cigar ash on a virgin's recoiling body, women breaking each other's bones over a man. He heard the slither of a whore's buttocks backing against a brick wall. He heard the heartless sputter of champagne corks from a cigar divan.

He turned into a narrow alley leading from the

Strand to the river that was cobbled with the bones of suicides. Currents criss-crossed like flagstones. The Thames was wide as the road of corruption. His head felt very light, every sense in his body flaring like a torch illuminating the darkest memories. He leaned against the jutting wall of a riverside tavern. The sounds of squabbling drunkards drifted out and sank like a brick to the bottom of the river stirring the drowned cries of self-murderers.

Full fathom deep.

Gabriel leaned his head back on the cold tavern wall. He breathed the murky river smell.

Fathoms deep she lies. The words ran through his head easily as a prayer. There was a smell of cheap perfume. The driftwood scent of the fathomless river. Full fathom deep. Five. The words lilting like a ballad. Five fathoms.

'Five guineas,' the woman said.

He opened his eyes. There was no sign of anyone. He walked on beside the mournful river.

'Give us five, sir!'

He looked at the vast black drop of water. Lethe's depths. The row of gas lamps could not light up its darkest places. The black water was hard as glass; there were bubbles like the distortions in window panes. He looked in vain through the glassy water to see if there was black drop for sale. Words bursting like bubbles.

'And for only five guineas, Gabriel,' the river sobbed mournfully.

*   *   *

After the black drop there were pipes of resinous opium heated to the consistency of treacle over a flame. He inserted a pinhead of opium into the hole in the bowl of his pipe and sucked contentedly. After a few pipes it seemed to take an epoch to pick up the pin, an eon to light the flame, a period of time as inexorable as the turning aside of God's face from the unrighteous to ejaculate opium into the pipe bowl. So he visited an opium den where Lascars lit the flames that were eternal as desire.

He slouched on a low divan in a narrow cubicle. Virginia floated in the ochreous air that was sweeter than full-blown roses. Virginia was elusive as smoke, wavering in her fidelity. Her hair was yellow vapour, her eyes the greenish pills a traveller, lately returned from eastern climes, offered Gabriel in the desolate intimacy of the den. He ate her eyes like a delicacy and at once he saw tangled limbs, sweating bodies, infinite ecstasy. The past rolled before him like a diorama. He heard Ginnie's last uncanny cry to him, he saw and heard it all as though the past were unfolding in the interminable present.

Laid out on his low divan in an East End opium den Gabriel saw all, heard all and felt nothing.

He woke in Bell's bed, the fresh sheets soaking with sweat. Someone had let the blinds down. He remembered stumbling back through an ashen morning and, recalling the delicious languor of opiates, reached blearily for the phial of black drop that he'd stowed in his waistcoat pocket. Perhaps in his stupor he had already drained the dose because his pocket was empty. He went over to a small cupboard Bell had used to keep clothes in and looked for the small loaf of opium he had stored there in its red wax paper. But though the sweetish scent of the drug lingered in Bell's linen, he could not put his hands on the hoard. Those thieving whores must have stolen it.

'Kathleen!' he roared. He limped over to the door. Damn them all, sluts and bawds who'd steal the very life from a man!

The landing was dark and Gabriel was astonished to find it night again. 'Kathleen,' his voice seemed to float, frustratingly linger like a ne'er-do-well, in the narrow passage, defeated by shut doors and winding stairways. He went in search of the woman; across the landing, past tall vases of flowers that reached out to brush him with silken hands in the darkness. He brushed a bloom aside impatiently and it came away with a rich, waxy submission, cool and fragrant in his hand. He bent his head and sniffed the flower, crushing the petals with his fingers, releasing a stronger perfume. White flowers trailed over him as he moved along the passage. Then a woman in white, her hair strewn with orange blossom, drifted past him like an opium dream. Her breath was a cool shiver. He was about to say, do you know anything of my black drop, woman? when the vision wavered and vanished.

He felt his bad foot ache. His throat was shrivelled with craving.

Damn the whores!

Kathleen was half undressed, reading by the light of

a candle, her long hair spilling down to her waist. She looked unsurprised to see him, as if she were prepared for something.

'Who's taken my opium?' he said directly. *She* had taken it, she told him simply without evasion.

'Well you can slip down to the druggist and purchase me another loaf directly. I can't sleep without aid of a soporific.'

'You've slept like the dead all day,' she retorted, shutting her book. 'You've slept enough, it's time for you to gather your wits and start to think again.'

He looked at her stupidly. Then his eyes wandered and he stared vaguely at the jagged mirror on the window ledge, the low-ceilinged room, the still burning candle.

Kathleen reached out to him and made him sit down beside her on the bed. She picked up her hairbrush and began to brush his hair with soothing strokes, her other hand running lightly over his burning throat.

'Stop your nonsense,' he groaned. 'Get my opium.'

'No more opium, no more sleep tonight, Gabriel.' But he had to drift into sleep or he might remember disappointment, he might have to limp along that long, hard road that leads nowhere again . . .

She got up and walked over to the window ledge and fetched a jug of gin from behind the looking-glass.

'This is just the thing to rouse you, leastways it might make you fighting fit again and that's better than the somnambulance of these past days.' She poured him a small measure in a chipped cup and added water from another jug. He drank the cool bitter stuff that

240

slipped easily down his throat and made to pour himself another draught but Kathleen knocked the jug from his hand and the gin spilled over her dress.

'Now look what you've done,' he felt like striking this woman who stole his opiates and frustrated his thirst for delirium.

'I want you lucid tonight,' she said. 'I want you to mind what I say to you. But first things first, where's Bell's stash of money?' she asked him.

'Money?'

'Sovereigns, notes, her years and years of profits,' Kathleen explained as if he were a child or an idiot.

'Profits?' he said.

'Do you have to keep repeating what I say? Tin, coins, the stuff you buy and sell lives with!'

Money. Money that couldn't buy lost opportunity!

'Bell's strongbox was always kept under the boards in her office,' he said.

Kathleen looked at him the way God looks at a lost soul.

'Will you fetch it for me?' she said, gently.

Gabriel lay down and turned his face to the pillow.

'Fetch it yourself. And get someone to make me a pipe or send up some laudanum,' he moaned.

The wood splintered soft as gnawed bread. Kathleen lifted up the heavy ledgers, then the tin box. There was a lock with the key still in it. Bell's box was stuffed full with money and opened easily. With what Markham had already given her, this would keep them all well into a rosy future. And no need to open the bordello doors to any more gentlemen. Kathleen put the box on her lap and bent over to replace the floorboards, leaning over the gap in the floor. Something white gleamed up at her. She put her arm gingerly under the floorboards, scrabbling about on the greasy earth until her fingers closed on folded papers . . . Bell's will, she half thought for a moment, but they were simply letters addressed to Gabriel. Kathleen recognised the writing on one of them as Bell's. It was a cryptic note and Kathleen could make neither head nor tail of it. The words Portugal Street caught her eye though. She'd never heard of that place and wondered who lived there and what sort of business they had had with the bordello. Unfolding the second letter Kathleen read about hot vomit and demonspawn and bawds and Mattie's screeching plea for Gabriel to return her money to her. *Mattie Holton!* Wasn't it a Holton's Groceries where Gabriel used to lodge sometimes? The writer of this dreadful letter must be the prosperous widow Gabriel was supposed to have been dangling after. On her knees Kathleen reread the letter as if committing it to memory. Then very slowly, very deliberately, with not a trace of passion, she tore both missives into tiny pieces and scattered them over the cold earth beneath the bordello.

♔ EIGHTEEN ♛

G in roused painful memory. This attic room might be that other, low-ceilinged sloping bedchamber. He remembered charged details: a fading tracery of blue flowers on some old china, the clacking of a servant's pattens on the narrow stairs and the way the landlord kept wanting him to take his ale downstairs with the local yeomen. He remembered the interminable waiting and how Kathleen had pleaded with him to accompany her on a walk. But, hemmed in, confined as he was in the old-fashioned room, he couldn't bear to leave it for a moment, when any minute a message might be delivered to him.

Somehow he would find a way of getting Ginnie out of her prison. They would elope and damn all Markham could do about it. They could live on her expectations.

Expectations!

How he had tried to be patient and what a mistake that was. He should have hacked away the thorny briars growing around his sleeping princess and freed her before death snatched her away to his eternally sleeping kingdom. Now there was to be no rapt awakening. If only he hadn't abandoned her; he wasn't a man, he was a lily-livered knave who had lost everything. He should have stood up to Markham, he should have been as ready with his fists as a pugilist, as clamorous in his arguments as a costermonger. But he had tried to the last to play the gentleman and the code of honour had defeated him.

A sealed mouth. A noble mien. A half bow and curt withdrawal. He'd behaved to the bitter end just like a gentleman and there had been no infernal row with Markham. Markham could even admire the damned seducer's style. After all, the most chaste Sir Galahad might fall, in the service of a lady.

And how he had fallen. From love and from money. From ambition and from reputation. He had lost the chance of them all. But, waiting, in the few days before the dreadful news reached him, he had believed love and money at least might be salvaged and at heart imagined that when he left the valley of roses Virginia would be with him. But the girl went and died. And he had to endure the thought of what might have been.

A horse had neighed outside in the hostelry stables. Somewhere downstairs a drunk carolled. He had laughed and said: 'That joke's in poor taste, Kathleen.'

244

He said that because Kathleen smiled and he certainly didn't imagine the lilt in her voice — her real voice, wasn't that the merest shade of an Irish accent? — when she said: 'Virginia died of your fever, Gabriel!'

The sloping floor had heaved like the deck of a ship. He felt suddenly weak as if he too had fever again. His heart burned hot then cold. He sat down heavily on the edge of the bed.

Up and down, to and fro, the bed had swayed like a rocking-horse on hoops. Kathleen sat down beside him. To his bemusement she began taking off her clothes until she was completely naked; drawing the covers over both of them, easing away his nightshirt, she made love to him shamelessly. Made love as if her kisses were the last rites she could perform for him.

The bed rose and fell like tidal waves. He had felt a slight nausea like seasickness. He let Kathleen love him as in a dream where he was powerless and her embraces had all the inevitability of repetition. He shivered because he had done this before and he would have given all the world to have had another woman in his arms at that moment. He looked at his lover as through a sea mist. He was a damned fool to have left Virginia. A damned fool, but she was no longer alive to forgive him.

Kathleen's passion was heavy as floods. She dragged the white covers awry with her struggles. Still she went on, spreading over him.

'Is it really her you love?' she had emerged to sigh like a rain-whipped breeze over an ocean. 'Why aren't you my own dear lover?'

245

He said nothing. Simply looked at her. The cleft in his chin the same, the cold grey eyes watchful as ever.

Kathleen began to weep, the old wounds stirring.

Gabriel had begun to feel pain again, the new wounds opening an old one.

'My bad, sorry love, I've wept full sore long enough for you.' Kathleen's weeping was piteous. 'Must you bind your heart to another?' Then she began to love him again, furiously as if the devil were at their heels, as if the devil chased after them.

Kathleen had no pride. She would lay her brow beneath his scorned foot and surrender to him. She threw herself down at the foot of the bed, clinging to his stern boots. The heels bruised her mouth. He got up from the bed, winding the sheet around him. He limped away from her. He *limped*. She accused him:

'Why must you always keep those damn boots on? You never wore them when you were in bed with Virginia Markham.'

Tears filled his eyes like mist spumed out of the depths of the ocean. He stared at Kathleen mournfully as if she were the icy wastes of his destiny. He looked into her eyes and saw something unimaginable: a long road leading nowhere ahead of him. His face must have looked a question because Kathleen answered him, 'You've left us only a cold place to go back to, a cold place is the only place left for us, Gabriel.'

'And what is this cold place that is the only place left for me?'

There was a long unnavigable silence before Kathleen could answer him and then the words weren't her own but another's, a verse penned long ago but written as if meant for them only.

> 'O that is the mountain of hell,' she cried,
> 'Where you and I must go.'

The mountain of hell, he thought coldly. Yes, that was the place, the bleak summit from where he could only dream of this valley of thorns and roses.

The lopped tree outside the bordello was uprooted and a sapling planted. The premises were given a facelift with white stucco and paint. The black door was changed to dark blue and adorned with a Grecian goddess doorknocker. Inside all was renovated and made fresh with pale walls and floral carpets. Flowers everywhere. Some of the whores left with their share of Bell's immoral earnings. Corrie and Missy remained along with Gertie, gap-toothed from her fight with Tess, but still possessing the purest, the most alabaster beauty in London. She *would* spend a fortune on silk dresses. The others warned her to put some by for a rainy day, but she said the finery, like her face, was her fortune, and sink or swim, rich man or poor man, she was going to be married and respectable.

Bell's bordello, the hole in the ground, the Resurrectionist Club was reborn and baptised like a Christian. At the celebratory gathering champagne poured like grace down the throats of the residents. A brass plaque on the wall legitimised its new name with engraved letters:

COVENT GARDEN SPIRIT-POWER CIRCLE, the curious read as they tottered past, slipping on cabbage
stalks, scouting for street women.

'And what'll we do about his nibs, intoxicated wiv
drink or doped wiv poppy juice as he is, night and day?
Gabriel's gonna put off believers and grievers wiv his
diabolical behaviour,' squawked Missy.

Kathleen looked earnestly at her companions, her
partners in this business. They'd put up their share
of Bell's money to organise this venture. She had
to take their fears into account and assure them
of success.

'Give me time, and I'll find a way to cure Gabriel's
melancholy,' she promised solemnly. 'In the meantime
it would seem opium works better than gin with him.'
There was a silence as they all recalled last night when
a drunken Gabriel had smashed a new mirror because
he said he saw only a cripple reflected there.

'We don't want him spoiling everything by behaving
unrespectable. We've got a reputation to think about,'
Missy said.

'Leave me to worry about our reputation,' Kathleen
retorted sharply. 'Haven't I arranged everything,
placed advertisements in the most ladylike journals,
sent cards round to gentleman's clubs, taken out a
dozen lines telling readers of the *Illustrated London
News* about our activities? Haven't I had this place
decorated so even our old clients wouldn't recognise it?
Wasn't it my idea in the first place we should make a
living for ourselves as spiritualists?'

Missy had to agree with her. Kathleen had sorted

out everything. Given them all new names: Gertie became Lucrezia, a warm name to make up for all the years of coldness; Corrie was called Prudence, which Kathleen discovered was the woman's real name; Missy, who would on no account divulge her real name, was christened Virginia, so she could wipe the slate of the past clean and make a new start in life. And for herself: a name floated through her dreams, a name she didn't recognise though she found herself speaking it aloud, rousing herself from sleep one morning — Porphyria, Porphyria, Porphyria, she had named herself in her dreams.

'But all your hard work should make you more concerned about getting rid of Gabriel. Or p'raps,' Missy/Virginia said slyly, 'your love for him is your weak spot that'll bring us all down.'

Two flames like rouge on Kathleen/Porphyria's cheeks.

'As I said,' she went on quietly, 'opium works better, it quietens him. We must keep him safely supplied otherwise he'll head off for those dens in the East End and be given all kinds of poison. If I can keep him quiet, out of the way of our business for the moment, will you agree to let him stay until I have thought of a way to make him useful again?'

Gabriel and the devil both. Both had to have their teeth drawn. Kathleen marvelled at her own audacity.

But what to do, what to do? She had agonised over the suggestion that they shut up Gabriel in a room and let him sweat out the disappointment and addiction. But that wouldn't answer, Porphyria had finally decided. The doses of opiates should be weakened gradually, she declared: the laudanum diluted as well as the opium pipes reduced. 'Gabriel needs to be set down on the road that leads to beauty, not truth. Too much reality has destroyed him,' she explained to the others.

Missy/Virginia raised her eyes because in her heart of hearts she thought Kath . . . Porphyria was as potty as Gabriel. Then Porphyria had caught up her friend's tiny hand in her own and said fervently, 'I must find another dream for him to dream if he's going to live a new life and opium will at first be necessary, it'll help him fall into those strangest of swoons where dreams are plotted that can change everything.'

Virginia had had enough of this daft talk. She liked let's pretend to be put in its place. Confusing the fake and the real only led to madness, she thought.

'Do what you like about Gabriel,' she said gruffly. 'Only don't blame me if he spoils everything. Now, if you've finished I'm going to lunch on the biggest haunch of mutton I can find in London.'

After she had left them Porphyria said, 'She's even more touchy since her illness isn't she?'

'Certainly can't seem to abide Gabriel near her these days.'

Porphyria screwed her eyes up thinking hard. There had been something she wanted to ask Corrie before she approached Gabriel.

'I've been wondering Cor . . . Prudence. D'you know if Bell ever did business with anybody in Portugal Street?'

250

The other woman's mouth fell open. She gave a hard laugh.

'I thought for a minute you asked if Bell knew some-one in Portugal Street,' she explained her surprise.

'That's right! Portugal Street,' Porphyria insisted.

'Well, she might be making the acquaintance of someone there now,' Prudence chortled darkly.

'What do you mean?' Porphyria asked.

'No one *lives* in Portugal Street dearie. There's no houses there. Just a place to bury paupers and corpses from the fever hospital. Portugal Street is a *cemetery*,' Prudence explained.

The country bloom drained from Porphyria's face.

'Holy Mother of God! Now I begin to understand,' she said.

There was a sour beery smell in the Slaughterman's Arms. A woman was drawing a wet filthy rag over the flagstones. Porphyria picked her way daintily between the barrels. Jess eyed her suspiciously.

'What d'you want girl? I ain't got no call for barmaids.'

'I've come about Gabriel,' Porphyria said directly.

'No use looking to me for my help if a brat's on the way. You can throw yourself in the Thames or find someone else to supply you with enough gin to shrivel the seed inside you.'

'I don't want to get rid of any brat,' Porphyria said.

'Well I won't be able to persuade him to marry you neither,' Jess said. Porphyria was about to say she didn't want Jess to get Gabriel to marry her either, when she remembered her immediate purpose and replied smoothly: 'Don't you remember me?'

'Naw!' the crone replied.

'I came here with Gabriel a while back,' Kathleen reminded her softly.

'The one with the fancy speechifying?' Jess asked, recalling the woman's dulcet tones rather than any aspect of her person.

'Ave you had a falling out with the varmint?'

'Gabriel's sick.' Porphyria explained how his sickness was one of the spirit which Jess, born and bred to unremitting bodily labour from dawn to dusk, had a hard time understanding.

'Tell him to shift his gammy leg down ere sharpish and I'll make sure he won't have time to feel sorry for hiself. Always thought those daft books'd lead him to madness. Mind you,' she shrugged, 'his ma couldn't spell her name let alone read real books and that didn't stop her going round the bend neither. P'raps it's something in the blood,' she grunted.

'Gabriel's not mad,' Porphyria said indignantly. 'Just a little . . . melancholy, not himself, that's all and I want to help him.'

'Women should help themselves and let men alone. Men don't help us when we're going half crazy with brats tearing at our petticoats and the scum drinking all their wages as soon as they get em.'

'You helped Gabriel once,' Porphyria pointed out.

'He were a child,' Jess protested, 'and there were none else to look out for him. I had no brats of me own, no, nor a man neither. I keep me eyes open in me head. I see too well in this place how most poor women get treated. But a young lad, why, I could help him but he could help me too, best pot-boy I ever had were Gabriel.'

'Then for old time's sake won't you let me help him?'

'Help you to hook him so you can be just like the other poor women who get trapped in their broken nests!'

'I won't be trapped,' Porphyria responded grandly. 'I have my own business. I'll not need to rely on Gabriel. I can support myself and him too, for that matter.'

'Until you get a brat,' Jess responded triumphantly. But Porphyria waved an imperious arm and responded airily, 'If he wants clothes on his back, food in his belly, Gabriel will have to look after any babies.'

Jess looked at her as if she were a madwoman.

'What d' you want then?'

'I want you to tell me everything you know about the life Gabriel lived with his crazy mother before he came to you,' she said.

Prudence/Corrie, soberly attired in plaid merino, sat next to Porphyria to support her. Missy/Virginia, draped from head to foot in diaphanous garments, hid in an alcove. Gap-toothed Gertie/Lucrezia, who had acquired a sealed smile and wore a lavender silk gown, collected donations from punters as they entered through the hall. As a prosperous middle-aged woman and her servant passed into the room, Lucrezia batted furiously blazing eyes at Porphyria who at once left her position and drew Lucrezia aside into the privacy of an adjoining room.

'What's wrong?' she asked the trembling ex-whore.

'We're done for!' Lucrezia gasped how the game was up because the seeming servant who had accompanied one of the sitters wasn't a real maid at all. She was only Sairy.

'Sairy,' Kathleen frowned. Where had she heard the name before?

'Used to be one of us. Bell threw her out because she went and got a dose of ladies' fever. She never would keep away from the gin stews and when she were sozzled anyone could have her.' Lucrezia inserted her tongue anxiously through the gap in her teeth. Seeing Kathleen's puzzlement she went on, 'Sairy were the youngest, most reckless whore we ever had at the bordello. If she's of a mind for revenge or mischief she could spill the beans on our true identities. What'll we do to keep her mouth shut?' she panicked. Veins knotted on the medium's temple.

Lucrezia half thought she was going into a trance there and then as Kathleen at her most Porphyria-like swayed and said in a hollow voice: 'We must trust to it this Sairy seals her own mouth. Remember if the game is up with us it must be up with her too.' Then she glided back to the darkened room where the circle was already forming.

The female sitters were bleary with grief or trembling with excitement. There was a gentleman who looked curious, another was sceptical and frowned through an eye glass. Porphyria ran through the procedure smoothly, despite the odd moment of nerves, using most of the tricks Gabriel had taught her. She'd hoped to involve him in the séances but his apathy was like a brick wall she couldn't scale so she was obliged to develop her own repertoire, using observation of the sitters' responses to decide what would entrance her audience.

Women clients thrilled to ghostly voices and the manifestation of dimly veiled wraiths who sang dirges. The materialisation of spirit-hands weaving over their heads sent them into delirium, as did fragrant gifts of spirit-flowers bound with semi-transparent white ribbon like ectoplasm. The men prefered touch. Even the most cynical gentlemen succumbed to the lightly frisking embraces and tickles of mischievous spirits who dared more than their stolid wives in the matter of roving intimacies yet whose spectral touch was innocent as air, for how could a spirit conceivably be *carnal*?

Lucrezia, a keen apprentice to the occult art, noted that the spirits were capable of malice. Should a stout fellow get up from his chair and wander round the room looking for tricks and trap-doors, he would be punished on his return to the circle by a veritable Pandora's box of gifts from the other world. One brute of a fellow had horse piss rained on him from another dimension. A shifty gent who wanted to feel under Porphyria's petticoats to see if she had a succubus concealed there was offered juice of the asphodel flower to drink from an unearthly vessel; when he swallowed, the stuff tasted suspiciously like brimstone and treacle and other less recognisable poisons and he was laid up for a week with stomach cramps. One jeering fellow was repeatedly slapped by disembodied spirit hands that hovered over the table. Knowing nothing of notions of chivalry, souls called over the great divide did not discriminate between the sexes in their attentions. A well-bred lady, who had come only to sneer, had to endure the levitation of her horsehair wig snatched from right under her bonnet. Another was mortified to hear chuckling devils make the most personal comments about her physical habits and appearance. Other devilment other ladies spoke of never after.

But the devout had their beliefs massaged with breezes cool as the sighs that blow over the Styx, their nostrils assailed with the most heavenly fragrances. Some swore they were granted visions of that summerland forever England where their lost ones gambolled in parks resembling the Cremorne Gardens presided over by the Lord with a crown and a sceptre like Queen Victoria's.

Autumn rain could be smelled on the sitters' clothes. The audience had gathered sedately after Lucrezia had deposited their donations in an empty leech jar in the hall. Sairy, as a mere servant, sat at a little distance from the circle and was expected not to make a nuisance of herself. The sceptical gentleman had crossed his legs irreverently and, assuming a superior smile, held hands limply with those seated next to him at the table. Porphyria suspected he might be a reporter set on writing an exposure of these depraved spiritualists who batten on other folks' suffering. She had to be careful. She was sure Virginia would be as quick, darting and elusive as a real spirit but hoped the robes in which she was draped weren't too long. She didn't want any slip-ups to prevent the spirit making her getaway through the concealed door in the alcove that led to the room beyond rather than the great beyond.

The woman with the servant looked expectant rather than supplicating. The bereaved widow was easy to spot. She was the one who'd worn a dark veil over her bonnet when she was admitted, the one who fingered her wedding ring hopelessly, the one whose white hand fluttered to her tight throat in the attempt to strangle at birth the sounds of heartbreak. They had placed the widow at the best vantage point to observe the wax dummy (saved from meltdown after an exhibition to commemorate the Battle of Waterloo). In its past incarnation the model had represented that Hardy whose kiss Nelson craved in his last moments. Now the wax dummy was everyman or everyhusband, ghastly in a shroud made of old petticoats. As a glassy-eyed corpse it would show briefly at an auspicious moment before an invisible Virginia hauled it away again. Money for old rope, Porphyria thought gleefully as the superannuated Hardy glided in and out with such deft grace the sceptical gent didn't have time to investigate. Now the widow was sobbing and her misery floated over them as the usual inchoate narrative, reinventing a marriage in which never a cross word was said and the only smack was one of lips kissing.

Porphyria was just imagining how Virginia would pour scorn on the widow's maundering later and was about to rouse herself from the fake trance when she felt suddenly sleepy, suddenly so weary of the strain of acting. If only Gabriel would rouse himself from misery and help take some of this burden from her. Her petticoats were as heavy as water. Her thighs were soaked, as with sweat, although there was no heat this morning. She was inexplicably wet but there was no resisting this delicious dream that was making her drowsy, drowsier than Gabriel with his opium-slaked desires . . . desirous, desiring . . . 'Oh Gabriel.' The words drooled from her mouth. Prudence nudged Porphyria and frowned at Lucrezia.

'P'raps we should leave our medium time to recover herself,' Gertie told the assembled company.

'I could pinch her awake,' the sceptical gentleman suggested.

'Sal-volatile!' The widow was rummaging in her reticule when Porphyria began to speak again in a dreary voice.

'Gabriel, Gabriel,' she muttered. Her face was bloodless. Her breasts heaved and shuddered.

Prudence broke the circle, got up and cautiously opened the blind a little way to let a measure of light in on the proceedings so everyone could observe the medium's lips turn mauvish as Porphyria began to scream blue murder: 'Gabriel, Gabriel!'

The hollering could have woken the dead and even roused Gabriel from his laudanum-soaked slumber. Opium called him with a thin penetrative voice, opium pulled him like a string of soft toffee, drawing him downstairs, along the ground-floor passage. His heart stopped as a wraith with hair like limp muslin flitted past him in slippery garments that fell fast from her receding form. He was about to follow the phantom of Virginia down the dark corridor that led on to the court beyond when a door opened rudely on his ecstasy and he was dragged forthwith into the drawing-room.

'Now clear your head and see if *you* can quieten her.' Someone led him across the room. He was dimly aware of an audience. A voice squeaked, 'Why, Gabriel's still turnin tricks ere,' then fell silent again.

His arms were placed firmly around Porphyria's heaving chest.

'Speak to er. Go on. Quick. Only yous can do it. Say who you are.'

'I'm Gabriel,' he said. And the woman became suddenly very heavy in his arms that strained to support her.

'This is Rosie, remember me,' the woman in his arms whispered in his ear.

Rosie? Gabriel could only see a woman with hair like fog. Prudence was wondering whether she and the stupor-dazed Gabriel could carry Porphyria off to have her fit in privacy when the medium began to speak — or, more accurately, sob — a message.

'For only five guineas,' the medium moaned, aloud this time.

The sceptical gentleman was looking curious.

'I have a message for Sairy,' Porphyria said, her eyes still shut on reverie.

The servant, who had sat on the edge of the proceedings, jumped out of her chair and, forgetting her place, tried to knock her mistress aside to get at the medium.

'That's me,' the servant said as her employer attempted to restrain her.

'Lawks a mercy!' Prudence muttered to herself. What the devil was Kathleen up to?

ᔆ NINETEEN ᔐ

Porphyria's arms struggled, pushing away waves that were as engulfing as desire; but her body was limp in his arms, swelling slightly, seeming to float in some tide of ether beyond Gabriel's clasp until he thought he held a drowning woman. The circle gasped as a plaintive voice bubbled upwards through the surf of emotions.

'I'm sooooooo sooooorrrreeee Saireeee' . . . breath ebbed and flowed.

'Sairy! I'm sure I don't know why spirits are giving messages to those who haven't a proper place in the circle,' Sairy's mistress complained, giving her servant a shove with her elbow. The blood drained from Sairy's peaky little face.

'That sounds like me cousin Rosie's voice,' she quavered.

The spirit moaned something with a voice filled with bubbles.

'Where are you, Rosie?' Sairy wailed.

'In a watery grave,' the spirit's aqueous voice swam towards them.

'Oh my gawd,' Sairy sobbed. 'Ave yer gone and drowned Rosie?'

'At the bottom of the Thames, I am,' the spirit confessed. 'I could stand no more of it,' the lost soul continued.

'Lawks!' croaked Sairy.

'Ask hhhhiiiiiimmmmmmmmmmmmmm why . . . fiiiiive . . . why five for a life . . . for love . . . ask whyyyyyyyy?'

'Five what? Ask who, what?' Sairy bleated.

But the spirit, sunk in its own obsessions, never heard her.

'My red dress spoiled with black water . . . all the rouge waaashshshed away,' the watery voice rushed over stronger currents gathering volume and beginning to crash like rapids approaching a waterfall. 'But I dooooon't care. I only wanted freedom and he soooooold . . .' anguish cascaded over the voice and the circle shrank back as if torrents splashed them.

'Who sold what?' Sairy screamed, jumping out of her chair again, casting off the restraining arm of her employer.

But the only words they could hear tossed up in the spray from the whirlpool of desire were: 'Freedom! Down, dragging me dowwwwn the muddddddeeee Thames. I jumped to the bottom, down down away from men to freeeeeeddooooommmmmm.' Then the waters closed over Rosie's torment.

'She's done for!' a flushed Lucrezia announced to the circle. But it was Gabriel not Porphyria who had fainted away so insensibly that smelling salts couldn't revive him as they did the medium. Porphyria opened her eyes and coughed up phlegm like words that choked her.

The sceptical gentleman, looking convinced, clapped and said 'Bravo Porphyria!' He bent towards the charming young Miss Lucrezia with her gap-toothed smile, who sat next to him, and said he would write them a puff in *Hearth and Heaven* (a periodical for young ladies of evangelical persuasion) and the Covent Garden Spirit-Power Circle would double the size of their séances overnight.

Sairy, who had thrown herself at Gabriel and the still floundering medium, was dragged out to the hall by Prudence. Living up to her new name, Prudence gave the ex-whore some of the cash from the leech jar and urged that never, as long as she lived, should she breathe a word of scandal to her missus or indeed to anyone about any of them.

Sairy's bonnet had fallen back over her shoulders, dangling by its ribbons, revealing how her spiky hair had been tonged into crisply burnt ringlets. Dressed with all the dowdy discretion of a housemaid, she was trembling with a grief as dishevelled as her old wildness, wanting to come back for another séance to discover the truth behind her cousin's watery fate. For Sairy was convinced it was indeed Rosie who had spoken to her; ready now to believe that these purveyors of flesh could turn to hawking spiritual wares, she wanted to know why the lovely creature, her own lost cousin, had been driven to self-murder.

'My sweet Rosie,' she sobbed. But her old colleague reminded her that any of that nonsense about returning for more sittings and Sairy's mistress would be getting a letter of recommendation from whores who'd worked alongside her parlourmaid. And did Sairy know what *that* would mean?

Sairy did. Sniffing, she protested she had earned her place in a respectable household by allowing herself to be saved by the Seven Dials Sisters of Temperance. The Sisters had rewarded Sairy's new-found sobriety by finding her this position as a servant; fifteen pounds a year all found and no deductions for laundry.

'I'll find out what I can from Porphyria,' Prudence promised. 'If that poor soul comes through again I'll pass on any messages to you.' But Prudence was perplexed. Prudence was worried. Somehow the pretence was slipping away. The Lord moves in mysterious ways, she told herself. God was not mocked, she fretted, beginning to think anew about this ungodly fakery, this tampering with imaginary souls who could so disconcertingly cross the divide of what is real and what is illusory.

A little laudanum, just a little, Porphyria warned Gabriel. For herself a drop of brandy would suffice. These sessions were quite draining. She always felt light-headed afterwards; the dizziness lasted hours. A flux of emotions rose and fell, squeezing her heart. Gabriel was still overcome and the two of them regarded each other as if through a looking-glass charged with something volatile as mercury.

He was shaken but relieved that the assortment of ladies and gentlemen who'd patronised the séance had made their awed departures so they couldn't witness his discomposure on being roused from an unmanly faint. All he wanted now was to blot out the memory of the troubling episode with an opiate draught. Perhaps the lingering fog of opium had clouded his perception of Porphyria's trance. It was no doubt some residue of guilt over the Rosie affair that had made him as credulous as that foolish little Sairy. A mere freakish incident, that's all it was, he reassured himself. No doubt Rosie was entertaining a gentleman at a bawdy house at that very moment. Kathleen was working too hard and the séance had slipped out of her control for a time. She'd always been an hysterical woman and probably that meeting they'd had with Rosie in the Strand returned like a bad dream when she lost consciousness. He was a fool to have let her craziness unnerve him.

His heart calmed. His blood thinned and felt cool in his veins now. He would have liked yet more opium but the woman wouldn't let him out of the room. She stood with her back against the door and said, he must listen, he must shrug off desolation for a moment and register what it was she had to tell him.

He regarded her warily.

'Let me pass Kathleen.'

265

'I've told you, Kathleen is not my name.'

'Celestine.' He had to humour her. The whores had hidden his money from him in the misguided belief they were saving his sanity. He had to have more opium. But, he thought with cunning, calmness worked better than rage with women. He could seduce her into returning his purse of gold. Kathleen even more than most women could never resist him for all that she was shaking her head mournfully.

'You've forgotten everything!' she said. No, not everything, he thought. There were some things engraved on his heart that even opium couldn't erase.

'What is it that I'm supposed to remember?' he asked, he imagined smoothly.

'Only my name,' she told him.

'Kathleen, Celestine, what's in a name?' he said.

'You must call me Porphyria now. That's my name. It's important you remember.'

'Porphyria,' the word seemed to swing at him from a censer, spilling like myrrh on the air. 'Porphyria, Porphyria,' he repeated. 'Why must I call you this strange name that sounds as if it leaked from Pandora's box of evils?'

She frowned impatiently.

'It's you who'll open Pandora's box if you don't remember we're making a fresh start. Here, I've written down all our new names. You can begin by trying to forget about the Resurrectionist Club and learning that your new abode is the Covent Garden Spirit-Power Circle.' She handed him a piece of paper with something scrawled on it.

266

Damn the woman. She was speaking to him as if he were an ignorant child. He looked down at the list he was supposed to memorise but the words made no sense to him. The words snaked over the paper. He laughed inwardly at Kathleen's foolishness. He had no need to learn words: only open his fanged mouth like a serpent and swallow them. His mouth fell open and, as Kathleen waited for him to say something to her, he felt the words slide through his bowels.

It seemed like hours, then eons later and he was still in this pale room with the paler woman who was brandishing a quill pen like an angel with a sword barring the entrance to Paradise.

'Have you heard a word of what I've been telling you?' The long swoon of time fell away and all at once, he was lucid.

He smiled smugly.

'Porphyria,' he repeated. Kathleen ran her fingers through her hair impatiently. 'Listen to what I'm telling you,' she tiraded, 'or there'll be no opium at all. I should have heeded Virginia, and denied you as much as a sniff of the drug.'

'My Virginia!' The sweet name spewed involuntarily from his mouth. His heart pinched him.

'Not *your* Virginia,' she said dismissively. 'I speak of Missy as was. You must remember our new names. Now you'd better get used to much smaller quantities of opium if you're going to participate in our séances.'

'Séances?' he said. This Porphyria wasn't an angel, she was a witch who had done away with quaint little Kathleen. He'd need all his cunning with this one.

'As a spectre. We need a male ghost. A dummy won't suffice if we're going to outdo our rivals.'

'Rivals!'

'Spirits are rapping tables from St John's Wood to Blackheath,' Kathleen explained. 'We have to keep ahead of the game if we're going to run a profitable business. I thought we might construct a large box where the medium could be sequestered in order to materialise spirits. We could have the medium tied up, constrained in some way so the audience would know she couldn't be dressing herself up as a spectre or getting up to trickery. We could maybe invite the sitters to participate by having them secure the tapes and seal the knots that bind the medium. What do you think of my idea?' Kathleen appealed to him.

Gabriel said nothing. His attention had wandered.

'If you could only abstain from poppy juice a while you might get your imagination working on more tricks and illusions for us,' she said crossly. 'We'll have to rehearse you tomorrow but before I let you pass out of this door, tell me what you're supposed to be.'

He looked at her blankly.

'I don't know what I am,' he said.

Porphyria bit her lip angrily.

'What are you?' she threatened.

'I'm a ghost,' he said.

An interminable night. They hadn't allowed him enough opium and by dawn a black bird of panic was beating its wings in the chilly chambers of his heart.

'Virginia!' He spoke her name aloud to reassure

himself he was alive still, and sane, not mad, in this freshly papered room that looked nothing like Bell's old bedchamber any longer.

Again he followed the wraith down a dark corridor of recollection but as in life his desire soon erased her. Was that apparition he had come upon in the downstairs corridor really Virginia Markham or merely the overwrought creation of his opium dream? He was finding it hard to distinguish between what was real and what was a figment of his drug-deadened imagination.

In a cold sweat he relived the séance where Kathleen had drowned and Porphyria snatched Rosie's ghost from the muddy Thames to haunt him. Women's names like flowers wreathed sinuously, binding him, clinging like reeds to his memory, strangling hope: Kathleen, Celestine, Porphyria, Virginia, Ginnie, Virginia; names falling like petals.

He had a long sleep but too soon it was morning and he dragged himself sullenly downstairs. He had to earn his opium Kathleen . . . Porphyria had said, and never mind about getting his own money back, they were saving it for him and he'd be grateful later when he was on his feet again, she had added without irony.

All morning he had to practise looming like a spook from a shadowy corner. A wax dummy was denuded of women's petticoats and these were draped over Gabriel. Lucrezia shuddered when she saw him so attired.

'You've lost weight Gabriel. There isn't a pick on you.'

'Well, you don't want a spook looking too substantial, Missy,' (he *would* not think of her as Virginia) he declared. She was disguised as an apparition and his heart had sunk on seeing her when he realised how foolishly he had mistaken the whore for the shade of Virginia as she slipped past him in the corridor.

Before the actual séance Kathleen had prepared just one opium pipe and it helped him stay calm throughout the proceedings.

He took little interest in the sitters or the whores turned spiritualists and the cloud of poppies in his eyes made the room limitless so he no longer felt confined. Agitation lifted until night fell and the whores locked him in Bell's old room with a dose of laudanum.

As a ghost Gabriel was adequate; as a man, a mere shadow of himself. It suited him being a ghost. Ghosts floated. They were not crippled. Ghosts weren't required to swallow food that lodged in the belly like stone. Ghosts were expected to be melancholy, not manly. Gabriel could wail like a banshee or weep colourless tears with impunity. He was applauded in séances when he gnashed his teeth with misery and desolation. He was loved for being pale, and frail as famine, yearned for by widows and orphans. He was everyone's lost father, son, brother, husband.

But nobody's lover.

Love.

Does it end? Like God does it have no beginning? When was the *real* moment of seduction — not that instant when souls, straining through *mere bodies*, mingled, but the occasion desire spilled like grace into the heart changing the nature of everything?

Where does love lead a man?

To the unholiest places.

And had it begun in Markham's valley of roses?

Or with Mattie's flour-dusted gold?

Or back further, back, way back: now he must limp through Seven Dials, slipping out from the barrel where he'd sought refuge in the Slaughterman's Arms, back to those curses that rained from a mouth slack with hate.

Ah hate. Hate sown like a seed flowering into the white poppy of fear.

He hated her. He wailed for love and was weaned on hate, his heart twisted like his mangled foot in her deformed embrace. That was how fear began then.

With curses not caresses.

That was why he could never find love. Turning over every stone in pursuing the secret, he discovered only the crawling things that spill from a worm-eaten heart.

It was stifling in the cupboard, the box contraption. His breath misted the small window. Through the thick glass he could see the woman who was monstrously fat. She stared imploringly at eternity, yearning for the son she had lain to rest quarter of a century ago to come back again.

'Mother,' he mouthed.

'My baby,' the fat woman cooed. He watched her forage for a handkerchief, her black bonnet bobbing with grief. 'I'd never have guessed how you growed in eternity. You was the littlest dumplin when the Lord

271

took you,' she began to sob plump tears. Her chins collapsed with grief. 'Speak to me son,' she exhorted. 'More than twenty years I've waited for the day we'll be reunited.'

He said nothing. Pitilessly he slipped away back to nothingness through the false back of the occult cupboard.

The fat woman returned to the circle on a number of occasions and each time he taunted her with his silence.

There was a regular who saw in his gloom the morose husband she had buried twelve months ago. None of your yearning nonsense there. She merely wanted to discover where the miser had stashed her inheritance.

Another widow wanted him body and soul, wanted him so much her need was painful to those who witnessed it. This was the time when Porphyria's reputation had grown to such an extent that she had audaciously proposed that Gabriel venture out of the box (where as the passive medium she was gagged, bound hand and foot); he could then demonstrate Porphyria's powers to materialise spirits by posing as her spirit guide and walking amongst the living audience.

'Why do you need a spirit guide?' Lucrezia had wondered.

'Because according to the *Spiritualist's Monthly*, a certain Miss Temple of Hackney has managed to materialise a spook who can be felt and touched just like real flesh and blood. Miss Temple goes into her trance secreted in a cupboard. Then, after a moment or two, out steps a woman in exotic dress who says she was a handmaid to Cleopatra. The gentlemen in the audience can give her a squeeze and she cuts off locks of her hair to pass them round to the ladies. Because of this plump houri Miss Temple's admirers have swollen and she has to rent out an East End theatre to meet the increase in audience size. She's raking in a fortune,' Porphyria concluded.

'But what if they discover Gabriel's a real man?' Lucrezia had worried.

'What is real?' was all that Porphyria had replied, smiling secretively.

Then Porphyria began to fall into swoons that made her face sickly white and her features look mouldy as old cheese while sitters were invited into the box to marvel at the spirit guide she had conjured for them. But they were instructed not to interfere with the medium and they had to allow her to remain bound like a bundle of lucifer sticks as they strolled arm in arm with a fully materialised Gabriel out of the dark box.

Women grasped his hands, ran their fingers over his thighs, much as they had in the gaff, with little squeaks of ecstasy. Soon Porphyria thought it was safe for Gabriel to speak to sitters. A few lines were all his lack of concentration would allow him to learn: 'Remember me,' or, 'In the arms of Jesus we will be as one again,' or, more horribly, fixing his icy glare on mere *mortal* sinners, 'Depart from me ye accursed . . .' For some folk would pay good money to feed guilt.

*   *   *

In this world of wavering surfaces, where Gabriel fed on drugs and materialised as dreams, Missy taunted him like the vision of opium trance. Not Missy but Virginia?

When she shut her squawking mouth, in that sealed box where her hands were padlocked, her thighs strapped to the chair (because Porphyria had claimed it was too exhausting for one person alone to be spirit medium at their relentlessly popular séances), with her pale hair tumbling, wearing what was indeed one of his own Ginnie's muslins, Missy might well stand in for that now unearthly shade, Virginia Markham.

And all the opium in the world couldn't hallucinate desire as piercingly as love could.

In that small dark world, the specially constructed box, from which he was about to materialise as the shade of Lord Byron for the delectation of a group of literary spinsters, in the moment after Missy had cunningly opened the false back of the cupboard with the heel of her dancing-pump, pressing on a certain lever, to permit him ingress, in the instant before his face seemed to float behind the window facing the audience, he was stricken.

Because, with her gagged silence, her fragile presence without words, as he came upon her in the gloomy interior, Missy might have been *his* Virginia.

He forgot his duty to go Byronically a-roving.

Whatever's keeping Gabriel? Porphyria hoped the

lever that manipulated the false back of the cupboard wasn't somehow jammed, the audience was
getting restive.

But Gabriel didn't witness the disappointment of the
audience, he never received the beribboned posies the
literary spinsters planned on pressing upon the deadly
demon lover of their romantic fantasies. He sensed only
the suspended moment.

Like the prince in the faery tale he kissed the
immobile women.

Missy struggled silently, her wrists rubbed raw from
the cotton thread with which they had fastened her,
the gauzy skirts of her dress ripped, powerless to
restrain this man gone mad, ruining everything! When
Gabriel ripped her gag off, she gasped for air.

But only sucked in his mad breath that was hot
as Hades.

Missy/Virginia swooned like a virgin.

She seemed to melt away beneath his hands, the dress
falling to pieces, the threads and tapes snapped, muslins
dissolving like water, ghostly garments vanishing at his
whim until only flesh touched his flesh. Until, only a
woman, not a dream yielded to him and passion died.

Her scent was not *the* scent, her skin not soft as the
pampered skin of a lady; her breath was flinty, not
sweet as rosehips; her very coolness had the bone-chill
of the streets, not the shivering thrill of a silver stream.
Her body spoke another language. She was not *his*
beloved and he could not love her.

In the end the incident didn't spoil the reputation of

the Covent Garden Spirit-Power Circle. If anything their standing was enhanced and the astonishment of the literary spinsters, who could bear the suspense no longer and had risen as one to fling open the door of the occult cupboard, was matched only by their thrill of amorous excitement at what their shared desire had conjured that decorous Monday morning.

It was *their* fantasy that had wrought this seduction of the medium by the shade of an infamous poet.

'Let that be a lesson to yous all,' Prudence had admonished them, 'to leave Lord Byron roasting in hell, not dragging him back to strip innocent women naked, bruising and scratching them, knocking them insensate with his infernal passions.'

And Lucrezia swore she'd never forget the heart-stopping moment when the twittering ladies opened the door: there was Virginia, bloody, bare, bowed but apparently not quite *ravished*; and no sign of his satanic lordship.

Mad bad poets were henceforth considered too dangerous to be called up from the other side to grace that drawing-room in Covent Garden.

For some weeks Gabriel's services were dispensed with and the only comment he ever made on the matter to Porphyria was: 'Appearances always deceive you know; whores and ladies *are* different under the skin, Kathleen.'

They had to send Virginia to Brighton for a little holiday.

When Gabriel failed even to try to rouse himself from the drugged lethargy of disappointment and bereavement, Porphyria decided it was time for harsher measures. Awakening on the bleakest of mid-winter mornings, Gabriel found his door locked. And only the merest drop of laudanum in a jar at his bedside. With his bad leg he couldn't risk escaping out of the window. He kicked the door with his good foot. He hammered with his fists but a bolt had been drawn on the other side and sterner bolts swung across the whores' hearts.

'Not in a month of Sundays,' Prudence declared stoutly.

'Its for your own good,' Lucrezia's words whistled blithely through her gap-toothed mouth.

He could tell when Virginia walked past his room by the bitter silence.

None of the whores would let him out.

Gabriel sat at the edge of the bed and carefully tilted the small brown jar. There wasn't enough laudanum left to drown his thoughts, just enough of the soporific for him to bob hopelessly on the currents of nightmare. He drained the unsatisfying draught and lay down to a fitful sleep.

He thought he was still dreaming when the door opened at last and that woman who changed her name as often as her dresses came in.

'Sweetheart, drink this!' She held the glass to his lips and he swallowed the wine that was cellar cold.

'I need something to take the pain away,' he mumbled.

'It's the guilt, not the pain, that troubles you,' she said.

Guilt. A profligate emotion!

'We Catholics have a cure for that,' she went on. 'It's called Confession,' she said. 'You must give your past a proper burial or it'll be forever erupting like the fever corpses in those overcrowded city cesspits they call graveyards.'

A proper burial.

'And how do I bury the past?' he asked grimly.

'You say a prayer over it.'

'What prayer?'

'The prayer of resurrection.'

'Tell me the words.'

'You begin by repeating after me and then the words find *you*. You say after me:

'Mother of God.'

'Mother of God.'

'Hear me.'

'Hear me.'

'Now.'

'Now.'

'And at the hour of my death.'

'The hour of death.'

'At the hour of all deaths.'

'All the deaths.'

'At the hour of corruption.'

'Corruption.'

'Make me clean again.'

'Clean.'

Gabriel began to sweat heavily. His clothes stuck to him.

'Bury the past,' the woman was saying, 'in consecrated ground.'

'Consecrated,' he echoed her.

'Not in a charnel pit.'

'A charnel pit.'

'Not in Portugal Street.'

'Portugal . . . ?'

'Who or what was buried in Portugal Street,
Gabriel?' she questioned him softly. 'Remember this
is Confession. You only speak to a presence who is
an absence,' she reassured him. 'You can tell me
everything.'

And, as if her question were a catechism whose
responses he knew by heart, he had no choice but
to answer her.

'The corpse of a pauper woman that that fool Cutts
brought here,' he confessed. 'I paid men to remove the
thing but it must have left some traces behind it which
contaminated Missy when she cleaned the basement.'

'Why did Cutts bring a dead woman here?'

'Well, she was just about alive when he procured
her and he brought her to the bordello because . . .
because Bell paid him, not dreaming he'd produce such
a desperate creature.'

'Why did she pay him?'

'Because a man paid her.'

'Why did the punter pay her?'

'Because in his own way he was a desperate
creature too.'

'And what did this desperate man want that could
not already be purchased at the bordello?'

'The truth.'

'At last,' Kathleen said.

And so Gabriel explained how Jeremiah Cutts had had the notion that the basement at the bordello would be the one room in the house given over to reality.

'To accommodate men who had no imagination. Men who weren't interested in games and fantasy such as the Resurrectionist Club was noted for,' Gabriel told her. 'Men who, like vampires, thought they could control death, or like werewolves, demonstrate you can never overpower the beast in a man, or as with ghosts, through their ghastly presence cast a chill over the living. The aim was that most things that were played out in the bordello above could be acted out down below with one difference.'

'The difference being?'

'Why, as I told you, in the basement all was to be real. There was to be no fakery,' Gabriel said. 'But from what Bell told me it seems Jer was too greedy, too reckless, pocketing the money Bell had given him for expenses; instead of investing in sound stock he bought cheap: shoddy goods that were tainted.'

'With Irish fever?'

'Presumably. Perhaps Jer was reckless enough to tout for business amongst those starved wretches who spill off the coffin boats and congregate in cellars at the back of Oxford Street.'

'Perhaps,' Kathleen said softly, 'he was simply spoiled by the sheer glut of the supplies available to satisfy such rare demands.'

Gabriel gave a hard laugh.

'Well, whoever the punter was, his appetite must have been well sated on a dish served with such piquant sauce.'

'Sauce?'

'Death,' Gabriel explained, 'whose inclusion at the feast sharpens the bittersweet flavour of everything.'

'But what happened when the woman died?'

'Then I imagine her too rapid decay alarmed Jer so, instead of coming clean with Bell at once, he panicked and went to drown his fears in a gin shop. By the time he'd come to his senses and staggered back to make amends, Bell had found out the horrible truth for herself and, anxious to escape contamination, left me to clear up the business in the basement.'

'But it was too late.'

'Too late,' he echoed her, 'to revive the Resurrectionist Club from the fate of all things mortal.'

⁓ TWENTY ⁓

And when did he move from the embraces of skinny little Kathleen to the hot-house of Porphyria's uncanny desire? It was hard for a ghost to organise a narrative with beginnings and endings. In truth, ghosts were haunted, they did not haunt. Ghosts were the echo of a moment endlessy repeated with no progression, knowing neither the origin nor the fate of their yearning.

Gabriel tried to recall the moment Kathleen's cold thin arms let him go and, falling into an ardent embrace, he became Porphyria's lover.

There were Rosie's drowning desires that had unmanned him and there was the long famine when the whores had locked him up and forbidden opiates. He had hungered too long for the flower that drowns pain and memory. Was it then he had weakened? When day and night blurred and past and present became entangled like sweating lovers he tried to return to certain moments as if they were beads on a rosary, sifting them through his endlessly repeated desires, calling upon names that were useless as prayers because they were the same empty words that could be a formula for anything.

When he called Virginia, another woman's voice floated back to him along the corridor. When he wanted to tear Kathleen's hair out for denying him black drop he found he had to grapple with an amazon, not a skinny wraith whose bones would snap if you as much as stroked them; it seemed as though she grew stronger as he weakened, flourished as he wrecked himself, became terrible Porphyria as he searched for the adoring submission of biddable Kathleen.

How the devil had he become only Porphyria's Lover?

'You can come out and ave a pipe and a small drop of laudanum if you conduct yourself like a gent, and no more roaring or screaming mind! Just sit quietly with the punters in the circle and if you're good you'll get your reward,' Virginia of the lewd voice had squawked at him through the keyhole. He remembered that because it heralded the second time he had fallen into a womanish faint at a séance. The whores had thought he should have a rest from being a spirit guide and join the audience where he could learn to control himself.

284

The prospect of his reward kept him sitting quietly in the circle. He had conducted himself sedately enough, until Porphyria, almost coming to a close in the proceedings as the circle were unlinking hands, gave a delirious yell and clutched her stomach.

'Demons . . . demon,' Porphyria had panted, hair streaming, kneading her rumpled skirts.

'Merciful heavens,' a female sitter shrieked as a moist red stain began seeping through Porphyria's petticoats to blemish her dove-grey satin morning gown. The medium was panting, exhaling air in methodical gasps. Gabriel watched her with a sinking feeling. Just when the damn show was about to come to an end and he could find blessed relief with an opium pipe the woman was going overboard with her shenanigans. He remembered his eyes had shifted wearily to the ormolu clock set down next to the carved parian bust of a veiled bride on the mantelpiece.

'She's bleeding!' a stout gentleman wheezed distastefully.

Porphyria screwed her eyes up, she doubled over in her chair.

'Ugh! Owwww! Mercy! I'm ruined! Help me!' The circle shifted uncertainly.

'Demon!' gasped Porphyria. Gabriel was irritated. Get on with it woman, he thought.

'Hot,' foamed Porphyria. 'Demonspawn, hot vomit pushing out of my stomach. Molten seed. This . . . child, this . . . horror tearing out of me. A curse on your loves! Liar! Whoremonger! Your stone of a heart, your demonspawn . . . tearing . . . too soon tearing out of . . . *killing* me.' When the last terrible words had wrenched themselves from her lips the medium tilted back in her chair and the appalled circle watched with mouths agape as Porphyria's stomach, before their credulous eyes, swelled horribly. So transfixed were they, one and all, by the spectacle, they never heard Gabriel whimper, 'Mattie?' before he fainted.

Porphyria had given him opium afterwards and in the weeks that followed she carefully measured out limited doses. And he had never more needed its calming properties because in those wretched weeks, debility, bereavement and disappointment must have conspired to swell terror, like Mattie's misbegotten child, within him; to which other terrors were drawn like succubi battening.

'Mama, ma . . .' someone was sobbing. Such a womanly, a childish cry. It couldn't be Gabriel!

The spirit gifts of flowers in which the sitters so delighted didn't rain on them from the celestial ceiling of the drawing-room; instead, a yellowish dust, then a chafing atmosphere. All the sitters were choking and his own throat was dry as . . . straw! Sticks of straw were floating across the room.

'Eat your dinner, Gabriel!' some devil was chortling. The other sitters were bemused.

Then the ghastly sound of bones breaking. An infant wail!

It was as if his own memory spoke to him, but it seemed the other sitters heard ma's coarse admonishments too so he couldn't have imagined it.

'Don't want the neighbours to see me son's a bleedin' cripple, do I? Got to keep him chained up so he can't wander abroad an have folks mocking us,' the voice of the devil who lodged in Porphyria's throat grunted as the eyes of an elderly gentleman and a dowdy woman of middle age slid away from him with shocked embarrassment.

'Perhaps we should try to rouse the medium. This is going too far sir,' a young clerk in mourning black had whispered to Gabriel.

But that was only the beginning!

After sitting through a succession of séances where blows, cartfuls of straw, rotten food, cockcroaches and curses were rained on him, Gabriel felt he could endure no more. Each haunting session left him weakened and distraught, dreading the night where the horrors returned in dreams so he was afraid to be alone and begged Porphyria to sleep with him.

The séance where he found himself bound by unseen hands to the leg of the table while abusive voices demanded he swallow straw as, long ago, his ma had bidden him, brought back that last hellish morning of childhood when Jess had rescued him from his crazy mother. The landlady of the Slaughterman's Arms had turned up to haul her barmaid into work and found the demented woman waving a sheaf of straw at a manacled Gabriel.

'Expecting oysters and champagne, were yer?' Mrs Feaver was addressing her infant.

Gabriel was scrabbling about in the filthy straw, 'Just like a little rat,' Jess said afterwards, when they carried off his tormentor to the asylum. Then Jess had rubbed his ankle with goosefat on the sore spot where the rope had chafed; she had asked him what he'd like, thinking a bowl of milk perhaps or a crust of bread with a piece of herring. But the starved brat couldn't eat at all.

'Tell me a story,' the tiny fellow commanded the woman who had rescued him.

'Why?' Jess asked him.

'Because I can hide in it,' he had confided.

When Kathleen untied the rope binding Gabriel, at the close of the séance, he was weeping. Gabriel shivered until the medium wrapped her arms round him.

'What's to become of me Kathleen? Hopes dashed. Love . . . lost. Demons dogging me!' He wept helplessly like an infant. He buried his head on her breast. 'I can't fight any more horrors. Take . . . take the pain away Kathleen.'

Was it then he sensed the very scent of her was not the same? The feel of her different? Her voice was wonderfully light and soft as she led him away from everything.

Cradling his head on her breast, she guided his stumbling feet up the newly carpeted stairs.

'Is there opium in your bedchamber?' he had wondered. But the woman said nothing and drew him into her room, drawing him down on the feather mattress.

*   *   *

The bed rocked to and fro like a rocking-horse on hoops. There were some flowers in her hair that possessed all the perfumes of Markham's valley of roses. She looked nothing like Virginia. It was Missy who looked like his dead love. But when he tasted Missy's lips they had been cold as marble.

This wasn't Kathleen!

The woman's dress was white as ectoplasm. Her mouth was moist as a dawn flower. Her arms were strong and held off phantoms. He buried his head in her thick hair that hid him from ma. Then his bare flesh was pressing bare flesh and there was heat like delirium.

Past and present merged like sweating lovers. And this had all the comfort of repetition.

He felt like a child who had wept all night and woken to a world that flooded his senses. There was only the eternally present moment. He could feel the sodden weight of everything as if the world had drowned in his own tears. The tall flowers in their vases flaunted clammy, swollen blooms that pressed against his fevered brow as he groped his way down the unlit staircase. He felt the pressure of his own weight on the groaning floorboards. There was a burning in his heart and the recklessness that was loss of hope filled his lungs like salt water so there were no gaps for fear to flood in.

He opened the door as if he were dreaming. He sat down in the airless drawing-room.

The people who sat around him were like effigies

weighed down with the gravity of their own desires, their dead history.

And this had all the familiarity of repetition.

As if he had done this before he knew what to do. He knew what was going to happen.

The medium's earth-brown hair was gold with light. He seemed to breathe with her breath. The familiar virgin scent perfumed his own flesh. The voice when it rose was thin and plangent. There was no need to say anything. Desire was speechless.

The other sitters at last rose up and drifted away from the circle. He was alone with the medium.

The medium had a voice like broken glass. Her breath was spiked with the briary scent of roses.

All her celestial body was speaking to Gabriel.

He got up and pressed the limp body close to him. He covered the woman with kisses.

'I knew you'd come back to me. Never leave. Never leave me again. Haunt me every day and night of my life, Ginnie!'

And the woman, passive as a corpse, yielded to him.

Porphyria soaked herself in the hip bath. The steam was fragrant with lavender oil and crushed rose petals and the scented water felt as luxurious as the silks she put on when she got out of the tub. Virginia Markham's white gown with its lace flounces revealed her bare shoulders. Cornflower blue glass beads at her throat glittered the same blue as her eyes. Her hair, dressed with an expensively perfumed oil, hung in symmetrical ringlets either side of her glowing face. Biting her lips until they were crimson roses, tugging at the low décolletage that squeezed her large breasts into brazen globes of fruitfulness, she smiled in the looking-glass. Womanliness spilled out of her.

'My own woman, at last,' she said.

And although sometimes she thought the draining performances would be the death of her, it seemed that with each bout of impersonation a little of the spirit was sucked out of the various incarnations and imbibed by her own hungry soul. She feasted on the shades of crazed, foolish or distracted women much as she dined every night with Prudence, Lucrezia and Virginia on roast fowl, rich sauces, fish and soup and fruit served with cake and ambrosial syrups. The repast made her sluggish while she consumed it but worked the magic of nourishment.

Only see how she was grown!

As she stared at the new woman in the looking-glass in her splendid dress she offered silent thanks to Henry Markham who had given her the opportunity to hone her skills of seduction and curtsied to the pitiful shade of Virginia Markham whose assets she had capitalised as ruthlessly as any entrepreneur.

Mattie and Rosie were given their dues. Porphyria knew she couldn't have succeeded without these phantoms.

And phantoms, in a sense, they were, even if something miraculous as a mass could incarnate them as flesh and blood again.

*   *   *

The miracle of money had restored Rosie. Porphyria trailed her back to a bawdy house one spring morning. The madam had bargained with the tenacity of a bulldog but agreed not to tell Rosie the name of the person who had purchased her freedom.

'You must make it clear to Rosie that part of the agreement is that she keeps mum about who put her here. Tell her she musn't open her mouth to anyone, friend or family, or say your men will find her out and fetch her back again,' Kathleen had insisted.

The madam had reached out a greedy hand for the twenty-five guineas saying, 'To tell you the truth I shan't be sorry to see the back of that one. Caused us a lot of bother, first the fellow who brought her here came back nagging me to give her a better place but he wouldn't put his money where his mouth was, not he! Then your Miss Hoity Toity gives us terrible aggravation, always throwing herself in the river because she thinks she's too good for us. Don't know how many times her minder has caught chills diving in the Thames after that mealy-mouthed troublemaker.'

Mattie remained as elusive as history and Porphyria never did clap eyes on her. It had taken some time to find the whereabouts of Holton's Groceries. And when she did locate the premises it was to discover they were boarded up. 'A disgrace! A scandal!' said the neighbour who answered her questions.

'They say Mattie Holton was having a child but though she made away with it she couldn't put an end to the gossip. The vicious talk got her down. That one prided herself on being respectable and couldn't hold her face up again hereabouts after a customer, finding no one in the shop and going through to the back where she thought she heard groaning, discovered Mattie on her back on the floor, and *blood* everywhere!' The neighbour lowered her voice. 'And Mattie Holton a widow for more than a year.'

'Where has Mrs Holton gone?' Porphyria asked with a shaking voice.

But the neighbour couldn't say: to a new life in one of the colonies it was rumoured.

A new life: already Porphyria had more work than she could manage to fit in at the premises at Covent Garden. She would soon have to rent larger accommodation. Lucrezia, with her exquisite beauty, was showing a talent for the art of mesmerism. Indeed, gentlemen of all ages and dispositions couldn't take their eyes off her and would pay good money just to be transfixed by the woman. Prudence was showing promise with administrative skills and, saying she was too old to perform, had set herself to learn accounts and reception duties. Virginia had developed a style of mediumship that appealed to a discerning male clientèle who liked their occult senses to be assaulted. She was proficient in spectral abuse and there was talk of her touring gentlemen's clubs in the provinces.

Kathleen Celestine Porphyria Mangan smiled at the woman in the glass, a woman who looked as if she had too much life in her to be a mere reflection.

Her heart grew warm even as she recalled how it was to feel half perished and that set her thinking about how lying with Gabriel for the first time had seemed to banish the cold that had been inside her for as long as she remembered. And now when he was cold and forlorn couldn't she give back to him his own warmth again?

A warm night and she only needed a light shawl over her finery.

Her trailing flounces swept the floor. She opened the door and softly descended the stairs. In the flower-decked hall Gabriel was waiting for her, a mere shadow in the darkness. She ignored him when he said he felt too faint to go out and he thought he had a chill coming on because he couldn't stop shivering.

Slipping her arm through his, she urged him out of the house into bustling streets.

'Where are we going?' he asked her.

'Where the best toffs and the finest whores go,' she responded.

'The Venus Rooms?'

'The Grand Hotel.'

'It'll cost you a fortune,' he said, bewildered.

'I have a fortune. Don't you know how much money we're raking in?' But he only stared at her, his oppressed mind too weak for calculations.

The Grand was all and more than Porphyria anticipated. 'As if I've died and gone to heaven!' she sighed over the ices, the sorbets, the coffee in tiny cups, the cognac served in gilded glasses. But Gabriel, as ever, had no interest in food although the music the band played seemed to clear the darkness from his expression. When at last his companion wanted to walk home he followed where she led him. For hadn't he begun to grow accustomed to following the woman on all her little jaunts, pleasurable excursions? Having no mind of his own, he fell in with her in everything.

Even shopping!

Where other men swore and hurried their wives through the Ali Baba caves of delight that were strung along Oxford Street, Gabriel loitered, palely, trailing Porphyria like a servant, bearing her endless packages. For she had discovered in herself an addiction to spend‑ing: pearly trinkets for Lucrezia's pale beauty, chocs in boxes for Prudence, perfumes with pungently spiced tones for Virginia, bath powders for herself and deli‑cate underthings. Then contrivances for the kitchen, appliances to help the maid with the housework, a mahogany desk, new beds with feather mattresses, lamps with wicks guaranteed to be smokeless. Not forgetting a smoking‑jacket for Gabriel in scarlet; she didn't like him in dark clothes, she insisted. Flowers and angels in any form or substance: dried flowers, their scents preserved with orris and arrowroot, wax flowers under glass cases, silk flowers with clips to fix in the hair, angels in alabaster, Florentine angels carved in wood painted with quattrocento colours, Venetian angels in glass with brittle complexions and then boxes and shelves to accommodate the trinkets. Oh the orgies of purchase! Porphyria was persuaded Paradise was an emporium!

But *God* is love, she remembered the nuns had taught

her! Even if, after she escaped their strict rule, the devil had often prompted her penurious soul to believe God was *money* because it was hell to be needy. And yet, wasn't the hunger always at her back, in truth, a guardian angel driving her onward?

Into the valley of love.

A vale of tears, the nuns had promised her; but they hadn't told her about the glaciers that shift when hot tears rain, when desire spills like a loch filling the ravines left by hunger.

But when, after they returned from The Grand, Gabriel followed her into the pantry and, watching her wolf down a plate of cold bacon, said with a pitifully empty smile, 'My thirst matches your hunger. Is there any wine in the house?'

Her appetite was suddenly blunted.

'Go to bed,' she told him. 'I'll bring some wine up directly.'

When he'd left her she looked round at the white-washed walls of the pantry, shelves groaning with delicacies. Stepping down to the scullery where the red wine was cradled in straw, she sniffed the smell of carbolic and the fresh laundry that was airing by a small stove. Fetching a tray from the polished-until-it-glittered rosewood chiffonier in the drawing-room, she admired the sets of porcelain lovers in blue and gilt ecstasy grouped on the mantelpiece. A scent of hot-house blooms thickened the air. The cat, which Prudence had acquired to purr reassuringly on the hearth, pawed her skirts skittishly but was too lazy by the dying fire to do anything other than stretch and roll back into dreams of contentment as Porphyria freed herself.

Setting out two fragile stemmed glasses on the tray and uncorking the bottle, she poured some wine into one of the glasses and sipped it slowly. She turned over the album that lay on a console table and read for the hundredth time, by candlelight, the newspaper and periodical reports on the wondrous, the uncanny, the *unaccountable* happenings at the premises of the Covent Garden Spirit-Power Circle, murmuring to herself, 'Well, if belief can turn wine into blood, it can surely turn devils into an angels.'

She swayed, a little drunk, on account of the cognacs she'd downed in large measures at the Grand tonight. She felt the bones in her bodice tauten. She pressed her hand over her swollen stomach; never cold again, the gaping chasm filled with warmth. No more hunger pangs. Then the woman who had dispelled the shadow of her former self picked up the tray and glided softly upstairs to Bell's old bedroom.

There was a light knock on his door. He turned lazily on his bed and watched as the woman entered. She carried a tray which she set down by the side of the bed and the first thing she did was pour wine into two glasses. He drank silently. He didn't bother to ask her for opium. When she came in the terrors of night subsided.

The gown slithered down her body and he caught the ghostly scent of some other woman, poignant as dead love. He tried to remember the woman's name but it was too late and he was too slothful and women's names were too perplexing a mystery, forever changing. The woman's hair sprung to her waist and fell over him as she drew back the bedcovers. A gleam of moonlight caught the flux of expressions running over her features. She might have been anyone. Excitement gripped him because he never knew where he was with this woman. She was scolding him gently and before he could stop her she had bent over him and was taking his boots off.

The bed swayed to and fro like a rocking-horse on hoops. The woman's smile cut through the darkness. She was lying over him now, her foot curving itself around his useless ankle. She was embracing him. He tried to whisper her name. His excitement was palpable. Any moment now she'd look into his dazed eyes and he'd try to say the woman's name. I know you, he wanted to murmur. And as if she guessed his thoughts she placed her fingers over his burning mouth but in love's play he bit them gently. As she took her hand away he laughed and thought, you don't fool me, woman. I know your name. I know you, capricious phantom.

'Oh love, . . .' Gabriel whispered.